CO|

C000264331

J. M. O'Neill was born [...] s a bank official in Ireland, England, Nigeria and Ghana (then the Gold Coast). Returning to the UK, he joined the building trade and supervised work in many parts of London and the Home Counties. In 1967 he established the Sugawn Theatre and Sugawn Kitchen (a well-known venue for folk music) in Islington.

He now lives in Co. Clare and devotes his time to writing. His plays include *Now You See Him, Now You Don't* and *Diehards*. He is the author of three novels, *Open Cut*, *Duffy is Dead* and *Canon Bang Bang*.

J. M. O'NEILL

COMMISSAR CONNELL

PENGUIN BOOKS

PENGUIN BOOKS

Published by the Penguin Group
Penguin Books Ltd, 27 Wrights Lane, London W8 5TZ, England
Penguin Books USA Inc., 375 Hudson Street, New York, New York 10014, USA
Penguin Books Australia Ltd, Ringwood, Victoria, Australia
Penguin Books Canada Ltd, 10 Alcorn Avenue, Toronto, Ontario, Canada M4V 3B2
Penguin Books (NZ) Ltd, 182–190 Wairau Road, Auckland 10, New Zealand

Penguin Books Ltd, Registered Offices: Harmondsworth, Middlesex, England

First published by Hamish Hamilton Ltd 1992
Published in Penguin Books 1993
1 3 5 7 9 10 8 6 4 2

The door bore the legend 'Colonial Industrial Development', which meant nothing: a heavy panelled magnificently furnished hardwood door. It led to an office of extravagant dimensions, perhaps forty feet by twenty-five, and windows running most of this longer side. From the windows one looked down and across a great expanse of watered manicured grass, shrubs, palms, parterres of brilliant flowers, everything symmetrical almost to the inch. A wide tarmacadamed drive came up from the extreme wall and its strikingly ornate gateway, two identical pieces designed and cast in Manchester: Victoria's ageing head on circular plates with delicate shooting sunrays anchoring them to the frames. Outside the gate were two impeccable sentries with rifles and fixed bayonets; and, inside, a relatively tiny office which was almost all window. A notice said, 'Stop. Inquiries.' The sentries and the man in the office were black.

The Industrial Surveyor, a tall military man – retired, in civvies now – with toothbrush moustache and grizzled tight hair, looked beyond the wall at the endless tangle of people and vehicles, a mile and a half or more of them; and at the lively waters of the harbour and cargo ships or cargo-passenger ships loading, unloading. The sun shone over it all, on the face of this Secretariat building too, but not on its windows shaded by ornate wooden canopies.

Only walking distance down the way were a dozen or more buildings, large stores, the bank head office, an insurance company. The stores were British, Swiss, French, Lebanese, Asian, Greek. There was a European hospital, a European club. A European residential area beyond it all. That was the nucleus. Then the miles of shanty-town congeries that, strung along the coast, north and south, and a mile or so back into the hinterland, were the accretion of a century: impenetrable miles of makeshift cabins of salvaged wood, tin, corrugated iron. Native clothes and European jostled out there but the faces were black.

There was a sturdy concrete jetty standing at right angles to the ageing stonework of the quayside, a wartime addition, the berthing position of the passenger ship now, which would have sailed down the Mersey fourteen days earlier. Near the jetty was the railway station, reaching out the four hundred miles through bush, desert, scrub, swamp; through rich mining country into the hills and northern territory. Trains departed each day, trains arrived.

The Surveyor – Industrial Surveyor – turned and looked back into his office: two desks on carpets; elsewhere dark wood that showed the gleam of decades of wax and polishing. Two ceiling fans, not above the desks, gently stirred the warm air. Framed maps mounted on soft insulation board were everywhere, and on them coloured pins made varying patterns. The desks had inkstands and blotters and swivel chairs, and orderly arranged bundles of papers and files. The light was electric and each desk had its telephone. There were guest chairs, waste paper baskets, a drinks cabinet. The office had an aura of importance.

The Surveyor's desk was farthest from the door and facing it. On arrival he confronted you; and, on your right, you passed the second desk as you moved towards the Surveyor's guest chair. Seated behind the second desk now was the Co-ordinator of Industry, a younger man by far; very fit, healthy skin beneath shining oiled hair, strong shoulders and arms. The holder of this incumbency, dubbed 'CO', had only recently arrived in West Africa from the UK.

'A Letter from a fellow called Lorimer,' CO said.

'London?'

'No, he's here. Somewhere.'

'Big C, small c?'

CO looked and waited.

The Surveyor laughed, went to a vast wall map. 'The Coast, big C, that's our whole territory, a couple of hundred thousand square miles of it, I suppose. Small c? That's the coast, the coastline, where the sea breaks. Here.'

'Then he's big C.' CO read from his letter. 'South Mining Area.'

'That's big C,' the Surveyor said; he tapped on a red pin. 'Two hundred odd miles up country. In the mines, is he? Gold, manganese. A lot of gold up there.'

'He's Public Works,' CO said. 'Bridge-building on the creeks. Biggish job, I'd say.'

'Ah, PWD. Public Works Department.'

'And he has labour problems,' CO said.

The Surveyor's interest was stirring, but coffee arrived: two polished trays with elaborate cloths, coffee and biscuits. He sat at his desk, drank and smoked, stretched, rang to have the trays removed. 'Thank you, boy,' he said as the door closed.

'You're interested?' CO asked.

'Yes, yes.' He went to the map again. 'Creeks here. Mines here. What they call a village here: a railway stop, bank, a store, a gaol, shanties shanties shanties. Some fellow hunger-striking in the gaol up there for three, four weeks, maybe longer.'

'Trouble?'

'Oh, he'll die and that's an end to it. A lot of trouble spots. Blue pins. You see them? They come and go.'

CO looked at the map and nodded.

The Surveyor said, 'Read the letter to me. What's his name?'

'Lorimer.'

'Can't place him. A lot of PWD bods about. Carry on.'

CO read, ' "This letter is by way of being a complaint and a request for information and action. I am erecting a bridge to span a major creek in this clearance area and for verification the PWD reference is FDR/218/31408. My work force varies between forty and fifty and the care of my plant, e.g. mixers, cranes, excavators etc., is vital. I am aware that these are troubled times in many parts of the territory and there has been a constant infiltration of dangerous propaganda from the coast ..." '

'Small c?' the Surveyor asked.

'Yes.'

'Carry on.'

' "... propaganda from the coast," ' CO picked it up. ' "We

also have a hunger-striker in the gaol, convicted of subversion and the organization of clandestine meetings. I'm sure you are aware of these facts and that the gaol has become a place of pilgrimage. The village and district needs additional protection of civil police, armed forces or both." '

The Surveyor said, 'The fellow must know there are troops at the mines.' He paused. 'More, is there?'

'Yes.'

'Press on.'

' "I feel that a major source of subversive activity in our area is a person named Connell. This may not be a correct spelling, or indeed the correct name. He has visited my site, threatened to stop work and damage plant, forced up labour costs. Who is he? He is white, 45–50, tall, dark, clean, European clothes, ran a school for blacks once, I'm told. He lives in the bush, deep in it, and has lived there for some years in what has become called a commune with African women – four or five, I believe – and children and grandchildren. The ground is tilled and he maintains a crude leprosarium for the dying. I have heard it mentioned that he has been there since 1922. Perhaps Immigration Authorities would have his entry on record. My own place of birth and home is in the County of Antrim, Ulster, Northern Ireland, and I can assure you that he too is an Ulsterman, perhaps even from my own county. He is known to the Africans as Commissar Connell. I think he should be investigated and, if possible, I would like to know the results of your inquiries ... yours etc...." '

CO put the letter on his blotter and waited.

The Surveyor said, 'Damn strange.'

'Commissars and communes?' CO said.

'Yes. I'll ring for coffee. Give Immigration a tinkle.'

The Surveyor lay back in his chair, watching the vertical rise of cigarette smoke reach the ceiling fans' stratum of disturbance, curl, contort, dissipate. White man with African women, children, grandchildren. Christ! A clean young whore in your bed

4

for the night and have the steward turf her out at four o'clock. That was routine for single bods and grass widowers. Good little performers, most of them. But *living* with them. Definitely over the top, outré. The coffee came. They smoked, drank, waited. CO's phone rang; he raised it and listened for a little while. 'Thank you,' he said, 'thank you.'

'Immigration?' the Surveyor asked.

'Yes.'

'Anything?'

'Nothing. 1920–25, slow traffic. A few missionaries and regulars. Not a Connell, not an Ulsterman in sight.'

'False name?'

'Might be,' CO conceded. 'But no blanks. In, out or dead. No loose ends at Immigration.'

'Lorimer?' the Surveyor pondered.

'Ring PWD?'

'Yes.'

The Surveyor was pleased. Here on the coast were miles of shanty-town sprawls and villages, always little explosions, unpredictable, gone. Cars burned, overturned, windows broken. Police work. Nothing else. But now and then a big one stirred. You waited, you got him! The Surveyor had shut the door on quite a few; and in the past decade had allowed himself, modestly of course, to be included in His Majesty's Honours List. He attended the Governor's regalia parties. A bad climate, a good life. A big one, he thought now, and a *white* one!

On Whitehall's records the Surveyor and CO were listed 'Colonial Internal Affairs'.

CO disturbed his reverie. 'Public Works Department,' he said. 'Alexander Lorimer, born 1923. Professional background, Masonic School, Ulster Special Police Force 1940–49, Queen's University, Belfast, 1940–44. Graduated 1944. BE, BSc.'

'Masonic School,' the Surveyor said.

'And "Mid-Antrim lodge",' CO added.

'Mmm.' The Surveyor considered it.

5

'A letter?' CO suggested.

'Two letters,' the Surveyor said. 'Our thanks to Mr Lorimer, of course. Will be in touch, kind of thing, you know?'

'And Belfast?'

'Yes. Police HQ. Belfast. Chief Inspector CID. Strictly confidential, urgent. Give him all we have on Connell, or whoever he might be. We await his reply. Urgency.'

'Should we hold on to Lorimer? A line of communication?'

'No,' the Surveyor said, 'I have a listening post up there. Bank manager fellow. Freeman. Haven't used him since the war years. He looks a very bad spy but doesn't miss much. I'll get him to have a look. Express registered airmail to Belfast, you know.'

'Yes.'

The Surveyor unlocked a desk drawer and began to record in his logbook, 'Today, 18 August 1950 ...'

CO's letter reached its Belfast destination at midday on 23 August 1950. It was the retirement day of the Chief Inspector CID. At fifty, he had put in thirty years, man and boy, from uniform to plainclothes, and step by careful step to his present exalted position. He had no regrets; in fact, in truth, he was amply satisfied with himself. At a lodge meeting, only days before, he had been taken carefully aside: have a month's break, had been the gist of it, and a lucrative security post was awaiting him. Plus his pension. It was a good day: this evening, a dinner in Royal Avenue, presentations, a few speeches, champagne and Black Bush whisky. He looked forward to it all.

He carried a little too much flesh at jowl and hips and belly, but he was strong, with ugly hands; and, when it was in repose, an unforgiving face. A church elder, an active lodge member, he had chosen carefully and well. In thirty years he had fitted-up and cleared the streets of dozens of these papish thugs, had maimed a few, left them toothless, damaged in balls and kidneys.

He had shot two of them, killed them. A good career, no regrets. He sat at his desk, clear and polished except for an ashtray and empty baskets. He smoked.

There was a knock on his door and a detective constable, in a cheap utility suit, stood there. He had a long white envelope in his hand.

'Yes?' the Chief Inspector said: he made a point of never being overly approachable.

'I'd like you to read this, sir,' the DC said.

'Yes?'

'It's from West Africa.'

'A bit off our patch, isn't it?'

'I thought you might remember something, sir.'

'Well, give it here then. Don't go.'

It was a plain envelope. The Chief Inspector looked at the typewritten name, address, stamp, postmark. Undelivered, a return PO box. He opened out the letter, studied the letterhead, the date, 'very urgent' in the upper left-hand corner. It said, 'Sir, Our department is concerned with the surveying and co-ordinating of growing industrial potential in this territory and labour relations and costs fall within our remit. In seeking your assistance we hope we do not encroach on your valuable time ...' Well, a civilized letter at any rate, the Chief Inspector thought, and read, 'The matter is a complaint regarding the fixing of labour rates by threat of stoppage and damage to the contractor's plant, which we would normally deal with in a routine manner except for exceptional facts in this case. Those facts are as follows ...' The Chief Inspector, without looking up, made a drinking motion with his hand and the DC went to bring tea. '... The facts are as follows. A fellow countryman of yours, an Ulsterman, Mr Alexander Lorimer, BE, BSc, from ...'

The Lorimers!

The Chief Inspector knew the Lorimers, solicitors, Mid-Antrim lodge, an hour's drive up the coast road; a son in the business never had good health but was a staunch churchgoer

7

and lodge man. Alec – for a little while at any rate – was the engineering one in Africa. The Chief Inspector remembered: hard, sober, as Lorimers were, a great healthy hatred for Rome and its papishes. And he had been a 'Special' too: a part-time police officer since his college days. He had rank now, of course: that was a privilege of the Lorimer class. A few months should see him back.

There had been an 'incident'. The Chief Inspector was calm, compassionate. Over-enthusiasm, you could call it. A bit nasty, of course, but in Ulster these things blew over. Fortunes of war.

He turned back to the letter. Interest was growing.

'... Alexander Lorimer has complained of interference by a person named Connell. This may of course be a false name, or perhaps incorrectly spelt. Mr Lorimer states that a person, Connell, a.k.a. Commissar Connell, is most certainly an Ulsterman, 45–50, and very possibly a fellow *countyman*. Immigration here has no record of his entry to this territory. It occurred to us that he might be a fugitive. He has spent approximately thirty years here and 1922 has been mentioned as a possible year of arrival. Connell is tall and well-made, originally dark but now greying a little. He is a disreputable character, living with African women, intimately, and has a number of children and grandchildren. We would like to be rid of him. Could you check Liverpool Emigration for West Africa? We would be greatly obliged ...'

The detective constable returned with tea.

'All records checked?'

'Yes, sir.'

'Unsolved?'

'Yes, sir.'

'Missing persons?'

'Yes, sir.'

'Nothing?'

'Nothing, sir.'

'Ring Liverpool Emigration. Switchboard will get it. 1922

first. Then two years either side. *Connell*, the letter says, but there could be a variation, you tell them. No forenames available.'

The DC was talking to the switchboard; he put down the phone. 'They'll ring. Switch will ring us.'

'1922. Bad times,' the Chief Inspector said. 'Bad records too. Or none.' He drank the tea in silence, thinking, finished it. He lit a cigarette. Minutes dragged past. The telephone rang. He listened to the DC briefing Liverpool.

Connell, he thought, and crept a little closer to it.

West Africa passengers few in the early twenties, Liverpool say.

'Good.'

'Back to us soon.'

'Good.' The Chief Inspector thought of Connell: it meant something. He drank the warm sweet tea. 1922, he thought. He had joined the Force in 1920, did his pavement-bashing, learnt the paperwork. The twenties had been dangerous times. And the thirties and the forties. Always dangerous. He had stood at a few gravesides, he remembered, and looked at weeping families. He still did. Bloody papist scum. A thought crossed his mind like a cloud shadow. He wondered, looked at the hard confident eyes of the DC opposite. He carefully put his teacup on its saucer.

'All records checked?' he asked again.

'Yes, sir.'

'Killed in the line of duty?'

The DC was silent.

'No?'

'No, sir.'

'You should have remembered, shouldn't you?'

'Yes, sir.'

'Ring personnel.' He pointed to the internal phone. ' "Fatalities 1922." They'll bring it to me. You'll go to check the other years. '20, '21, '23, '24, '25. You should have remembered, you know.'

9

'Yes, sir.' The DC made the telephone call and moved away.

When he was at the doorway the Chief Inspector said, 'Don't worry. It's my last day. We'll forget about it.'

'Thank you, sir.'

The Chief Inspector sat alone, remembered the war years: sneaking bastard suitcase bombers here and on the mainland. Murders, captures, hangings. Bombs in London's Underground, in pillar-boxes. Christ!

There was a knock on his door, the file placed silently on his desk, and he was alone again. He opened it with deliberate slowness. 1922. They had lost ten officers. He examined each sheet: victim/s, assailant/s, known, unknown, suspected, killed, apprehended, hanged. Hanging was the thing, he thought. Let them sweat out the minutes and seconds. And then the drop. Cowardly cringing bastards when the end came. He stopped. There it was! Connell! Suspect: Connell, John. He took out the sheets and read what was relevant.

'23 June 1922. Weather: persistent rain, heavy. Sergeant ★★★ and Constable ★★★, both armed, left the Station at 6.30 p.m. on foot patrol. Patrol would take them through often deserted areas of warehouse and storage space, areas partially demolished for redevelopment. It was a poorly lit area. Their duty ended at 8 p.m., but they failed to return. Twenty-four days later, 17 July 1922, at 10 a.m. approx., the bodies were discovered at the foot of a drainage manhole by Corporation workers (their statements appended). The drainage manhole was adjacent to partially demolished workers' dwellings, only 200 yards approx. from a main thoroughfare. It is assumed that the murders were committed on the demolition site and the bodies dragged to the manhole. There would have been a considerable amount of blood and the drag-marks of the bodies. These were almost completely obliterated by the days of heavy rainfall on the relevant 23 June and the four or five days following. The victims were positively identified by their personal cards and possessions, clothing and what fingerprints were available. The faces of the victims had been almost entirely blown away by a shotgun fired at close range (forensic report attached), and the bodies were found in a decomposed state. In addition there was mutilation by sewer vermin. The murderer/s is/are at large. Details of a possible suspect attached.'

A filthy breed, the Irish, the Chief Inspector thought. Time would weed them out of this decent land of Ulster. He remembered the name Connell. When the hue and cry had been dying, someone had matched Connell with the killing. A long time ago, 1922. Twenty-eight years. He leafed through the statements and 'forensic' and found 'History and Movements of Suspect'.

He read, 'On the morning of the date of these murders, 23 June 1922, a funeral took place in a rural area of County Antrim, some miles from the town of Ballymena (full details on map attached). The charred remains of a Catholic schoolmaster, James Connell, were interred. He had been trapped when his house had caught fire. The Coroner's verdict was of accidental death (Coroner's report attached). Following the funeral his family dispersed. The widow and two daughters moved west, to reside in Londonderry. A remaining son, John Connell, travelled by train to Belfast where he had recently taken a Bachelor of Arts degree and hoped to begin a Master's course in the autumn (1923). He has not been traced after months of inquiry and search. It was noted that he had a relationship with a fellow student, Elizabeth Orr, of good Presbyterian stock. She stated that she had not seen him on 23 June 1922 or for some days prior to that when he had learnt of his father's death. Also, reliable sources in the Ballymena area say there was Catholic whispering of discrimination and even arson. This, the Coroner pointed out, was an infamous slur on the overwhelming Presbyterian and Protestant populace of the County of Antrim. However, there is a distinct possibility that John Connell committed the murders and absconded. A shotgun was missing from a garden outhouse and cartridges discovered there were identical with those found in the manhole. Our Agents in the non-British part of this Island have been alerted and the family house in Londonderry is under discreet surveillance. Emigration Authorities at Liverpool and mainland police are co-operating . . .'

Mainland police were lazy bastards and Liverpool Emigration was a mess now as in 1922, the Chief Inspector thought. His telephone rang. It was Liverpool Emigration.

'Yes?' the Chief Inspector said.

'1922. John Connell?'

'Yes?'

'He boarded for West Africa, cargo passenger vessel, SS *Niger*, 24 June 1922.'

'24 June 1922?' The Chief Inspector checked. 'John Connell. C-O-N-N-E-L-L?'

'That's it. Any help?'

'Indeed.' The Chief Inspector thanked him. 'A pity you weren't there in 1922.'

'I'd be twenty-eight years older, retired, maybe six feet under.'

The Chief Inspector laughed. 'You have a point,' he said, and hung up.

What a special way to end his career, he thought. He felt a flood of power, a great afflatus. He telephoned the Chief of Communications. 'Private and Confidential,' he said; he recited the address. 'Night rate, West Africa, "cable as follows. Apprehend C for return to UK. Express letter follows."'

He ordered tea and smoked, wrote a full, meticulous report which he addressed to his Chief Superintendent, put it under cover, sealed it, inscribed 'Private and Confidential'. He wrote a shorter explanatory letter to the Surveyor at Colonial Industrial Development, marked 'Express/Registered'. He put both letters in his outgoing post basket. He would call it a day, call it a lifetime. He smiled. He would drive home and change for the evening.

The detective constable knocked and stood in the doorway. 'I couldn't raise anything, sir. Any luck with 1922?'

'Just vague possibilities,' he said. 'Thank you, constable.'

'Thank you, sir.'

The Chief Inspector took the 1922 file and, on second thoughts, both his letters. He returned the file to Records and handed the letters to the chief postal clerk.

Freddie Freeman's desk, polished, uncluttered with paperwork, faced the barred windows of his office so that, standing, he could look out at the entire desolate shambles of buildings comprising the village. Three shed-like stores of provisioners, Asian, Swiss, British, were there; a church and what was called 'Hookers' – for Europeans of a kind – and a post office, were all shrunken breeze-block buildings with asbestos roofs. The rest were shanties: tiny dwellings the African had raised from salvaged timber, corrugated iron sheets, the flattened tin of kerosene drums.

Except the lock-up, the gaolhouse for thieves, overnight drunks, the not infrequent killers: it was a sturdy box, concrete, with slits barred beneath projected eaves. For how many days Freddie couldn't remember now, a shoulder-to-shoulder ring of hardcore diehards had kept a vigil about it; and from every sweaty track protest came, a straggle of bodies, gathering, swelling, coalescing, a kind of strange withdrawal of aimless labour bringing paralysis neither to the village nor to the surrounding mines.

The bank too was single-storeyed, but of late Victorian stonework, dignified, even ornate, still with a quiet confidence in dominance and prosperity. It might have fallen out of the sky into this jungle clearance.

Christ, Freddie thought. He lit a cigarette and pondered the long trek to sundown and a drink.

In the gaolhouse, some politico-johnnie protested with his gut: no food, no chop-chop. Hunger to the death. Well, Freddie wished he'd get on with it. You tired of these damn things; it had had its run.

13

Freddie looked at his watch. There they were, gathering out there, already pushing in from the surrounding gullies and creeks – nothing better to do, a bloody holiday – to cram the village.

And the noise! The torment of godawful drums, flutes, tin cans, clappers, horns, rattles, brass pans, all through the midday sun, and on and on to the chilling small hours before dawn ...

The telephone tinkled unevenly on Freddie's desk and he looked at its metal and ebonite handset, a cranking handle, a glistening hardwood cradle. It tinkled again.

He raised it. 'Yes?'

From the post office the one-man exchange said, 'Call from the coast for you ... sah.' That delayed 'sah'.

A hint of cock-a-snook, Freddie thought. The ceiling fans pushed hot air from place to place, made a tired sound. Freddie's face glistened, his forearms. He wore a shirt and tie, sleeves rolled up, flimsy palm beach slacks. White. His socks were white too, and he had black leather shoes.

Outside, a few Africans, even in the morning sun glare, sat in shaded places: later, in normal dog-days, they would sleep and loiter and sleep again. But now there was a quiet restless air of foreboding.

The village sat on slightly raised ground, a baked rock-hard ground in late September oven heat. Ninety-five by midday, Freddie thought; humidity a bloody hundred. The bank looked out on an amorphous open space with a single thriving palm tree, and beneath it, squatting, an ageing bearded wraith with tribal marks. The palm tree leant forward, making a kind of plumaged baldaquin for this man of learning. He had a typewriter more ancient than Freddie's telephone, with great looping hammer-head bars. It sat on a draped wooden crate. He was 'Big Man Letter Writer'. Those with need but not the skill to communicate by the written word could, at a price, purchase his magic.

Freddie wondered at his repose.

The telephone earpiece was full of distant sounds and echoes straining to reach out across the long simmering miles to the coastline, the jetties, the dense fringe of crawling humanity down there. The sweat of it.

Freddie dabbed a handkerchief inside the neckband of his shirt. He was a quiet and, he thought, reasonable man. The Surveyor's description of 'bank manager fellow' or 'listening post' would have irritated him.

After three minutes he said, only in a muted chivvying voice, 'Hello, hello.' The echoing silence swallowed it up. Another minute and, unprepared, he was juddered by a birth-cry from the exchange.

The voice said, 'Am I hearing you?'

Christ, Freddie thought. He said, 'You could be seeing me if you don't move your bloody arse! The coast, you said. There's a call from the coast.'

'Ah, you remember, sah. Here it is.'

Freddie sat and mopped his forehead: the hours would drag their feet through the day until the sun dropped over the rim of the world, he thought again, and it was time to sip whisky and feel no pain.

There was the final tear of telephone static. 'Freeman? ... Freeman? ... ' he heard across the great space of two hundred miles.

'Yes,' he said.

'You know who this is?'

'Yes.' Freddie remembered.

'I sent you a letter yesterday.'

'Letters take four days to get here.'

'We have *our* man on the train at all times now. Night and day. A white person, of course. One of *us*. Delivers by hand to the army. They do the legwork.'

'Marvellous,' Freddie said.

The black army. Twelve miles up the bush there was a white captain at the mines who slept most of the time.

'You know who I am, Freeman? You remember, don't you?'

'Of course I remember,' Freddie shot back at him. 'That was '39–45. This is 1950. Five years. Remember?'

'1950, yes! Troubled times on the west coast.'

He was an iron-grey Secretariat blimp on the Governor's staff, CB bloody E or something like that, Freddie remembered. He had met him only once. That was '39. An MI some digit or other, Freddie supposed. Internal Security it had been in the war years. 'Listening posts and weather-eyes at strategic points, old man. Don't use phones or post offices. Can't trust these blighters, you know. I have a man on the train. He moves up and down. A tight ship, you know. We need you, Freeman. Unlikely types are best, you see. Inconspicuous.'

'In-bloody-competent,' Freddie had said.

'My dear fellow!'

Freddie remembered him.

'You're still there. I keep tabs, you know,' he was saying now.

'Yes,' Freddie said.

'The letter? Has it arrived?'

'I haven't looked at my post yet.'

'Then have a skim through, there's a good fellow.'

'Don't patronize me.'

'Not intended, old man.'

With a damp palm Freddie fanned out a half dozen letters. There was a plain long envelope, unstamped: 'Personal. Frederick Freeman Esq.'

'It's here,' Freddie said.

'Good. Read it.'

'When I have time.'

'Of course.'

'I have a shipment in forty minutes.'

'Of course, of course. Read, shall we say, at the first opportunity. And respond. All right, Freeman?'

'Yes, I'm all right,' Freddie said.

'I mean have you got the picture?'

'And a shipment out of here in forty minutes,' Freddie told him.

'Keep the letter on your person until you can read it. Destroy it of course. Reply ASAP. All the old rules. Understood?'

Freddie blew smoke into the mouthpiece. 'Yes,' he said eventually. He replaced the handset on its metal hooks.

Groups were jostling through the village now to join the encircling devotees on their endless circuit of the gaolhouse: a strange concrete Kaaba and its pilgrims.

He pocketed this precious envelope and went into the general office with its public counter, brass grill, sloping desks, parquet floor. And staff: Africans, there were three, a chief clerk, two juniors in their twenties. The chief clerk was greying, important in European clothes. Freddie gave him the routine head office 'daily' and nodded at the juniors.

'Get them working, Mr Koffee.'

'Yes, sir.'

The main doors were still locked but at the counter there were four native soldiers: tall, silent, impassive, smart in khaki shorts and tunics, puttees, black glittering boots; they wore tasselled bright red fezzes. Freddie saw their rifles stacked in the corner.

'Good morning,' he said.

'Sah!'

As usual he graciously accepted their salute; he liked their smartness.

'The safe, Mr Koffee.'

There were two combination dials. Mr Koffee, shielding with his body, found his numbers and retired. Freddie completed the unlocking.

He said, 'The door, gentlemen.'

The juniors swung from the door-handle until the massive bulk moved on its hinges.

The door had been a wartime embellishment leading to an extended safe: a great steel-barred cage surrounded by breeze-blocks and roofed with steel plate and concrete. It jutted out from the rear of the building and might have been mistaken for a temporary urinal by a newcomer unaware that the African peed when and where he chose; and faeces were a precious manure. It amused Freddie. It could be taken with a pickaxe and a hacksaw.

There were twenty boxes of gold ingots inside: reinforced boxes, double-padlocked, sealed, hemp rope handles. And there were diamonds in a package large as a tome, heavily wrapped and taped.

'Line up a squad out there, Mr Koffee.'

The soldiers were fixing bayonets to their rifles; they went out into the sun and stood on guard before Freddie's bank. Mr Koffee marshalled labourers, twenty-two of them: two files of ten stretching back to the bank steps; and two to haul out the boxes from the safe.

Everything was ready and in waiting.

Freddie smoked and let time waste; he went and stood in his private cubicle at the counter, where he would attend from time to time when summoned by Mr Koffee and diamonds were to be purchased. Only Africans had licence to prospect and they came, a couple in a day perhaps, rarely more, with the minute brown pebbles in tiny bottles or in matchboxes or pieces of coarse rag. Freddie's technical apparatus was here too: Anglepoise lamp, tweezers, magnifying glass, hydraulic press and plates to test the suspect ones. Small brown pebbles for industrial cutting edges; and sometimes a rare 'brilliant' among them, bright as a pinprick orphan star.

Freddie smoked and listened.

Somehow the shuffling feet, like sand-dancers, were an audible scratching accompaniment to the whole percussive dissonance. A single voice pealed out a litanous verse and the response was thunderous. The village roads and streets, dry dirt tracks, teemed with black flesh, discoloured feet.

And beyond the village, volcanic miles, a crumpled sheet of paper: ridges, cones, waves, soft undulations, clefts, bush, scrub, jungle. A fifteen-mile radius swung round the frail old Letter Writer would circle gold mines, five in all. They dug, panned, hydraulicked, separated the precious stuff and made the ingots to fill the boxes in Freddie's safe. Britons gathered the gold and sent it home to entrepreneurial fortresses and for King and Country. Freddie smoked. The same fifteen-mile radius would encompass the creeks, his own bungalow high on a volcanic plateau, the cricket club with its bar and almost without cricket. And Connell's commune.

Freddie Freeman was a kind person, aware of the importance of showing some flinty imperial carapace and hardly successful in achieving it. A big man at forty-eight, healthy, agile, with just the first gathering of flesh at chin and waistline.

He had been born in India. Parents were dead and buried out there in colonial soil; dead more than thirty years in the wake of influenza's great post World War I pandemic. They had sent him 'home' to England before his teens – a reputable school, he was told – and he was at the end of no mean academic journey when the news of their deaths had come. Death and burial. He was seventeen.

'There isn't much money, Freeman,' the headmaster had explained. 'And relatives, if they are somewhere, haven't come forward. But you mustn't worry. Colonial banks. That's the answer. They'll find a place for you.'

Freddie looked out at the village. Colonial banks. Christ, he thought.

Mr Koffee's juniors were at their sloping desks, on stools. Mr Koffee had a table, an upholstered chair. Like Freddie, he smoked. He stood and went to mid-office, held his cigarette aloft: the smoke rose in a vertical thread for a moment and was sucked and blended into the spent humidity.

He said, 'Ah, it is coming, sir.'

Freddie listened.

'The train is coming.'

'Yes, I hear it. Get them loading, Mr Koffee.'

19

From the safe Freddie took a lightweight mackintosh; there was a 'poacher's pocket' for his parcel of diamonds. And there was a revolver in a thigh holster. He strapped it on. 'Hold the coat open while in convey, let the gun be seen' was the bank instruction. Bloody marvellous! If there were some lunatic blitz, those professional johnnies with bullets and bayonets out there could get on with it. Freddie smiled at his own specialized surges of misanthropy.

The job was under way. Freddie stood on the steps. He looked at his gun; he felt the hand-delivered letter from the Secretariat panjandrum in his pocket.

All this Bulldog Drummond stuff!

The loaders carried out the ingot boxes from the safe, swung them high with a neat rhythm on to the padded heads of the labourers. Legs, neck and shoulder muscles moved into balance. It was a fifteen-minute bustle of sweat. Those poor bastards up front, Freddie thought; how many pounds sitting on their 'coconuts' for a quarter of an hour before take-off?

From the bank, through the village, through the great tightening mass, a roadway had been cleared, two hundred yards of gentle slope down to the railway stop. The train from the north – there would be a special coach, gold already aboard – sat, hidden, engine turning over in its own vast orgasm of steam.

At the bank the soldiers deployed themselves, two on each side, arms shouldered, bayonets fixed.

Freddie descended the steps, took the rear position, called out his command. 'Move!'

The steady careful march began. Male groups emerged to jeer, spit; banners, a red flag here and there. '... Imperialist pig ... big shitman ... go home big shitman ...' But women and children laughed, waved, cheered: the magic of soldiers and gold and the hoarse breath of the train awaiting them. Stalls were cluttered at the foot of the hill: mango, yam, plantain, pineapple, coconut, flies; vessels too, gourds, brass bowls, trays. Huge blinding mammy cloths hung limply, side by side, and below them baskets and toe-grip sandals. Refuse tips too, ravaged by flies and vermin, gashed and probed by vultures, tame as London pigeons. Freddie looked at the bald obscene heads and necks of them.

The bearers mounted the steps now on to the wooden platform. In a few minutes the cargo was loaded, diamonds handed over, documents signed. The custodian, from a branch in the north country, white of course, would escort the accumulated loot to the coast for shipment to home. A steel coach for gold and diamonds. He snapped the door shut.

'Cheers, old man,' he said.

He was a young man. I could be his father, Freddie thought.

'Cheers, old man.'

The labour gang, disbanded, was on its way back to the bank, where Mr Koffee would pay them their hire. Freddie watched the train out of sight, stood on the empty boardwalk platform, looked north and south at the glittering steel convergence.

He went back past the refuse stalls, pushing uphill through the crowds, to Hookers. A quiet façade, discreet. Discreet inside too, soft lighting, carpets, bar, billiard tables, a welcoming place. But it was a knocking-shop, a bordello. Hooker, crippled in the mines – amputated toes, both feet – had set it up, was boss, barman, chief bottle-washer. Bloody wise man, Freddie thought. Back home, he had told Freddie, he'd be a non-starter. Even in this love nest of white man and black whores he was a man of business, right? And in a land of cheap drink he could drink his share at cost. That was all he wanted: booze and an African tart when he felt jazzy. His name was Hooker so he called it Hookers, without apostrophe, smiling as he flip-flopped about on his clubbed feet.

A smart east London river beerhouse Hooker had aimed at, and he was close. No plywood, peeling paint, concrete floor for Hooker. It was a smart pub, almost a club. Stepped-up white miners felt important there: 'workers' in Durham, Leicestershire, Yorkshire yesterday; section managers, paymasters, even engineers today. In heat, without wives, Hooker bridged the gap of flesh and liquor. Expensive, of course, but Hooker knew that was their benchmark of quality. They needed a billiard table, a dartboard too, glass-topped tables with pictures of home, mock leather upholstery and Hooker leaning on the counter with his backdrop of booze. He supplied all. 'Clean women,' he would say quietly. 'Rubbers obligatory.' Trouble was a rarity, perhaps once in a twelve-month, and with a snub-nosed .38 in his reinforced pocket, he was his own minder. Customers paid at the counter and he allowed them through to his rest-rooms at the rear. Daytime was an ambling trade and nights were busy. Yes, mines had their own clubs, excellent clubs, but services didn't extend to procurement of ebony teenage nubile flesh.

Freddie's bank had financed Hooker's venture – 'club' it was designated on official forms – and it was a remarkable success. To the respectable of course it was out of bounds. Bank manager Freddie Freeman, respectable, without blemish, was the exception. What was out of bounds was within the bounds of business protocol. Freddie called on all his business liaisons and, if more frequently on Hooker, it was perhaps that Hooker needed more guidance. Freddie would say logically, 'There wasn't a knocking-shop, Connell, so I built one.'

But for Freddie it was a place of talk too: gossip, rumour, fact, fancy, whispers rising up from the coast. Not an African there, not even staff. You bought your spirits, lagers, by the bottle, did your own pouring and legwork. Hooker's young whores were requisitioned as the need arose, from private huts in the village.

It was smoky now, almost always a little smoky and smelling of tobacco. Ceiling fans and roof lights had never won the battle. A foursome played snooker, between shots dipped hands in a flour box and towelled away sweat, but fingers left the green baize striped and untidy. They raised hands, smiled a salutation to Freddie as he passed. Their bank manager. Hooker in the red, they probably thought, drinking too much.

Freddie went to the counter, rested his elbows on it, faced Hooker.

'Mr Freeman. Nice to see you.'

'Thank you, Hooker.'

'Soda, ice, a speck of angostura?'

'That's it.'

They spoke quietly; noise from the snooker table isolated them.

Hooker said, 'A pricey little cargo you took down to the puff-puff.'

'Yes,' Freddie said.

'Set us up for life, eh?'

'Cleared the place out, Hooker.'

'Wise.'

Freddie smiled. Drums and clanging rhythms were growing outside; he nodded towards it. 'What's the pulse, Hooker?'

'Very high,' Hooker said. 'High fever, you could say.'

'Down on the coast?'

'Everything. Troops, troops, troops, like flies on a turd.'

'Yes.'

'Release our prisoners ... imperialist, you dead man ... all that crap. A few stores alight. Cars too.'

'Dead?'

'Six.'

'Africans?'

Hooker nodded. 'Six wogs.'

'What about here?'

'You saw it, didn't you? Dicey, wouldn't you say? Me? I'm to close shop. Lay off their whores or they'll have my balls off.'

'Unpleasant,' Freddie said.

Hooker smiled a brave smile. 'Inconvenient. Don't mind leaving me bloody toes here. But a joke's a joke.'

Freddie laughed, drank back his angostura-soda, on impulse nodded to Hooker. 'It'll pass, Hooker,' he said.

Hooker raised a glass from behind the counter. It was whisky.

23

'Early,' Freddie said.

'I was thinking of my toes,' Hooker said. And then a little louder. 'Come in the office, I'll leave you with the ins and outs.' In privacy he said, 'No girls now for three days, Mr Freeman.'

'Afraid to come?' Freddie asked.

'Bloody terrified.'

'I'll just sit for ten minutes,' Freddie said. 'And move off.'

'You never drink in daylight, do you?' Hooker asked.

'No.'

'Angostura and soda? Again?'

'Another time,' Freddie said.

The sun was getting up fast now; the glare was blinding, heat bounced off the iron ground and slapped against Freddie. Noise enveloped him, the crowds: a sullenness, lowered heads and eyes as they scarcely made way for him.

At the gaolhouse, the single chain of protest was a huge broad-rimmed wheel now; seemingly invertebrate bodies, swaying, arching, chanted as they shuffled this beaten track. Freddie's soldiers from the station, bayonets still fixed, stood one at each corner of the gaolhouse building, impassive sentinels.

Freddie walked to the bank, shouldered a passage through them, pushed recalcitrant ones out of his way. He could see Mr Koffee's face behind the barred window, so that when he mounted the steps the door opened before him and was quickly shut and bolted.

'Nervous, Mr Koffee?'

Mr Koffee was looking out at the shifting crowds. 'This is not good, sir,' he said. 'Special people from the coast here, strange people, strange people for the village. Plenty big palaver, sir. Big trouble.'

'Bloody Marxists,' Freddie said.

Mr Koffee raised his hands at the world's inexhaustible

madness, a suppliant biblical servant. 'Yes, yes, Mr Freeman. And freedom from work for everyone.'

'Not a bad idea,' Freddie said.

Koffee shuffled in confusion.

'Joking, Mr Koffee,' Freddie said. 'Joking. Where are our juniors?'

'Gone, sir.'

'Gone?'

'Afraid, sir. They are afraid, you see. A kind of strike everywhere. But please, they are innocent. Afraid, sir, that is the cause.'

'Yes,' Freddie said. 'And the caretaker? Afraid, is he?'

'He too is gone. An old man, you see.'

Freddie walked to the rear windows, looked out beyond the village at the bush and scrub and palms falling downhill. Twenty yards away, a man knelt before a palm, held poised a long honed machete. On the palm trunk a four-foot glittering snake was coiled and motionless as if, unblinking, they watched each other. Then in an instant the machete was launched, lodged quivering in the wood. The snakehead dropped away first, then the body coils loosened, slipped away. The man held it up by the tail: the beautiful glittering green mamba skin. Belts were made of them and they would shine on the hotchpotch stalls down by the refuse dumps and the scavenging vultures.

'We open for business now, sir? We can manage.'

Freddie listened to the clangour of the village, the beat-beat of it, looked at the crawling mass. It was a token gesture, he knew. 'No,' he said. 'Lock up and go.'

'Tomorrow?'

'Tomorrow is another day,' Freddie said.

'Yes, sir.'

'And thank you, Mr Koffee.'

Freddie went back to the privacy of his office and sat. There had been a King Koffee up in Ashanti when Victoria was still wetting and fouling her royal bassinet. With a vast army he had decimated the strutting invincible little British force: officers were beheaded, the heart and flesh of General MacCarthy distributed to chiefs and warriors that they might chew, swallow, ingest such courage. Down on the coastal strip, eight, ten degrees north of the Equator line, steamy, most infested miles in the world, Freddie thought, Danes, Dutch, Portuguese, British had raised their trading posts then. Britain had outlived them all, bought them cheap.

Outposts of the Empire. For how long? In a corner of his office where a monster beetle had died a great relentless snake of ants were carrying off brain and viscera. They would leave a polished perfect shell. Empty. Freddie lit another cigarette.

He listened to the shooting of bolts, the rattle of keys, as Mr Koffee made fast. Then a gentle rap on his door.

'Yes?'

Mr Koffee placed the keys carefully on the desk. 'I should go now, sir?'

'Yes.'

He was a thin ageing man, in palm beach suit and black shoes like European Freddie.

'Mr Freeman, sir?'

'Yes.'

'You are respected in the village, in the mines, everywhere. This,' he nodded towards the uproar, the imbroglio of the village, 'this kill all my joy, sir.'

Freddie nodded. 'Feed my heart and flesh to the juniors, Mr Koffee.'

'Feed the juniors, sir?'

Gently Freddie said, 'Another joke, Mr Koffee, that's all. Thank you.'

He listened to the heavy snap of the outer door as Mr Koffee left. For a moment even the thunder of noise was far away and he was an entombed body, left alone at last. He cranked the telephone, lifted the handset, cranked again. A dead line.

'Am I hearing you?' he remembered. Stupid bushman. He

26

took the ring of keys and put them in his pocket, felt the letter he had received from the coast. He had forgotten it.

It was carbon-copied on flimsy tissues: pale blue anaemic carbon ink, headed 'F.F. Confidential'.

There was a dreary preface: a potted history of the years since '45, somehow composed in a histrionic whisper of self-esteem. 'Care, infinite care, Freeman, you know ...'

He read, '... there is little doubt in our minds that though hostilities may have ceased in '45, the encampment of erstwhile allies in Eastern Europe is merely the creation of a vast land base from which further to encroach on the West ... in Britain ... the USA ... grave disquiet among more sensitive observers ... and now Westminster in the hands of illiterate leftist workmen ...'

Freddie skipped through it.

Espionage was rife, it seemed ... defection, treason, dangerous government, ideologies ...

Christ, Freddie thought, all this waffle: of course there's spying and skulking and all kinds of bastardry. But it wasn't Freddie Freeman's pigeon. He went to the window and looked, like a prisoner, through the bars. People, dirt, heat, disease. A bloody mess.

When he returned to his desk again he looked at the last sheet of flimsy paper.

'... the situation as pertinent to our protectorates and colonies and overseas possessions as to Britain itself. Vigilance ... infinite care ... subversives ... black subversives ... strange faces in the community ...'

Freddie laughed, looked towards the window. Strange faces, he thought. Bloody strange faces, even Freddie Freeman's sweaty blob! And then he saw *Connell's* name!

'... a person, Connell or Conner, in your area? White, European, Irish perhaps. Immigration a blank. Does a person Connell/Conner exist? Important. Reply at once.'

Freddie crumpled up the tissues, threw them in a brass tray,

27

set them alight. They flared for a moment and were dust. He wondered if he should break a sacrosanct rule and pour himself a gill of neat malt. Did Connell exist! Ask five African wives, a score of sons, daughters, grandchildren and who else. Freddie guffawed. It was so bloody funny. Connell! Did he exist? He steeled himself against the beckoning drink.

Connell was fifty, fit as a greyhound, an Irish greyhound – 'African', Connell would say – and he had built a shanty hospice for lepers and shambling ghosts when there were hardly roads. Emerging Africans had dubbed him 'Commissar' and his patch of reclaimed bush the 'Commune'. The surrounding mines, between wars, in the lassitude of the twenties, were great sleepy uneconomical dumps.

He was Freddie's neighbour. From Freddie's hilltop bungalow, eight miles from the village, he could look down over a mile of bush at Connell's almost hidden agglomeration of shanties, formless, clean, limewashed; and the surrounding plots of vegetation. Distanced a little from them, a burial ground. Two hundred or more wooden crosses, precise, straight lines of them, might have been an incongruous patch of Flanders. Did Connell exist? Christ!

Oh, he existed, Freddie smiled. Colonial Secretariat wallahs, swanning about air-conditioned corridors on the coast, would vanish without trace. But Connell would leave a mark: wives, children, a great dynasty; and corpses if nothing else.

The heat swelled, the noise swelled, the doors were locked, the empty day stretched out before him. Tobacco, that was the solace till sundown. Connell, a spy! He should go down and find that Ringmaster CBE in his swivel, spell him out a few home truths. Bloody time-wasters.

He spread out the few remaining letters on his desk. There was a Private and Confidential, UK franked, Staff Office EC3.

'Dear Freeman,
    In these five or so post-war years it has been necessary to

28

reappraise our entire overseas structure and I am personally writing to you in deference to your sterling service since 1937 in such an isolated and difficult posting. Your work has been greatly appreciated.

The Bank, in these circumstances, is offering you generous terms of retirement which I wholeheartedly support. Though your status has been an 'acting-managerial' one, this letter automatically gives you full status and your pension and sizeable gratuity will be commensurate with that rank. At forty-eight of course you are a relatively young man and you might contemplate returning to London for administrative duties. But it is an overcrowded field at the moment, I should tell you, and I would not recommend it. Overseas commercial organizations, on the other hand, often value people of your experience, and I am sure you have many friends to steer you in that direction.

If you have immediate plans we could get a replacement out to you at short notice, but the date of departure will be at your discretion and at any convenient time in the next six months.

Again, let me reiterate the Bank's appreciation of your service. Kind wishes to your family. If you are in the UK I would expect you to call so that I can give you lunch ...'

Silence encapsulated Freddie for moments. Some faceless hyphenated bod had signed it. Retired? Fired! He went to the window again. He felt a great happiness. There were a dozen red-fezzed custodians surrounding the gaolhouse now; faces and bayonets shone in the glare, the Letter Writer before his magic machine seemed to drowse in the shade; the village was teeming, bristling; long 'crocodiles' had formed and chanted and swayed in this ludicrous charivari. Christ, Freddie thought, they had pushed him out at last! And in the right direction. Eighteen years in London but they had never posted him. Not up to the mark? It didn't fool Freddie. Married in '27 and Lucy, in an agonizing pregnancy, had brought forth their daughter within a year. It was a Saturday: he had been with a dozen other naked bodies in the rugby-bath when the news came. Good old Freddie! The unbearable dreariness of a furnished flat in Highgate (use of garden), the creeping discovery of Lucy's dead sexuality.

And then the impending war had reprieved him. It was 1937.

'Thirty-five, aren't you, Freeman?'

'Yes.'

'Wife thirty-one, daughter nine ... ten?'

'Yes.'

'We need people on the Coast. West Africa. Starting a bit old, you know. You understand? Thirty-five. Not easy.'

The young ones were on call-up for Hitler's war, Freddie knew. 'I was born in India,' he said. 'A colonial; heat doesn't worry me. Came here when I was twelve.' He smiled. 'Empire blood in the veins, you could say.'

No return smile on a bleak face. 'Yes. Hard on women out there, you realize. The Coast. Children too. Opposition, do you think?'

'No,' Freddie said.

'You could go out for a year, test the water, accommodation, all that. We'd send them out.'

'Yes ...'

This steaming pestilence had been escape from the awful suburbanity of London. Well, it was time to break a rule. Retirement! He took a bottle of malt and a glass from his cabinet, hidden from the sun. He poured a careful measure, not too much, and downed it. The chill graciousness of the letter. The The chill graciousness might have had the terminal lash of doom administered in the cosy permanence of an upholstered surgery. But it was freedom, a sudden realization of escape, escape from the tunnel. Death was life. He put the retirement letter carefully in his pocket and locked away the rest.

Freddie took a white felt hat, a little fingered and soiled, and stuck it on at its usual forward tilt. With his keys he treble-locked the bank's main doors behind him. He stood on the steps, a strange symbol of supremacy, looking out on the frightening untapped ebullience of energy.

There was a concrete lean-to annexed to the bank, where Freddie's car was insulated from every angle of the sun. A year ago he had bought it and wondered, even to the last moments, about extravagance and impermanence. Its deep blue, in shadow, the metal strength beneath its beautiful lines, comforted him now. He could use it where he was going; he was free. It was a Humber Snipe, almost the last of its breed.

He pushed into the crowd that would normally have opened out a road for him but now had to be hooted at, almost bumped.

He saw Connell walking up the hill from the markets, standing in the same shade as the Letter Writer. Connell wore full-length cotton slacks, a multi-coloured African shirt hanging loose at the waist, toe-grip sandals on bare feet, a straw floppy hat that he might have made himself. Connell was fifty. In the distance and glare, this tall limber figure might have been more than a decade younger.

Freddie edged in and parked on the uncluttered ground of the Letter Writer. Connell looked at him, at the closed doors of the bank, and waited.

Freddie stepped out; he said, 'Cleared the lot this morning. Twenty boxes only. A few pebbles too. They're windy down there on the coast. Plenty palaver.'

Connell nodded. 'Palavers today, cadavers tomorrow.'

'You think so, Connell?'

At close quarters Connell's face, though still having youth, showed the wear and tear of twenty-eight years of wet heat and pestilence. But you looked at him and felt his strength, hardness.

When Freddie had come out in '37 he had spent long months stop-gapping: the beginnings and ends of furloughs, appointments, illness, retirements, until they had found him his village bank, hardly more than a holding shed for ingots and brown

31

pebbles, and his bungalow, finally rid of an ailing predecessor. It was a small appointment and he knew it. Once a month they had sent him notes and coin for whiteman's cheques, blackman's pebbles and wages. In '38 he had come to stay and Connell had walked up the mile from his strange little patch of reclamation, swinging a bottle of Scotch. The sun had just vanished and palms were black against a yellow strip of horizon. When light came, they still sat on Freddie's verandah, empty beer bottles, the whisky bottle too, scattered between them; and when within a year Lucy and Jane arrived, he had, during Freddie's bank chores in the village, settled them in, showed them the ropes.

Connell was a friend. Who is Connell? ... That damned idiot down at the Secretariat ...

Connell now was looking at the heaving village, the soldiery by the gaolhouse, arms at the slope, the eternal moving ring of pilgrimage.

'Times have changed, Freddie.'

'By God, they have.'

Connell was silent.

'Lucy's on her own out there.' Freddie nodded towards the distant hills. 'Looks a bit below par the past week, wouldn't you think, Connell?'

'Yes.'

'Sent her up north in July, remember? High ground up there, cooler. Give her a break, I thought. With friends for a while, you know. English. Surrey, I think. Pictures on the walls, garden tools, forks, rakes, a poodle like something you wind up, all that bloody rubbish. But a nine-hole course there. Reservoir. Cold showers. Like home she said. Christ, home!' Freddie paused, remembered it. 'It seemed to do the trick,' he said. 'I looked at her. A1, I thought.'

Connell said, 'She's on her own out there now?'

'At the bungalow. She's on her own.'

Connell waited.

'Jane?' Freddie asked.

32

'Yes?'

Freddie's affection showed for a moment and then a faint irritation. 'Well, she's sparking about with some engineer fellow from Public Works, Connell. A bridge out on the creek and he whips her off today to see his handiwork. A Scot, I think. Out there for the dry season. Near the end of it now.' Freddie looked at the grey burning sky. 'Can't remember his name. But there's something sour about Scots, gets up my bloody nose.'

'Lorimer,' Connell said. 'I met him. Once.'

Freddie examined Connell's face. 'You disliked him, didn't you?'

Connell was silent.

'Forget I said that, Connell. Fathers and daughters, you know.' Freddie laughed.

Connell said, 'It's five miles to the bridge, the creek. You could pick her up.'

'Half an hour on that bush track to the bridge. Maybe more. And back. Murder on springs and "shocks".'

'To the bungalow,' Connell said. 'Back to the bungalow.'

Freddie was suddenly aware of the disruption of the village, the howl. He and Connell had been face to face to make themselves heard.

'I should pick her up, should I, Connell?'

'Yes.'

'It's not safe any more?'

'Anywhere.'

A little spark of alarm showed in Freddie's eyes. 'And Lucy?'

'Lucy is safe.'

'You've seen to it?'

'Yes.'

Freddie nodded. 'Thank you, Connell.'

Connell's bicycle was propped behind the Letter Writer's tree: an ancient indestructible Raleigh, gear lever on the cross-bar, a gear case, a great cowling over the chain drive, a bell, even a carbide lamp.

He rolled it out and stood before Freddie. 'You shipped everything out, did you?'

Freddie nodded. 'Gold and pebbles.'

'Banknotes?'

Freddie stared at him. 'That bad, is it, Connell?'

'How much?' Connell asked.

'Twenty thousand, maybe. Cheques to meet every day, black-man's wages, pebbles across the counter . . .'

'Wait,' Connell said; he took a few paces and sent a small boy, swift as a bat, towards the market stalls.

'I have a call at the gaolhouse,' Connell said. 'Soon. Fifteen minutes with the dying.'

'Dying?'

'Yes.'

Freddie looked at the restless skin of humanity. 'Christ, how do I get through that!'

'Get your daughter,' Connell told him; he held the huge heavy coil-springed saddle of the bicycle, looked at Freddie's car. 'Lucy is all right,' he said. 'I'll be drinking your whisky when you're home.'

Freddie looked at Connell's bicycle now, its age, its weight. 'Eight miles to the bungalow, to Lucy, Connell.'

'On tracks, two wheels are faster than four.'

The small boy was suddenly back with a large crocodile bag, and gone as quickly again. A son, a grandson, Freddie thought.

'Get your notes,' Connell said. 'I'll wait.'

He watched Freddie's progress, slowed, impeded, as he tacked against the current to the bank. The Letter Writer raised himself up: tall, fleshless, a gaunt bearded face. He spoke village dialect to Connell.

'Dying by hunger. He has courage.' He bowed imperceptibly to Connell, a gesture of deference.

'Yes,' Connell said.

'You are going to see him now? The last time?'

'The last time.'

34

He rubbed his fingers along Connell's palm. 'Touch his hands for me. My respect.' He slid his typewriter on to a padded handcart and secured it. 'He will die soon?'

'Tonight,' Connell said.

He held out to Connell a small snakeskin wallet; then moved through the crowd without effort. It closed about him; he was gone.

Connell opened the wallet. There were pale blue carbon-copied flimsy sheets folded inside. A letter without provenance or date. 'F.F. Confidential.' Without even signature. He glanced at the final page: '. . . a person, Connell or Conner, in your area? White, European, Irish perhaps. Immigration a blank. Does a person Connell/Conner exist? Important. Reply at once.' 'F.F.' was Freddie Freeman, he supposed.

Freddie had closed the bank door and was pushing across with his laden holdall. Connell came out of the shade to meet him at the heating metal of the car.

'Twenty-two thousand, near as dammit,' Freddie said; he put it in the boot, locked it. 'It's serious, Connell, is it?'

Connell said, 'The beginning, I suppose.'

'Of the end?'

'Your guess and mine.'

'That damn brainless Scot taking Jane out there.' Freddie held out his hands. 'Times like these. He must know the goddamn score.'

'His name is Lorimer,' Connell reminded.

'And Lucy?'

'Hurry,' Connell said. 'I'll be drinking your whisky, remember.'

For moments Connell watched him inch his way across the village: it would take a long time. He walked with his bicycle, unimpeded as the Letter Writer, to the gaolhouse. A soldier hammered with a rifle butt. The doors opened for him.

★

Connell stood inside. The village lawman, gaoler now, adjusted bars and bolts. A fat man; he disliked Connell who mixed his blood with their women. The air was a stench. Away from the glare, there was a kind of twilight imprisoned in the concrete box. Only at eave-level did heat and light force an entry and remain in suspension.

This was the gaoler's office: bare concrete, a table, a chair, a naked light bulb, a metal drum for food refuse. For other refuse too, Connell knew: always there were the empty palm wine jars beneath the table and the acid tang of inspissating urine. There was a sanilav thunderbox in the corner, but in long mosquito hours to midnight and after, it was easier to pull the metal drum between fat legs and let the bladder empty itself. One could let the day's heat dispose of it too.

The lawman-gaoler was a man of power in piping days, but they might be crumbling. He listened to the village, looked at Connell. On this interminable surveillance he had folded and put aside the weight of his King's uniform and trappings, for bare feet, shorts, a string vest. Flies settled on the thunderbox lid, seemed to scrape at the metal for whatever stale excrement was below. Behind him was an iron-framed door to a passage-way, three barred cells.

'It used to be quiet here, Connell, remember?'

'You could sleep,' Connell said. The village dialect was a lilting monosyllabic gobble. 'You should empty that shit-box, wash out that drum, pass the time.'

'Leave my gaol door open?'

'There's bayonets out there.'

'For who?'

Connell shrugged.

'How long more,' the gaoler squealed at him. 'How long more, Connell! How long this bastard live, live, live! How long your bastard live, Connell?'

Connell waited for energy to flag and there was a kind of panting silence. '*Mr* Connell,' he reminded him.

The gaoler measured him. 'What did you say?'

'Mr Connell.'

'You Mr Connell?'

'I am Mr Connell.'

'You go shit, Connell. And your mongrel dying bastard blood in there. You go smell him.'

On the table there was a service revolver, clean, shining. Connell saw the creeping movement towards it. He brought the sudden force of a hammer fist on the paling fingers. The gaoler squealed again, in pain now. A pig squeal. Connell swiped the revolver across the grinding concrete.

There was a knocking at the entrance door of the gaolhouse. Connell opened it.

The uniformed man said 'You all right, Mr Connell?'

'Yes, sergeant.'

The sergeant appraised the fat man at the table.

'Everything is fine.' Connell watched him go; he bolted the door, looked at the gaoler. 'In what field is the enemy?' he said. 'Hard to know.'

To the lawman-gaoler, colonial servant, Connell was white 'nothing', a great shame across the infinite distance to His Britannic Majesty: Connell naked astride his tramp women from the bush, black tramp women, filling their bellies with his mongrel spawn; filling his white shacks out there with cast-out rot and sickness.

The gaoler was his Majesty's servant, clothed, paid to obey, to punish. But he listened to the village tumult again and was in fear of it. If madness came suddenly, which way would the bayonets point?

Connell nodded at the door behind. 'Open,' he said. 'I want to visit.'

'I could say no visit for no one. My power, you see?'

'You could,' Connell said. 'You've said it a lot of times.'

'Come back when he's dead for skin and bone.'

'You could say that.'

'I am saying it.' The gaoler donned his tunic coat, a drape of authority. 'You come every day. How many days? Forty days I let you in. You bastard. I count them.' He sprung the fresh authority of whiteman's lingo now. 'Out there, every day, more noise, more shout, more shit because what? Because this!' He pointed back towards the cells. 'You nothing, Connell. I man in charge!'

Connell nodded, moved towards the exit door. 'That sergeant doesn't like you,' he said. 'Thinks you're too loyal, maybe,' he said. 'When killing comes, Mr Gaoler, how many soldiers will the King have?' He began to unbolt the door, looked at the gaoler's fat buttocks. 'I could tell him where to put his bayonet. Twelve inches.'

Connell paused; there was almost silence inside the concrete box.

'Ten minutes,' the gaoler said. 'You have ten minutes.' He opened his cell block, turned away his head from the sudden effluvium of death and slammed the door tight on it.

Connell faced three open-barred cells. He had known the smells of death for so many years; but the dreadful odour of starvation halted him; death was very close, he knew. He took cigarettes from his shirt pocket: dark indigenous weed of tangy bitterness. The cigarette packet showed a grinning blackman's face with dangling fag and curling ropes of smoke. Connell drew on the cigarette, drew it to soddenness, ground it out. Two cells were empty, even of a pallet.

The third housed an army camp bed, a basin of liquid disinfectant, vapid, subsumed in death. There was a wooden stool. Connell looked at the near-death's-head bound in brittle glass, it might seem, lying on the pillow he had brought him a long time ago. Beneath a pale grey sheet there might not have been a body: skeletal head, shoulders, arms, that was all. A dry skin in steaming heat.

Connell placed his hand on the forehead: the coolness was

creeping death; the fingers stirred; the eyes, in their deep pits, diminishing, strove to focus. Connell leant above him, battled with the rancid breath. He had watched him die each airless day, from times of fear and uncertainty, the first rapid loss of weight and then the slow diminution; the days of a cold body battling back to moments of warmth as if rallying forces against the iron resolve to perish; the body consuming itself, its own sustenance, until now there was nothing. Connell had sat with sleeplessness, delirium, the agony of starvation, unbearable grips of pain in the emptiness. Only the brain, almost untouched, would survive to the last hours. Connell rubbed the cold hands.

'The Letter Writer,' he said.

He sat and drank from a metal flask, drank again; he smoked the stained bitter tobacco; he listened until the village clamour pervaded and seemed to distance him even from his own breathing. The body on the camp bed trembled in a moment of convulsion; and then stillness again.

1950. Strange, Connell thought: this, the half century; and this, a son, not half the half century yet, twenty-four years born, already at the end of his journey.

As if death might put conquerors to shame!

'Five minutes!' the gaoler was shouting from his office. 'Five minutes, you hear?'

Some deep shame in the bowels of conquerors? This death's-head had been handsome once: mulatto skin, hardly a coarseness of nose or lips; a body, tall, balanced, fashioned for hardship. Its mother had come to Connell, a child. Sixteen years, perhaps, standing naked, beautiful before him; taut jet black glistening skin, laughing, waiting for the game to be played. That was her 'love' for him: laughing, tumbling, opening her body's doors to him. She was old now; women were old at forty: flesh gathered on thighs and buttocks, hung on them, breasts lengthened, flattened. She sat by Connell's stall at the railway halt now and traded; returned to share a roof with his other women, wept for her son then. Wives and children: children had grown and gone, but there were always children; in the suspension of the womb, crawling the earthen compound, searching the bush, running with the speed of hunters. He was their Connell; they worked for him, with him, made lives for themselves. Only his secluded hospice shanties were avoided in a wasted fear of the awful consuming malady he tended, horrendous faces they sometimes glimpsed. . .

Connell gazed at the dying wraith before him, listened to the village's raucous dirge for its sacrifice. . .

He had spent two years, part of a third, clearing his compound in the bush. A quarter of a century gone. Now half of it spent. He had laboured with his women, and bushmen who would work an erratic pattern of days for wine or tobacco: scrub and brush had to be hacked and roots dug out to let light and sunshine reach the earth, in patches bring grass to life. Clusters of wine-palms remained and were tapped: the birth of Connell's 'brewery'. The women brought goats and fowl. From where? The village, eight miles trek from them, was beginning to stir with discovery of manganese. The railway halt, a wooden platform and roof; provision stores, the gaol, missionary settlements, three, four sheds that served for churches: all these were, for Connell, his source of building materials. The primitive shelters gave way to one-roomed huts with doors and windows, corrugated iron roofs. Connell had marks to show for his enterprise, watchmen had marks too, when cowled disguised thugs came out of the darkness to thieve. Then two dying lepers had been left in his compound – omen of evil – and he had set apart their refuge and given them shelter. Their number grew and, unwittingly, they were his defence. The black and white blotches of leprosy, ulcers, grotesque faces, wasting limbs, drew a circle of fear about his compound.

It was then he had first visited the village in daylight. There were enough whites from the mines – almost obsolete, beginning to stir – goings, comings, new faces, that he could move without risk.

But the Letter Writer had bowed courteously to him. 'There is no danger for you here,' he said.

Connell looked at the strange dignity of his face, younger then but with the same mildly smiling eyes. The Letter Writer: a wooden case of rubber type, a composing stick, a brush of black dye, paper from where he might find it or filch it.

'Are you hiding?'

'Yes.'

'Have no fear.'

Connell nodded.

It was a day of clear sky and burning sunshine. Africans brought their produce from wherever there was an arable patch: yams, breadfruit, pineapple, plaintain, enamel basins of guinea-fowl eggs; they had already established their stalls by the railway halt. They came in idly too from the bush to wander, stare at new buildings, squat, to talk and palaver in the shade.

'I will get you a typewriter,' Connell said. 'Old but good.'

The Letter Writer had laughed. 'I will care for it.'

Not more than fifty persons stood or walked in the village; and perhaps half a dozen whites, mines foremen, an agent from a building site, a nondescript passing through.

Suddenly a white face was shouting, wobbling: he was drunk at midday, had stumbled against Africans, seemed to complete a strange morris-like dance as he fell to the dust. There was silence, little titters of laughter that were gone in an instant. He raised himself up, a great sweaty man. At random he picked an African and beat him. Not just a single punch or kick but a methodical savage attack. He left him bleeding, barely conscious.

'Dirty stinking wog!' He stared at the silent impassive onlookers, who didn't dare meet his gaze. 'Wogs. Filthy creeping wogs!'

Connell had for a moment been shocked and then rage had begun to take hold of him. The Letter Writer – a grip of steel – had held his wrist.

'You must let it pass. The whiteman is always right.'

41

'Christ!' Connell swore.

'Christ said, turn the other cheek,' the Letter Writer said. 'The Mission Schools teach it.'

'Police?'

'Black police, whiteman's money. They carry his gun. Kill a blackman. No questions.'

Connell stared at the Letter Writer for a long time. 'No one rebels?'

'A little flare on the coast. Once in a year, in two years. A few dead blackmen. No more.'

'A school,' Connell said; he had walked away across the village, into the bush, to find his track. They needed pride. Iron. A school...

Connell listened to the village and its anger. He thought of Freddie, in sweat, somewhere on the whorls and twists of the red dirt road down to the creeks for his precious Jane. Arrogant randy little bitch, Connell smiled. Hardly in her teens, more than a decade past, pert and well-made, she would watch him coming across the compound and stand naked on the verandah for him. 'Mamba!' Connell had howled at her once and sent her running for cover, hands on her buttocks. A spicy dish for escort, Lorimer. A Scot, Freddie had said; but Connell knew better. The past for Connell, beyond twenty-eight years, was distant as a fairytale but never erased. They weren't forgotten: the Presbyterian wariness of eye, the straight line of lip, the nuances and snaps of speech that a sliver of Scottish-Irish sea could make. Connell knew better. Lorimer was a loyal man of Ulster.

Long, long ago, Connell remembered, he had squatted on Ulster hills, where their Antrim skirts touched the sea, and in fair weather gazed at the line of Scotland's coast: behind him, his father's house, secure, its bow windows and dormers aglow. The house of the schoolmaster, the dominie. Inside, old cared-for furniture, pictures, brass, ancient polished timbers. And, rosewood-framed, Their Gracious Majesties George and the impeccable Mary Regina. The schoolmaster, a loyal man of

Ulster too, two dead sons, lost for ever in the Passchendaele mud, to prove it. And a Catholic! The Passchendaele mud of 1917. A mother and sisters had wept that day, he remembered. The dominie had stood in his doorway, stiff-lipped, perhaps a little proud. Connell, sixteen-year-old last of the males, had fled the grief, from cover watched the Catholic imperial face in the doorway. The house had been emptied of warmth that glory never restored, time was a featureless passage. Only the November day, Armistice, when Empire finally triumphed over evil, was stamped on his mind and retina. The schoolmaster had intoned a power of prayer at bedtime, a booming thanksgiving. There was weeping renewed, a mere shadow of happiness too, even a glass in the schoolmaster's hand with a cautious spoonful of malt. The world was right again. And while at Versailles were arranged specious lines and curves of peace, the schoolmaster had found for him, John Connell, the last of his male seed – with proper deference to his betters of course – a loyal place to pursue scholarship and excellence.

He had been happy then, he remembered. But peacemakers had come to arrange the lines and curves of Ulster too, and the blackguardism of decades and centuries had set course for putsch and pogrom. The parameters were set, the bonfires lit: red flames, songs of praise, incontrovertible bibles, terror. 1922.

The house of dignity was razed, the papish schoolmaster's house, and in the flames perished again the dead photogravured sons, Their Royal Highnesses; and, in the flesh, the dominie himself, immovable, found, a charred grotesque cinder, locked in shattered allegiance unto death in his study...

'You ready in there?' the gaoler was shouting.

Connell looked at the defiant cadaver before him, pale brown skin grown paler, sunken eyes where the body's fat had vanished, teeth and gums pushing out of a gaping orifice. A sudden shock of convulsion rattled agains the chain-linked metal of the bed, peaked and subsided. Stillness. But life gripped to the very bone. Connell listened to the village. The stench gathered about him.

43

He drank and smoked again. The gaoler shouted. Connell took out and read the flimsy letter; he read again, '... Does a person ... Connell ... exist? ...' Like Freddie Freeman, he set it alight. He watched it fall, almost like dust, to the concrete floor...

He had stood at the schoolmaster's graveside. A day of pouring rain, a handful of frightened people, a careful ambivalent curate, praying, aspersing. Women had been sent away. Connell had lighted a cigarette and dropped the burning match on the coffin's engravement. There was silence. He waited until all, even the gravedigger, had dispersed. 'James Albert Connell,' he read. 'Aged 60 years. May He Rest in Peace.' He took the shovel and backfilled the sodden earth, made a careful mound. There were no wreaths or tributes. And he had walked back a silent mile to the domicile of James Albert Connell, now a pyramid of rubble embraced in dwarf stumps of masonry still lodged in their footings. All that remained was a barn, removed from the dwelling, a lonely monument set against rolling hills and rock-land. Its annexe was a garden shed, a workshop.

There was a fowling-piece there, he knew: expensive, oiled, polished, beautiful. Before he had sailed out in the darkness for Liverpool he had left dead two Royal Constabulary men, their faces blown away, in some Belfast loyalist midden. Two barrels only, he had thought. There should have been three: two for Passchendaele, one for schoolmaster James Albert Connell.

The West Africa lines sailed out of the Mersey and at first port of call he had vanished into the unlit lanes and tracks; and then the hinterland, the bush, the scrub, the jungle, where Christ himself might have been lost. He had been eighteen days at sea. 'Does a person, Connell, exist? ...'

The gaoler shouted, 'I want you at the door *now*, see! When I open, you jump out! Jump out! I want no more coffin smell in my face. You hear? ... You hear?'

Connell rested his hands on the pale dying ones, put his lips on the forehead, cold now again. 'The Letter Man,' he said.

'You ready?' the fat man shouting.

Connell crossed and jolted his hip against the door. It was opened.

'Out!' The closing door sped past Connell's shoulder; the gaoler's face, his body tightened against the reek. 'I give you ten minutes, you take twenty,' he said; he kicked the empty wine jars by his desk. 'You give something too.'

'Advice,' Connell said. 'You have a village somewhere. Go home.'

The gaoler spat, opened his main doors on the village mass, let noise flood in about them. 'I am His Majesty's servant,' he said. 'I can kill. I am the judge.'

Connell took his bicycle from the shade and moved across the village towards the bush tracks that ran north and west. On the hillock by his palm tree the Letter Writer stood, unencumbered now by his precious furnishings and machinery. He had come to wait.

'Yes,' Connell said.

'You spoke my name?'

'Yes.'

'You have forgotten how to weep?'

'A long time ago.'

'He will die soon?'

'The cold hours after midnight.'

The Letter Writer held out his palm and Connell touched it, returned the snakeskin wallet.

'There is more,' the Letter Writer said. 'This too.'

It was a small scrap this time, folded to rest between finger and thumb. 'C known to you. Delay. Murder. Crown Forces. Ulster. 1922. Await warrant, escort. No reply.'

Connell looked at the sharp tightening profile of the Letter Writer; age was lessening him, enhancing dignity; from his hillock he gazed down across the village.

'From where?' Connell asked.

'Army.'

'You have friends?'

45

'The Army is my friend,' the Letter Writer said.

'The Army knows?'

'It is not message for Army. For Mr Freeman.'

'For Mr Freeman?'

'What Mr Freeman get, I get.'

'Yes,' Connell said. He took the long beautiful hands of the Letter Writer. 'They send whiteman for whiteman, you see?'

'Respect,' the Letter Writer said.

Connell nodded; he pushed his bicycle across to the perimeter road of the village where a funeral cortège, drawn into the pulse of noise, swayed, moved rhythmically along, the bare board coffin shouldered by young men towards the church. Ahead, a strange vanguard of strolling footballers – striped jerseys, stockings, studded boots – slid the ball one to another, or from head to head: the shreds of ritual, sending a colleague with honour to God. Respect.

It passed. Connell crossed the road, moved towards the bush, out of sight, to find his path. It curved and undulated, tunnelled through the scrub at times, but it was smooth from compacted decades, a century perhaps of bare leather-skinned feet. It was a silent track today, had emptied itself into the village...

Freddie Freeman's bungalow – eight miles of gentle pushing – sat on the plateau of a steep erupted hill. Connell left his bicycle and walked the winding road to the summit.

Creeks were dead-ends, almost stagnant fissures of water, dark, deep, or shallow, reaching down from the mainstreams even ten miles distant. The heavy bush and scrub crowded to the water's edge, canopied over it; plant life took root in the mud basin and its foliage gathered like slime on the surface. Creeks seemed to soak sunshine, without reflection, into their depths.

The banks had been cleared at the locus of Lorimer's bridge. Helmeted, in drill shorts, stout boots, stockings rolled down, a bush-shirt open to the navel, he seemed to stand on guard over his 'prisoners', surveyed every movement of the site. He didn't need foremen; frighteners, whippers, greedy renegades from villages far afield, did the job for him. Three stood behind him. He gave them each a pound note, a very sizeable 'dash', a sop: wages of a doss-labourer for one week.

'No one go from job, see. Savvy?'

'Sah!'

'No one go for village, no one go for bush.'

'Yes, sah!'

He nodded, pointed to palm wine calabashed in the shade, watched them drink in great mouthfuls.

They were greedy. 'Enough, you bastards. Enough!' he shouted.

Big fleshy men, clad like Lorimer; the black oily faces nodded, smiled. They carried bush-clearing knives, broad-bladed, cusped, feather-edged; and hardwood staves thonged about the wrists.

It took thirty men to do fifteen men's work in this wasted country, Lorimer thought; and lazy creeping ones needed a rod across their backs to stay awake. You arranged that they managed each other, that was the whiteman's trick. Water was being passed hand to hand from the shore, along the escarpment, to the tanks of concrete mixers. A small boy beat on a drum, a resonant monotony to ease the monotony of labour.

Lorimer's trio passed along the line, prodded and struck with their staves, the pain and profanity drowned in the hammer of machinery. For a moment the line was broken and an ageing man scampered away in fear, along the creek bank, out of sight into the bush. There was no escape. The trio stood and watched. Lorimer watched them. Screaming suddenly came back from beneath the distant tangle of growth. The drum beat faster, the five-gallon pails moved faster too from hand to hand. The trio spread out to bring the message of industry wherever it was needed.

Lorimer went carefully down the slope to the water; the

screams were lessening now. A minder shouted warning to him but he waved him away. He pushed meticulously, foot by foot, into the twilight of woven and plaited growth.

He saw the scorpions first, an army of them only yards ahead, giant scorpions, five, six inches of somehow repulsive segmented bodies, barbed tails curved above them, darting into shade and cover.

The almost naked labourer had crashed into this nest of poison, unspeakable pain. The screaming ceased, consciousness had been blotted out. There were moments of silence before the bush stirred again. How many barbs had struck, how great was the agony? In the green filtered light Lorimer was afraid. He looked at the canopy above him, at his feet, the burrows and clefts about him, and sensed movement everywhere. He turned and fled, fought back the scream that was rising, held it down to a whimper. The blinding sun and glare, reached at last, had almost a healing beauty. He stood and watched the water gang, the changeless rhythm; eyes looked past him at the bush, dead motionless eyes that could see his fear.

'Faster!' he shouted; he saw a minder in the distance, with shouldered stave, turn to make the journey back. The drummer boy quickened the pace again and watched the uneven stream of overload.

'Faster!'

Lorimer climbed the battered slope to level ground, the crawling scorpion army still in his mind. The sweat was cold on his forehead but he stood there, determined, intrepid commander, surveying the battle. He looked at the horizon; for days a greyness had been creeping along the distant line.

His bridge would be a hundred-foot span. On opposing shores stout concrete retaining walls and abutments faced each other; and the centre pier, in mid-creek, had begun as a rectangular coffer of sheet-piles, emptied near dry of water, shaped into a massive bulk: an agglomeration of reinforcing bar and concrete. The steel span, from abutment to abutment, would rest on it.

Lorimer walked back to his machinery stockpiles. Farther along, raised on concrete blocks, in deep shade, was his site office where Jane Freeman had kissed a finger, put it on his lips and said, 'Don't be too long.'

Lorimer was afraid of her. Clothed, she could smile, show tongue and wet lips, appear naked! Fourteen days since he had seen her down on the waterfront, on the coast: the UK ship out of Liverpool was berthed and she had come down the gangway, letting little flurries of breeze show her thighs and underwear. He was dazzled, confused, shocked. Big Freeman from the village bank had embraced her and she had looked over her shoulder and smiled. His twenty-eight-year-old puritan, perhaps virgin, soul was helpless in the face of damnation. In a few days he had called on her...

Jane Freeman had a special kind of beauty: tiny infinitesimal faults, shrewd humorous glances. You found her watching you. Brown hair came to her shoulders. It somehow amounted to beauty. Her body, quick and decisive, or graceful too, could turn heads. And she was unaffectedly amoral.

She lay now in his site office; she had invaded it. 'This is special, Alec, very very special.' A broad trestle table for a quire or more of dog-eared blueprints, kerosene fridge, hanging shelves of delph, cutlery, cooking pans; a bunk bed and pallet; tools of the trade stacked in corners: levels, pins, ranging rods; 'Very special, Alec,' she said, kicking off sandals, arranging herself supine on the bunk bed. She had closed her eyes and he had looked at the contours of breasts and hips and thighs. Bare shoulders, arms and legs, seemed to undress her once more.

He struggled without hope. Cleanliness, he thought; cleanliness, peace, a state of grace; the staunch impregnable Ulster heritage, its surrounding palisade of trees and sanctity, where elders came to sit with his parent patriarch; Sunday prayers, orations, lessons, the ineffable warmth of salvation: an armour...

But he had looked at her again, watched the smallest movement of body, heard the sound of clothing and soft skin.

He took a site helmet and dropped it on the wooden floor, and as he bent to retrieve it he had said, 'Sorry, I wakened you.'

'I wasn't asleep,' she said. 'I wanted you to look. Not bad, am I?'

He had fitted the helmet, stuck a dim-book and pencil in his bush-shirt pocket, anxious to move.

'You look like you caught your hand in the poor box,' she said. 'And you did look. I squinted once or twice.'

He let it pass. 'Don't you want to see the Works?' he had said.

'Yes, please.'

'The bridge, machinery, the creek?'

'Hurry back,' she had said. 'Put those black sods in top gear and hurry back ...'

Lorimer walked now and stood between the concrete mixers: great ugly sculptures of machinery, stained, oil-smeared, sending out the incessant hammer of their engines, the grind of the mixing drums. A crane swung out its half-yard skip of steaming concrete to the coffer in mid-stream, and a crew, balanced on uneven piles and timbers, shot the load on the pronged case of reinforcing. A vibrator clattered on and on, its long phallic poker, reaching deep down, settling the smooth mix, closing the voids.

Lorimer looked at the grey horizon again and watched the staves of his minders prodding, prodding, clouting when they saw need.

He shouted at the mid-stream gang propped above the creek. 'How deep?'

They lowered down a calibrated rod to touch the concrete: eight, nine feet still to be topped. Eight, nine feet was twenty-seven yards cube, give or take, he knew. Twenty-seven yards was fifty-four mixes. Restless, he watched the loading gangs at the hopper, shovelling sand and stone, breaking in the heavy paper bags of cement. 'Faster,' he said. 'And keep it fast.'

He thought of the dead fugitive down in the bush and looked at his scattered gang of moving bodies: sly, lazy, ready to sleep;

a whole vast country under their feet since the beginning of time and only mud huts, spears and knives to show for it. Work was discipline, the purpose of things: they had lessons to learn.

Their sloth rubbed off on the weak too, the unwary. He thought of the site office, the arrangement of desire, the rubbing of flesh and flesh, the rustling of clothes. For him, lessons to be learned.

Standing back from the window of the office, Jane Freeman watched him. A fine stallion, she thought. Tall enough, erect, shoulders and calves pushed back so that hips and pelvis jutted; he had the features, handsome, of a pious prig; beneath the helmet brown close-cropped hair seemed bleached in the heat. It would be strange, exciting to lay this wary beast. He had begun to walk towards the office.

She positioned herself carefully again on the bunk. No longer supine, she was reclining against a mound of garments and a pillow, some bodice buttons undone, one leg, instep arched, pointing at the door; the other drawn up, knee high.

Lorimer might have had righteous words of reproof at the ready when he opened the door but he was halted as if by sudden ictus at this wild sensuous abandon.

'Oh my God!' he said.

'Come here, Alec,' Jane Freeman said prettily. 'Come and sit beside me. And a little kiss. That would be nice for starters.'

Lorimer was rooted.

'Well?'

Lorimer said, 'Surely you must be aware ... surely ...'

'Nonsense and rubbish,' she said. 'You're a big big boy who can eat whole Africans with a pinch of salt and you're afraid of poor little me.'

'You must be aware of our position here.'

'I took a great deal of care with my position, Alec. I wish you'd do the same.'

Lorimer went to the window. This exposition of warm carelessly draped flesh, and within reach, was unbearable. He threw off the site helmet that had soaked in the heat. There was a holy trick of contemplation to drench desire with ugliness: he gazed at the slime of the scarcely moving creek, watched the great vomiting discharge of concrete from the drums: two labourers squatted side by side, on their haunches, to defecate and converse, shaking their heads and buttocks when they laughed; their legs were scarred and wasted. He thought of the poisoned disfigured man in the scorpion nest.

'Alec,' she whispered.

Suddenly, reflected in the window, he could see her, both knees drawn up now and thighs exposed; a shimmering image, a smiling magnificent succubus. He closed his eyes, remembered the stony or sandy beaches of home, instants of sunshine and then the grey filter of cloud again; the female undressings under drapes or in rented boxes before they scuttled, knock-kneed, to the cover of the sea; wind and blue-blotched skin, sagging costumes or blubberous ones, amorphous monsters...

'Alec!' she said.

He heard her bare feet moving on the floor. He turned. She stood, her back to the door.

'I'm going to shatter our colonial image, Alec.' She was smiling at him.

He said, 'Don't you worry what *I'll* think of you?'

'Later.'

He remembered decent words to recite. 'We respect our women, see them coming to us with dignity.'

'No fun?'

'Fun?'

'Mater and Pater, Alec? After a day's honest toil, a tumble?' She leant forward to whisper. 'Upstairs for tricks on the bedside rug?'

'Oh God,' he said.

She let her dress fall to the floor, stepped out of her dainty pants. The beauty, the soft pale cream flesh in the heat and humidity seemed framed in an almost-visible aura.

She held the door ready to open. 'I'm going to step out there now. Just like this. And run. And you'll come to save me, Alec, won't you? Those animal drooling men, savages. And your minders. You'll catch me, of course, and I'll struggle a little. And you'll drag me back for punishment and obedience.'

Lorimer shouted at her.

'They'll enjoy it out there, Alec. Sad sad whiteman has to strip his woman and tie her down! They'll like to think about that when the big stick falls on their backs. No pain at all, only sorrow for poor Master Lorimer.'

She turned with catwalk grace and commenced her exit. He rushed at her. 'No!'

She wriggled, slapped, groped, in her sham battle to escape; everywhere his hands touched flesh, slid along it. Virtue was taking flight. He pushed. She did a little tripping caper and tumbled on the bunk.

It was over. The battle was lost. Won.

He threw his clothes down, kicked them away. He was the stallion now indeed, rearing above her in his huge leather boots and socks.

'Alec,' she said. 'Haven't you forgotten something?'

'Forgotten?'

'A rubber, my precious.'

'A rubber?'

'A rubber, a sheath, a condom, a letter, you arsehole!'

'I don't carry them,' he said. 'But I'm going to give you everything I've got. Won't that be nice?'

'Jesus!' She was out of bed like a wounded spirit, a sheet wrapped round her, a ranging rod like a broadsword to ward him off.

'And you can scream your tits off,' he said. 'No one hears, no one cares.'

And then came the blessed sound: Freddie Freeman's car arriving on site. They glimpsed its roof as it passed down towards the mixing plant.

'Oh Christ!' Lorimer shouted. 'Oh Christ!'

Shorts, shirt, underwear that had fallen away at the prospect of sin were props for slapstick comedy now: boots suddenly grown larger, a lost and found shirt, inside-out sleeves, tangled underpants. He fell and pulled himself upright, dragged at his shorts. Everything was somehow awry, even his cropped hair.

He made for the door. To waylay Freeman, win time, was the tactic. 'Get dressed! Get dressed!' he shouted.

'Your helmet,' she said; she handed it to him. 'I *am* dressed.'

He looked at her calm undisturbed propriety; hardly need for tactics now. She was covered and modest, combing her long brown hair.

When he was on the threshold, she said, 'Your flies, Alec.'

He had a hand for each: the door, the zip. He pulled them with equal venom. She heard the great bellow of surprised pain, entanglement, the groans of field surgery. Quietly she would get that animal. He would pay.

She opened the door and said, 'I hope you lost three inches, you bastard!'

Lorimer gritted his teeth against the nether pain that he might endure for an hour or more; and thought of the tender days ahead. He limped a little. Freddie Freeman had left his car and stood at the edge of the escarpment, gazing about in search of white skin. He had heard Lorimer's roar but it came only as another sound, muted, scrambled, tossed into the confusion of the site's voices and machinery.

Freddie turned and saw him then: a bit knocked about, he thought. 'Jane with you, old man?'

'In the office. She'll have heard you, I imagine,' Lorimer said.

'Everything all right?'

'Of course.'

Freddie had seen the slight limp, the straight pained lips, untidy dress. 'A spot of trouble, had you?'

'Part of the contract.'

Freddie showed a trace of admiration. 'Call yourself the only

54

operational set-up for a hundred miles, Lorimer.'

'Alec Lorimer.'

'Alec, yes. Mines, villages, everything, every place, a full stop. The fellow in the gaol is going downhill by the minute, you see?'

Lorimer looked at Freddie's gleaming shoes; slacks, shirt, tie. He tidied himself: stockings, bush shirt, the shorts, gently, carefully.

'The hunger-striker fellow, you know?' Freddie explained.

'I know.'

Freddie looked at the clusters, the buzz of industry, the crane jib swinging out with its mess of concrete, the grinding 'revs' of the mixers: there was unreality in such discipline with the uproar of the village still in his ears.

'Don't know how you do it.'

Jane Freeman had come up suddenly behind them; she hugged Freddie's waist, slapped his buttocks. 'Putting on weight, you booze hound,' she said.

He kissed her; he was grateful. 'Things getting a bit tricky everywhere,' he said.

'I was in good hands.'

'Thank you, Lorimer.'

'Call him "Alec", Father. A special privilege. He's dining with us tonight. Mother is aware. Aren't you, Alec?'

'Fine,' Freddie said. 'I just told him he runs a tight ship. All this jabbering mob. Don't know how he does it.'

Below them the drummer boy kept the beat and the water gang took and passed its pails with infinite patience. Then, a pace of two from Lorimer, on the edge of the steep batter, a pail was dropped. The water was sucked into the hot ground, the pail rattled and bounced down to the buffer of the creek slime. The rhythm faltered, the drummer fought to bring it back; the culprit stood in confusion, gazing at Lorimer, unaware of the next bucket held out to him. He turned away, making little nervous laughing sounds of apology.

'Stupid bastard!' Lorimer planted a heavy boot in his buttocks, sent him staggering, scuttling in the path of a minder. He hobbled back; the line was intact; in moments the drumbeat restored peace and drudgery.

Jane watched, seemingly without concern. Freddie's disapproval showed only for an instant and as quickly was masked.

'Like that,' Lorimer said.

Freddie stared.

'A tight ship,' Lorimer said. 'That's how it's done.'

'Ah.'

Freddie found smoking in the heat unpleasant but he took time with his silver cigarette case and the tapping down of overstretched tobacco. He lit the cigarette but hardly smoked it, held it wasting in the hot air rising up from the ground. 'I thought I'd run Jane home. Safer. Less worry for you too, old man. Though I wouldn't drag my feet if I were you ...'

'Start a job, finish it.' Lorimer dismissed it without any great deference to Freddie. 'Not just locking an office, you know. Two hours concrete, then we break. Before the rain breaks.'

'Yes,' Freddie said; he looked at the faint flickering lightning on the horizon against a deeper grey now; and at the parched ground beneath him. 'Might be the last dry day for weeks.' He studied it. 'Rain before morning, I'd say.'

Jane said, 'Oh, Alec will speed things up. He's coming to dinner, remember?'

Lorimer could see her po-faced humour. 'You go on,' he said.

'But you are coming,' Freddie insisted.

Jane gave him her smile: he would be remembering the awful gaucherie of his exit and the whiz of a self-inflicted wound. He would remember other things too. And she would remember. She smiled her 'forgiving' smile. 'You are expected, Mr Lorimer.'

'Yes,' he said.

'But don't mark time, Lorimer.' Freddie knew the score. 'These johnnies can turn like mad dogs. Bodyguards with pounds and palm wine too. Not a place I'd sleep tonight.' He saw a flicker of unease in Lorimer's eyes.

'Before sundown,' Freddie said.

'Yes.'

'We'll expect you.'

'Yes.'

As Freddie manoeuvred out on to the scabrous bush track of road they could see Lorimer shouting his instructions to the crane driver, pacing out across the site, still limping. 'Looks like he sprained an ankle or something.'

'Yes, sprained something or other,' Jane said. 'He tries hard.'

Freddie had leant a little on the throttle: more heavy braking at twists and turns, he knew, but with a little speed he could ride the endless spread of corrugations.

'He doesn't have a lot to say, does he? That Lorimer fellow.'

'Now you must call him Alec,' Jane said, tongue in cheek. ' "Lorimer" sounds like a junior clerk or a tradesman.'

'I'll try to remember,' Freddie said.

Midway to the village he turned away on to other tracks, to leave brush and jungle behind: open scorched ground now, outcrops of rock, indestructible anthills, isolated palms, but some semblance of surface beneath them.

Jane said, 'I shouldn't have left mother alone, should I?'

'Connell is with her.'

'For days now. Better than nothing, I suppose.'

Freddie didn't reply; he thought of this cloak and dagger message from the coast. Connell a bolshie spy! He was angry.

It was cleaner country now: hills, tall trees, even great patches of withered grass that the rains would restore. He joined at last with the made-up dirt road that strung the village to his bunga-low and fanned out to the more distant mine reservations.

Ahead was the cricket club, still a three-mile journey to Freddie's bungalow. The cricket club was a joint brainchild of the mines, where top brass – and honoraries like Freddie and his ilk – could meet their peers. There was an impressive bar and lounge; and a burnt pitch that showed hardly any signs of wear and tear.

Freddie liked to play; he liked to drink too. But once a week his gardener, Josiah, travelled down the three miles or more to the club. It was a sharpening-up exercise at fielding and stopping: he would bowl from all angles at Freddie. Josiah was a shade over the top but he enjoyed outwitting Big Master Freeman: high one, low one, one out of reach, one straight at the midriff. Josiah's face would have a glow of youth; and he had a pound for his trouble.

'Josiah's at the club. Cricket work-out,' Freddie said. 'But no cricket till this damn war-dancing and spear-throwing is over.'

'You'll pick him up?'

'Can't leave him there, swanning about.'

'In, out, remember! No bar,' she warned.

Freddie smiled. 'Ten minutes with Josiah, that's all. Give him his pound. Good fellow. And he enjoys it.'

'No bar,' Jane said again. 'I have to scrub this grime off, change, talk dinner with Mother. We've invited Alec, remember?' She looked at him, smiled. 'No bar. All those bumbling bores in there. Cross your heart.'

Freddie pulled into the club compound. 'No bar,' he said.

'Ten minutes and I'll drive off! You and Josiah can stretch your legs.'

Freddie was laughing. He skirted the clubhouse to the pitch that was burned almost sand-dry. No Josiah. Strange, he thought; and then he saw movement at the groundsman's shed.

'Josiah!'

Josiah emerged. Freddie paced across to him. 'Ten minutes only, Josiah. Miss Jane is waiting out there. Get some balls.' Freddie paused, looked at him. The fellow seemed odd. Damned if he wasn't afraid! Not the time for that caper, Freddie knew. 'Get a move on, there's a good fellow,' he said.

'Sah.'

Josiah hurried away behind the shed; Freddie loosened his tie, rolled up his shirt-sleeves. The pavilion verandah was deserted but, in the stillness, the drone of European voices swelled out to him. Well, no work, they might as well drink, he supposed. Not a bad idea. Jane of course! And that Scots fellow Lorimer. Didn't care much for him. Not the way things were done. The boot, the minders. A lot to learn.

'Josiah!'

The damn fellow was wasting minutes back there. Needed to be put back on the rails again. Freddie rounded the shed. Josiah had gone. There was some scrub stretching away, palms, a few trees, a lot of open space. Josiah had vanished!

Freddie went back through the pavilion to the clubhouse bar and lounge. No staff; they were serving themselves; bloody chaos. He left.

It was a steep spiral climb to Freddie's bungalow; but the bank maintained the surface clear of loose stone and detritus, rolled it firm enough for Freddie's car to take grip on its daily journeys. Freddie's gardener, Josiah, kept the grass verges cut and trim.

Connell made the climb without rush, an effortless unhurried progress: the pace that heat and damp and indigenous fevers had enforced since some primal daylight. You watched the African, learned: things took a little longer or were impossible, that was all.

He thought for a moment of Freddie's letter that he had burned – a kind of schoolboy desk-to-desk espionage – and how Freddie might respond to it. React to it. It was hardly Freddie's kind of thing. Freddie had a certain ebullience at odds with silence, watching, listening. *You* watched Freddie, listened to *him*.

Connell liked him; he was a friend.

Visits to the gaol hadn't helped, he supposed; but you didn't stand apart to let a son die without dying a little with him every

59

day. He would be alone now, locked away from the fat drowsing gaoler, the smells of waste. Connell had twelve children, five of them sons; and grandchildren had arrived, were arriving. His clan gathered about him and his cabins. His hospice did its work of mercy: wasted dismembered dying shells were abandoned on its doorstep. Some hobbled to it and knelt in pain.

He reached the top of the hill, less than a couple of acres, square, flat as if its spire had been sliced away in whatever bursting upheaval had created such absurdity of terrain: a pox of hillocks, stone and soil, strangely isolated plateaux left behind in a disintegrating cluster. They rose to rocky or jagged peaks, all of them, strangely, except Freddie's precious plinth where Victorians had planted a dwelling.

At three hundred feet there was sometimes a stir of air, rarely a breeze, but the same hot spent vapour was everywhere. It was a young world, Connell thought. Freddie's bungalow had been raised up sixty, seventy years perhaps, a wink of an eye, when hills and high ground were deemed beyond the reach of malaria: malaria, bad air, seeped from the poisoned ground, they said, killed; but perished itself only a few feet above its source. Such a godsent simplicity. A remedy from God.

Fever lived on in swamp, valley, hill or plateau, indestructible, to take its unremitting toll of the African and his whiteman teacher. Only time and death led them to creeks and stagnant pools where mosquitoes bred. Now they had lessened death with a daily tablet but at sunset the mosquito was stirring in the darkness of her daytime recess, emerging for the night's sustenance. She came silently, 'stung' only when she left, drawing out the little needle-like proboscis from the skin. The male came to drink too but he was a bungler, noisy, paid the price sometimes in a tiny squash of blood and tissue.

When Connell, long ago, had left the coast and first trekked inland – close on three decades now – he had escaped the poison of fever for months. And then it had almost killed him. He had reached the village, small now but then only the bank, an Asian store, a few huts and the railway halt. There was labouring work at the mines but he had never reached them. A strange dry coldness had seized him, weakness, pain in muscles and limbs. Where now stood his home and hospice, there was nothing: a track, a tiny clearing. He had fallen on his knees, crawled a few yards and succumbed. Consciousness came and went but he remembered a roof above him and African faces. They cared for him through dryness, cold, shivering, sweat, head-bursting pain, thirst: for how many days had he lain, spent as a weak old man? He had never reached the mines. He had reached 'home'.

He looked down from the plateau towards it now: it was hidden, only little wisps of smoke rising from the bush marked it. At night-time, when kerosene lanterns were lit, they would glimmer in the distance.

Connell turned. The plateau of this steep hillock was Freddie Freeman's compound, its periphery neatly fenced with stakes and cladding; the bungalow too was further raised on stilts, and wooden handrailed steps rose to its main door and to its veran-dah. Josiah, the gardener, kept shrubs and grass in trim, even grew limes and avocados and pineapples. Freddie's house staff extended to another four: steward, cook and cook's small-boy assistant; and a watchman who came at sundown, an old man carrying a folded deckchair for sleeping all night outside Fred-die's garage. Engaging a watchman who never watched was merely a kind of blackmail assurance of the ethnic honour among thieves.

Connell crossed and mounted the verandah. Folding doors, almost the entire width of the gable, were thrown open to show a spacious lounge and dining area. It was in shade: the jutting eaves held off sun and glare; open steel windows ran the length of both sides but there was no escaping heat. One day soon perhaps electricity might reach out from the village and ceiling fans would stir the monotony.

Freddie Freeman's wife, Lucy, sat some feet back from the verandah. She had seen Connell's arrival in the compound.

Connell, such a habitual unannounced presence, scarcely needed salutation.

When he arrived on the verandah, she said, 'September is an endless month.'

Connell stood and looked out across tossed volcanic country and flatland to the horizon: the glare of the sky ended there at what was now a black-grey line of storm. In the compound, blue and orange lizards stood still as the air or suddenly darted over the dry ground to cover.

He said, 'It's like this always before the rains. A sudden death of sound. Not a stir. Once the village used to sit and rest. Waiting.' He looked across eight miles of ground that seemed closer in the shine of light and could see the blur of the village down on the plain. He looked at the compound about him. 'A garden of lizards out there,' he said. 'Dozens, dozens of them. They used to revolt me once. Blue and orange lizards. Not a movement. The eyes follow you everywhere.' He stood in silence, resting on the handrail for moments. 'Darkness will soon be on the creep,' he said. 'Up here night-time comes in from the horizon like a tide on flat sand. The village is a smudge already.'

'Yes, a smudge,' Lucy Freeman said.

She was an attractive woman, nearing her middle forties, suffering a time of sadness, regret, even anger: looking back to youth that seemed only moments ago, and the same moments would bring age. Old age. She still had fresh clear skin, hair trimmed short, quiffed with a kind of carelessness; and the merest hint of plumpness. But there was illness in her eyes. Connell could see it: features a little drawn and tight-lipped.

She said, 'We'll have trouble, of course. They've been hammering in the village for how many days' interrogation?'

'I was there,' Connell said.

'Worse than usual, would you say?'

'Crowded.'

'But trouble?'

'Possible.'

62

'You're not sure.'

She looked at the tall hard frame of Connell, skin a shade darker with decades of this heat and steam; and black hair, long, greying a little.

'Freddie enjoys it. Grouses but enjoys it.'

'The village is closed,' Connell said. 'The mines too. The hunger-striker, you see.'

'Blast these people!' Lucy was dismissive, then slowly gathering her thoughts. 'Freddie? Where's Freddie?' She paused. 'There was a letter for Freddie. Motor-cycle fellow. Red fez, black face, sergeant's stripes. Something out of a circus, I thought.'

'A letter?'

'Oh, some Secretariat bumph, sealing wax and all that rubbish. In his file. The sideboard drawer. I mustn't forget to tell him. And Jane? Where's Jane?'

'The bank has closed,' Connell said. 'Jane has an equerry. Mr Lorimer. Out at the creek. Freddie has gone to collect her.'

She was suddenly agitated. 'Lorimer, yes. Coming to dinner. Freddie wouldn't know what to do in a crisis except waffle about fair play! Absolutely useless!'

'They should be here very soon,' Connell said.

'I hope he doesn't bungle it. My God, Jane out there in that stinking place. Freddie in charge!'

'Freddie knows his way about,' Connell said.

'That Lorimer boy is reassuring.'

'Is he?' Connell asked.

Lucy's hands were restless, one clasped on the other. Connell watched. More than a month since she had come down from the hills in the north. Intermittent fever had left its usual listlessness, ennui, and in July Freddie had packed her off to her friends on high ground. She had spent weeks up there and returned bright, invigorated; but still the little nuances of regret, dissatisfaction, were always close to the surface. The palm of one hand rested on the back of the other and Connell watched the tightening and loosening of fingers.

'I'm having a drink,' he said; he saw her suddenly motionless, even the hands. 'Will I pour one for you?'

'No.'

Connell's 'personal' glass rested on the sideboard beside an array of spirits, liqueurs, vermouth, port, angostura: an array of colours and eccentric bottles. Freddie was a colonial. In the earliest days Connell had brought his personal glass to find a permanent place on the Freeman sideboard. Connell had insisted: however remote or impossible infectiousness from his doomed cabins of the dying, the dread of disfiguring illness, for most all, lived somewhere in suspension. Malaria and blackwater fever, the cargoes of insects, killed every day; the tsetse took its toll; reptiles poisoned. There was inevitability, certainty about them, these fragile airborne or crawling destroyers. But the timeless malady of Connell's village hospice went back to Christ and the millennia beyond without a pattern of hosts or susceptibility. 'Who selects lepers?' Connell asked Freddie. 'God or a germ?' Connell's personal glass sat alone, and in Freddie's kitchen it was washed apart from other vessels. Connell insisted.

Out of Lucy's vision now, he poured the whisky noisily and watched her jolt, the hands pushed down against her thighs. There was a little moment of fear in his eyes. He drank the whisky back, quietly filled the glass again. He could see her relaxing, loosening now. Except for the clasped hands.

'You liked it up in the hills?' he asked; he went back and took his stance on the verandah, looking away from her at the vast segment of flat jungle and swamp.

'After midnight, two, three in the morning,' she said. 'In the chill, I used to walk about the house. It might have been home. Pictures on the wall. Coniston, Isle of Wight and a mass of sails, the Thames with night lights everywhere. Cushions and rugs, porcelain figurines from Liberty's. Even in daytime the air seems to stir up there. You could see home for a moment.' She pondered it. 'We used to live in Muswell Hill, you know. Muswell Hill . . .'

'Yes, you told me.'

'Tall houses with balconies and beautiful chimneys, the surgery beside it. Sixty-seven, my father. Sixty-seven, still practising. My mother's letter every week. Come home. Come home for one leave soon. Just one. Come home. We won't last for ever. They were killed in '41.'

'This is 1950,' Connell said gently.

'Eleven years out here, Connell, and never once home. To kneel at their graves even.'

Connell listened, turned to look at her from time to time, watched her hands. He said eventually, 'The war years it wasn't on. German subs out off Freetown. A fifty-fifty chance of making Liverpool. Maybe less. Freddie was right.' He said quietly, 'South Africa was good for you. Sea and beaches. Shopping in Cape Town. He was thinking of you and Jane.' Connell remembered, 'Jane was a child then.'

'The war's been over five years, the subs are sunk or in the scrapyards, Connell! Still it's Cape Town, Cape Town, Cape Town. He hates England. Hates it.' Lucy paused, repented. 'I'm sorry, Connell. And I shouldn't talk about him like this, should I?'

'No.'

'He likes Cape Town, he'll tell you. That's why. Clubs, drinks, houseboys, all that. Reminds him of India, he says. All those years ago! In India, he was twelve!'

'Yes.'

'But I like home.'

'And he doesn't have one.'

'India?'

'A childhood memory,' Connell said. 'All our homes are memories.' He drank and watched Lucy turn away from him, her hands still agitated. Beneath the covering palm, he could see on the back of the clasped hand a small adhesive dressing. It had been there for days.

'Your home, Connell?'

'I'm an African.'

'You always say African. Like a party piece, I sometimes think.'

Connell smiled, was silent. 'Up in the hills was better than this heat and steam, wasn't it?' he said suddenly.

'I was happy for a while,' she said.

Connell went carefully. 'Pictures on the walls, figurines from Liberty's, telephones, running water, a breath of coolness. Even *pets*?'

For a moment, a split second, Lucy smiled. 'A poodle. A little toy. Small as a teapot. I fell in love with him.' She looked at Connell. 'Freddie hates dogs.'

'Yes.'

'India, I suppose.'

'Yes.'

'Hates Europeans in the hills too. "Useless wallahs, never where there's a job of work to be done."'

Connell nodded, tried to push away the almost certainty of her appalling illness.

She said, 'You know there'll be trouble, Connell, don't you? Danger too?'

'There's always danger.'

'Oh yes, there's always danger. Forebodings up in the hills every tour.' She gripped her hands as if she might be in pain. 'Pink gins and forebodings up there in the hills, miles from everything.' She paused and thought about it. 'Freddie,' she said, 'Freddie has cleaned and oiled his shotgun. God, he hasn't used it in ten years. Wild-fowling on the creeks was a kind of war-effort. I was dragged out there too, shaken to death in a little Standard car. He never got anything. I used to sit, wet, on hot leather and count the explosions. Hundreds of cartridges.' She was almost calm.

'Your hand?' Connell said.

She looked at the dressing, at Connell. 'Some flying, crawling thing, I suppose. Filthy country.'

'You're feeling better.'

She thought about it. 'Yes. Just now. It's almost gone for a moment. Like suddenly feeling lighter. It comes and goes, you see?'

'Fever comes back,' Connell said, with conviction, he hoped, 'for a flying visit sometimes, hovers about for days and never perches. A blood war. We're ravaged battlefields, all of us. Years ago, my head would burst. It was death.'

'It isn't fever,' Lucy said; she pondered over it, dismissed it. 'It's nothing. A bite most likely. After eleven years shouldn't I be impervious or puncture-proof, or something?' She looked at Connell. 'Do all our insects bite or suck? They seem to. At home they sting. More civilized.' She peered beneath the small adhesive dressing on her hand. 'A speck, now a spot. You said Freddie is on his way? And Jane?'

'Yes.'

'There'll be a halt for Josiah at the club, I suppose.'

'Wednesday,' Connell said.

She nodded. 'Wednesday is cricket. Thursday is callisthenics. Friday, the Rotary. Men are always busy out here.'

'In motion,' Connell said. 'Always in motion.' He gauged the coming night-time, the faint twilight mix, a single drop of shadow tinting the flood of glare. He crossed to the sideboard, poured whisky, noisily again, and watched her discomfort. The village was throbbing now, sending interminable pulses of sound across the miles of still air. 'I drink too much,' he said.

She ignored it; in a little while she said, 'The village. You hear it? Trouble, trouble. When will this fellow die?'

'Hours. Six, eight, ten .'

'Cheap trick, I think. Blackmail.'

Connell said, 'Twenty-eight years I've listened to drums. I hardly hear them now.'

67

'Twenty-eight years. Oh God!'

'Yes,' Connell said. 'A lifetime. In twenty-eight years there's always been trouble. But danger? Once or twice, that's all. Down on the coast, before the war, I remember, they chopped up a works inspector. He drove them too hard, hated them.'

'Savages.'

'*He* wasn't up to much. A stepped-up ganger.'

'White?'

'Yes,' Connell said. 'Blacks kill each other when they *have* to. Then out of sight, out of mind. An innocence about it.' He looked at her fingers rubbing along the dressing on her hand. 'That damn thing, don't you remember it? It's poisoned, festering, isn't it?'

He paced about, went on the verandah again. Life out there was cheap as the scattered mess of the market stalls, hardly important. But a manner of death was: sudden death or long unbearable horror. Connell's face was hard and chiselled, tight-skinned. He stood in silence; light, diminishing, would remain for a little while, the distant palms and trees stand in silhouette. Then in half an hour it would be black night.

Lucy Freeman said, 'Strange, I remember nothing.' She raised the dressing and looked at the festering spot. 'Nothing at all. A day or two must clear it.'

'It hasn't cleared in a week,' Connell said and pushed the words out at her again. 'Have a drink?'

'No ... no!' She was angry, distressed; then collected; it was a pattern. 'I'm sorry, Connell. Freddie and Jane will come soon. Perhaps then. Jane will be safe with that Lorimer boy, won't she? She was off at first light to meet him this morning. God, I thought, she's sickening for something.'

Connell smiled. 'You're feeling better.'

'She sleeps most of the day, Connell. Comes alive at nightfall. Freakish, isn't it? Oh, Freddie says she's true blue. A colonial! Women should sleep all the days, sparkle at night-time. India. He remembers it all. Sahibs, memsahibs, pegs, punkahs, chukkas,

68

all kinds of wallahs. Thirty-six years past. He remembers it all. This is the Coast, I tell him. The Coast! Here even sleep is threadbare.'

'Sleep,' Connell nodded. 'You can escape the glare of blue and orange lizards, the cracked earth out there.'

'And the smell of waste in gloomy village junk shops. Shops! Village! God! That tangled wilderness. A whistle-stop, a filthy little market of flies and black bony hands touching our food ...' Pain had arrived again and Connell saw her fight against it, rigid in composure, persistent. '... Strange how light and bony their hands are ...' She was silent for a little while. 'I seem to be waiting, waiting for something, Connell.'

Connell turned, looked out into the brief twilight now. He saw death down in his cabins, sometimes day to day, silent sleep-like death or groaning final pain. A time had come. There was always a moment of gratitude in brown yellowing eyes. They spent their short years with birth and death, without fear. Fear of pain only. Death was solace. Connell remembered churches and prayers of home, the dread of last illnesses and perhaps endless punishment beyond. The man-made god was a monster. In villages, beyond whitemen, deep in the bush, if pain was insufferable they killed it. He heard Lucy Freeman's restlessness again and thought of the merciless night ahead. He thought of Freddie. He thought of letters from the coast. He thought of the gathering peace in the fetid village gaol.

'Their hands, Connell.'

'Yes.'

He turned and looked at her, at the youthful prettiness that remained in her face and had once brought smiling young men, even big stricken Freddie Freeman, giant of Saturday rugby and summer cricket, gathering about her when there were clubhouse hops and soirées. She still looked smart and pretty, Connell thought, confined to the monotony of cotton skirts and tops; even her hair had withstood dampness and heat. He looked at the covered suppurating hand again and felt almost the compulsion to doubt his own knowledge of sickness and death gathered down the years.

He tried gently again. 'Waiting for something, waiting for the rains. An empty feeling in the guts. A year ago it was like this, coming up from the coast with "spirited" drugs and whisky, in the dead air,' he said. 'September heat. I should be used to it.' She sat, looking away from him towards the dry shrubs at the window. He watched. 'The train steaming in sweat and then the sky opened. Torrents of yellow bilge scouring past us, seeping in at the doors. Suffocating.' He could see her throat tightening as if she were close to tears. But she was dry-eyed. She made a small sound. 'Then it was gone,' he said. 'You could hear the sun slapping against the ground again.'

Dear Jesus, he thought, how awful; he waited for her to recover and went to the sideboard, out of her vision, to drink a little whisky. It would be a night to keep reality far out in the distant wilderness.

'Yes,' he said eventually. 'The women's hands are fragile too. Even beautiful.'

'I didn't think you noticed.'

'In twenty-eight years you've noticed everything and forgotten and remembered again. Fragile wispy hands. I don't see their greasy fingers in my food any more, or smell them, or hear the rattle of their voices, but I remember when I came back from fever, from the dead, all those years ago, a beautiful woman held out her hands to welcome me and they were weightless hands. She was twelve. I'd never seen a naked woman before.'

'Twenty-eight and twelve. She's forty now. Ageing.' Lucy was calm again. 'Is she?'

'Women are old at forty.'

'I'm forty-four, Connell.'

'African women are old at forty. Old at thirty, some of them.' Connell hid the compassion on his face, smiled, head-shaking. 'You look unhappy, not old.'

Behind her, around her, the lounge and dining annexe was a

70

masculine place, a den. It had only Freddie's trappings, as if he had laid claim to it and given her only houseroom. Or perhaps it was Lucy's own indifference, a grown fear that the merest semblance of home would be a surrender to this grossness that crept up to her doorstep. There was a table for what trophies Freddie had brought with him, a few gathered in recent years: cricket caps on the wall; a bat signed by so many people, standing in the corner; a cluster of England rugger rosettes; a few team pictures standing among the trophies, Freddie's younger eager face, unmistakable. Nothing more; the walls were bare; the furniture, as Freddie would say, went with the job: dining suite, cutlery canteen; in the lounge, easy chairs, rugs, drink stools, the sideboard. The curtains that could be drawn the length of the steel windows were probably Lucy's sole submission: they were dark as if to repel the shrubs, so close that Josiah cut them back, week in, week out. If, Lucy thought sometimes, this cage on stilts were abandoned for a single season, it would be swallowed in the jungle.

She said, 'I've rotted in this awful place. Poor Freddie. When we came out, Jane and myself, he was so attentive, so protective, never out of my shadow.' She seemed so at ease for moments now, Connell thought, remembering. 'Once in Benin, a big native boy waved to me, swung around, all teeth and grin.' She was smiling at Connell. 'He was peeing,' she told him. 'The empty hand raised in salute. With the other he directed his water in great artistic surges ...' Suddenly she was distracted for moments: oscillating pain, fear, seizure. Connell moved about, stood on the verandah. Darkness was perceptible now. He waited. 'Freddie,' she said eventually, 'Freddie followed him with a stick, threatened him with hell and damnation. "Never look at them," he warned me. "They do it on purpose, you know." That was '39. Only weeks to the war. Sometimes in the early days it was bearable.'

Connell said, 'It was younger.'

'The war changed it, Freddie says. And the mines. They used

71

to be sleepy fenced-off scrapyards, good for squash and cricket and their weekend booze-ups. But in a year they were frantic. They still are.' It all seemed a long time ago for Lucy; she said, 'Manganese is more valuable than gold, I remember that.'

Connell said, 'Gold is soft. Manganese toughens.'

'You haven't changed in eleven years.'

'I drink more.'

'Have I changed much? . . .'

The buzz of the Humber Snipe, pushing along the dirt road from the cricket club, reached them. Connell held up a hand, nodded towards the fading daylight. Lucy Freeman listened.

'Freddie,' she said.

'And Jane.'

'And Josiah.'

It was duskish now. Connell, from the verandah, could look down at Freddie's headlamps lighting up the bush at every swing of the road. When he reached the base of the hill he was changing down to a crawl for the last winding climb. In low gear, the whine of the engine was a lament of wasted power. The lights prodded out from the spiral roadway into growing darkness. Only far-distant palms were in silhouette and now the last tiny arc of the sun was showing above the blackness of the horizon. Lights flickered in the village too, torches or bonfires, Connell thought; and the jangled rhythmical sound reached them as a single throb growing with night-time.

Freddie drew nearer, his lights pointing skywards now until he seemed to flop over the edge of the plateau and return daylight to the compound. Their voices were clearer now; a door banging.

Jane was saying, 'Damn staff. What do we pay them for?'

Freddie prodded at the high-frequency klaxon on his car,

sending out spears of sound. He called for steward boy, Samuel, again, again.

Lucy wilted and recovered. 'Poor Samuel. Sleeping or visiting, I suppose. Samuel's job to put his car in the garage. Rules, rules, rules. Why doesn't Josiah do it?'

Connell glanced at her for a moment: since his arrival she seemed to have been unaware of the unbroken silence in the house. It was almost dark. Freddie and Jane stood in the beam of the lights. Freddie gave a final despairing halloo, bleeped the klaxon once more and said, 'Damnation!' He switched out the engine, let darkness return.

'Lorimer would have them scampering with his minders,' Jane said.

Lucy heard, showed her weariness. 'Impatience,' she said.

'Alec, Alec Lorimer in tow with Jane.' She paused a moment. 'Connell,' she said.

'Yes.'

'My hand. I won't mention my hand.'

Connell nodded. They were crossing the compound now, Freddie and Jane. There was no Josiah.

'Freddie is impatient with everything. Even pains and aches. Jane too. They never have pain and aches.'

Freddie's arrival in the lounge, unaccompanied by Jane, had his usual restless quality. He carried his crocodile grip of banknotes. Like a benign demagogue, he addressed them from the verandah, darkness behind him, the lounge in half light from the faint glow of mantled pressure lamps. He was rarely angry, but displayed a kind of heroic, almost humorous, acceptance of native inefficiency, stupidity. In the house, behind the lounge, Jane was banging doors.

'Where's Jane?'

Freddie nodded towards the house. 'Used the main door. Gone to have a scrub, I think.'

'My dear ...' Lucy began.

'Where is he? Where's that fellow whatsisname?' Freddie said.

'Samuel.'

Excepting Josiah, whose cricket affiliations bestowed on him humanity, Freddie's staff might have been innominate. 'Samuel or whatever. Where is the fellow? Should be out there, coming to attention, waiting. He can hear me a mile off. He knows the drill.' Freddie shook his head at the hopelessness of it, raised a hand in salutation. Evening, Connell, old man. Damnable journey.'

'Did I hear Jane?' Lucy said again.

'Yes, she's gone to scrub off grime.'

Lucy was impatient; illness brought an edge. 'You're quite late, aren't you? And Samuel is our *steward*. He supervises cook in the kitchen and keeps that small-boy pot-walloping. Didn't Josiah come with you? They can drive in first gear, all of them. Let Josiah do it for a change.' She looked at his bag. 'Not very sporty, is it?'

Freddie, a little puzzled, gazed at her. 'Money,' he said, and dismissed it. 'Josiah is our dogsbody. But not for cars.'

'Josiah is our *gardener*. Wednesdays you meet him for fielding or bowling or something silly. Remember?'

Freddie smiled, lifting his head to whoever God was, moved to the sideboard. 'Well, I've decided to give him the push, send him off with a rocket in his ear. Slippery customer.' He listened resignedly to the drumming for a moment. 'Damn the whole festering fifty million of them,' he said.

'Didn't Josiah meet you?'

'No.'

Freddie would be noisy at the sideboard: the clink of glass, the trickle of whisky, the choking cough of soda. Lucy stood for the first time and walked slowly to the verandah.

To Connell Freddie said, 'Extraordinary. I turn my back. A split second, no more, and he's off, Josiah, that gardener fellow.' He put his money bag in a compartment of the sideboard. 'The village must be a shambles. Listen. Noise, infernal waves of it, rolling out like a funfair. Couldn't hear yourself at the club, fellows in the bar having to shout for drinks, serving themselves! All kinds of drum-walloping and wailing. Not good enough, you'll agree, Connell.'

Connell thought about it. From the house, with a cavernous ring to it, Jane's voice could be heard calling out. 'Samuel, Samuel! Where the hell is he? Anybody here? Anybody home?' Moment of silence. 'Samuel, Robert, Josiah! Damn, what the hell is wrong? It's a graveyard!'

Lucy crossed to a bell-push; its rattle could be heard in the kitchen and corridors behind.

Freddie was pleased. 'Some things haven't changed. She's hardly back and she'll soon have them hopping.'

'She's not very brave, you know,' Lucy said. 'She might enjoy it of course. A colonial, I suppose.'

Freddie drank back his whisky, was forgiving about it all. Lucy wasn't at par, bound to be a bit edgy. 'I'll move the car a shade,' he said. 'We don't want that fellow Lorimer playing dodgems.'

'And when Josiah comes there'll be no sacking,' he was told. Freddie nodded.

'He's our gardener. Keeps everything perfect. We don't pay him for ball-playing.'

Freddie was out of sight, descending the steps to the compound; he called back. 'It keeps them lively, my dear.' He had taken his drink with him.

Connell's smile was a thought only; he looked soberly in Freddie's wake. Freddie would take the air, let little storm clouds pass over, return to less sensitive encounters. Suddenly he was filled with compassion for them all, the doomed, the survivors: Lucy would at last escape the changeless attrition of discontent and her journey had already begun. There was no return.

The door from the house was suddenly thrown open and Jane, smoking, naked, holding a towel at her crotch, was standing in the lounge.

She said, 'Where the hell is everyone?' and then saw Connell

75

turning away towards the verandah. 'Does he squat here?' she shouted, and made her exit. The slam of the door echoed through the empty house. In the silence the village drums crept back again.

Lucy said, 'She's not going back.' It seemed so incomprehensible. The noise had set the pain throbbing again. 'London is a refuse tip, a glory-hole, a cesspit, and I can't remember what else. It's maddening, Connell. Five years lumbering to a BA, a bad one at that, and now it's back to this sweaty rancid place.'

Connell said, 'Home.'

'This? Whites don't call it "home". We pass through, that's all. Fifteen months sweat, three months furlough. Fifteen-three, fifteen-three, for ever and ever.' She looked at him. 'You call it home, don't you, Connell?'

'Yes.'

'You're an African?'

'Yes.'

'That's nonsense, isn't it?'

Connell had heard the slapping of Jane's sandals in the house; a fast pace bringing rancour, disdain. It was the same exasperated entrance: a minimum of decorum. She wore a housecoat, had tied back her hair.

She looked from one to the other, took time over it, awaiting explanations. Connell went on the verandah. He could see the faint glimmer of his hospice lanterns through the bush. Lightning flickered on the horizon, a dancing interminable strobe. The movement of torches in the village was a muddled signal across eight miles of darkness. He saw Freddie, untroubled, resting on the perimeter fence, looking towards it.

Jane was launching her attack. 'Where are they?' She passed her hand before Lucy's stricken face. 'You're with us? The staff. Where are they?'

Lucy moved towards her chair.

'It isn't a time for putting your feet up. Dear God!'

Lucy battled with nausea, grasped at patience. 'Well . . . they're

76

in the kitchen . . . or the compound . . . they do move from place to place, you know.'

'They aren't in the kitchen. Or the compound. Or anywhere! Even Josiah!'

'Josiah was to meet with your father for his cricket. Fielding or bowling or something. I'm not sure. It's Wednesday, you know.'

'This place is derelict. Do you hear, derelict? We have a guest for dinner. Mr Alec Lorimer is coming to dinner, Mother. Mr Alec Lorimer. And you have made arrangements of course?'

Lucy was already moving, escaping, approaching the door to her kitchen. 'They're preparing dinner, they've forgotten something, they've gone to borrow it. Something like that. That's all it is.' A litany of Lucy's forbearance.

'All of them?'

Lucy left in silence; the door closed gently behind her.

Jane took aim at Connell's back. 'Staff, homeless persons, wandering about the place. Any place. Some place. They do move from place to place, she says. This whole place is a damned circus. God, I almost need a drink.'

Connell looked into the darkness, only intermittently heard the spiky self-importance. In the darkness cicadas were beginning to rejoice; there would be a great incessant clatter soon until the mind blotted them out. He heard the sound as Jane poured her drink, could feel her gaze on him. In the compound Freddie lighted a cigarette; the match flared: a burn of magnesium.

Jane said, 'Would you like another drink? I shouldn't worry, I suppose. You'll help yourself.'

Connell turned. 'Very soon,' he said. 'Are you happy to be back?'

'I've been back for days, you know. Every afternoon you and Mother wake me, clinking your glasses.'

'Unlikely,' Connell said.

He didn't show irritation or displeasure: the daily challenge of survival had priorities removed from those of boredom and sufficiency. But always he was aware of change. She had a bold assuredness, style, inevitable brashness. New people for new worlds. He would sip his drink and waste the moments in small talk.

She forestalled him; she said, 'No, I don't miss London. Yes, I got my degree. No, a very poor one in fact. Yes, I'm going to pierce dear Mother's heart and lie about here for years and years.'

A few moments of silence and Connell said, 'She isn't very well.'

'She drinks too much.'

'So do I.'

'And you're well?'

'Yes.'

Jane was amused. 'How do you manage it? I don't mean the outlay. Other people's booze is hardly exorbitant.'

'Hardly.'

'After a quarter of a century isn't the liver transmogrified or something? Blackman's magic, there's a secret, isn't there? You must tell us.'

'I enjoy it,' Connell said.

Lucy had returned from the kitchen and staff quarters; she closed the door gently as if noise might reinstate shock, weakness. She gestured to Jane for silence; her puzzlement was for Connell.

'Yes, quite deserted,' she said to him.

'This upset at the village. The mines too. Their protest,' Connell said.

'Some damn golliwog hunger-striker?' Jane said. 'It's so difficult for you all.'

Lucy said again, 'They've forgotten something and rushed off to get it. Don't you think, Connell? They're always trucking and dealing with each other.'

Connell was silent.

Jane studied him. 'You think so, Connell, do you? Shouldn't they come for Madam's permission?'

Lucy said, 'Oh, rubbish.'

78

Connell watched Lucy on the verandah, perhaps trembling for a moment, leaning forward on the handrail.

'Rubbish,' she said again. 'Robert and Samuel have done three tours with us. And Josiah. I trust them. It's just a sign of bad management if staff is forever being chopped and changed.' She looked at Jane: housecoat, tied-back hair, drink, poised cigarette. 'Why don't you go and dress?'

Jane curtsied. 'Waiting for Madam to decide on dinnah. Guest Mistah Lorimah coming for Miss Jane.'

'Oh God.'

'When he comes,' Connell said, 'he'll share our crust.' It was an unmistakable message for Jane.

Lucy said, 'Wear something cool and refreshing for him.'

'Muswell Hill evenings, by God! If we had a piano, Mr Connell, you could play "Come into the Garden, Maud".'

Connell said, 'I have a wind-up gramophone, of course. A lot of records too. But it's not the time. Death at the gaol, you see.' He looked across and paled Jane's amusement. 'Hardly decorous.'

'A wind-up gramophone, Connell?'

'Yes.'

'With a horn? A box of needles too, I bet?'

'Yes.'

'Stolen?'

'Of course. Prodigal Europeans. Too much money.'

'You're not European, Connell, are you?'

'No.'

'You're African.'

'After all these years, yes.'

It was almost dark in the lounge now, the pilot lights glowing like small glistening alleys. Lucy turned to face them from the verandah. Behind her, night-time was a backdrop, only the twitchy lightning at the horizon making the rim of the world. The pilot lights caught her face, leaving pools of shadow, making a death's-head. She looked at Jane. 'You said "Muswell Hill Evenings".'

79

'I said, Muswell Hill evenings, *by God*!'

'They were wonderful, Connell. People arriving. Excitement. New frocks, new suits, new coats. Staff in the dining-room. Melon, consommé, roast beef, peach soufflé ...' The words tapered off.

Connell brought her chair a little closer. Illness was gathering. But she was struggling with it. The tiny wound on her hand was an angry pustule in a deep red splash of skin. She grasped it and stiffened as if it had sent pain shooting to every fragile extremity. Even throat muscles tightened and jerked until the spasm had passed.

Jane, oblivious, listened for Lorimer's car. 'You've told it all before, Mother. Peach soufflé, cream sponge, cheese-board and coffee. Toilette and titivation for our nanny-goat ladies. To the men, the bucks, their hour of alcohol and heat. Then cards or a damn good rowdy at the piano. Oh, Oh, Antonio, Sussex by the Sea, Don't have any more Mrs Moore. God, what a life!'

'Your language is disgraceful. Street language!'

Jane looked with satisfaction at Connell.

'Muswell Hill was very beautiful, Connell,' Lucy said. 'I used to walk to Archway and then across to Highgate Village. The Green, the Park, the Cemetery, everything was magnificent. And it's all still there, Connell.'

'In Muswell Hill they sweep their own doorsteps now,' Jane said. 'Themselves. I've seen them. It was "once upon a time" when Mother lived there. It's bedsitter slum now.' Jane held out her drink to Lucy. 'You'll finish my drink, won't you Mother? I've hardly touched it.'

Connell watched Lucy's unsteady retreat to the verandah. He took Jane's wrist in a tightening grip, held out the other hand for her glass. She released it. Connell put it on the sideboard. 'She's ill, I told you. Don't be a bitch.' Connell's voice was scarcely a whisper.

'The drink,' she told him. 'I'll have it later, Connell, you'll remember that? It'll be quite safe there, won't it?'

'Yes,' he told her.

'Damn their stinking hunger-striker,' she said. 'Cold water, no staff. Washing, ironing, everything lying about.'

Lucy returned to them. 'It's getting dark,' she said. 'Turn up the lamps, but only a little.'

'Oh, leave them until we need them,' Jane dismissed it. 'They only draw insects about the place.' She was standing in the doorway to the house now, gazing at Connell. 'Yes, I'm going.' The slam of the door was a thunderclap that wasted over long seconds until the countless world of cicadas could be heard again. Lucy made her way slowly to her chair and rested.

'Freddie is out there in the compound. He doesn't like unpleasantness. Smoking, drinking, lying against the fence. He's happy here, you know, Connell.'

'Yes,' Connell said. He pumped the lamps, sent the hot kerosene vapour across the pilot lights to capture a degree of incandescence in the mantles. A brighter room materialized about them.

'Oh my God, Connell,' she said. 'That's worse. Blinding.'

'I'll dim them.'

'No.' She had put on metal-rimmed deep-smoked glasses with tapering side shades. 'It's better now. Sometimes I feel so strange, empty, Connell.' She rested a while. 'I'm sorry about Jane. Lost whatever manners she had.'

'Your hand,' Connell said.

'I'll have it looked at tomorrow. Don't you think she's lost her manners? You've known her so long.'

The door from the house was opened again and Jane's face was there. 'Not lost, Mother. They have bins for them in London. Even on Muswell Hill.' She paused, whispered. 'Alec is coming to dinner, you know. Whatever that will be.' She looked at Connell. 'Give him a drink when he comes. If there's anything left.' She closed the door gently now. The drums of the village beat into monotonous silence.

'Your hand,' Connell said again.

'It's not painful all of the time. Sudden shocks, seizures, and then nothing. My head aches. Blinding sometimes. You've been very good, Connell.'

'Is there something I can do?'

'You talk to me. Or are silent sometimes. You seem to know.' Connell smiled.

'Did I tell you we had a pear tree in our garden in Muswell Hill? Just outside the surgery. In winter I could see Alexandra Palace through the bare branches. It snowed one Christmas and I've always remembered how beautiful it was.' She turned the square, almost black glasses towards Connell. 'It can't have changed so much, can it? In a little while?' She lay back. Behind the black shades her eyes would be closed, Connell knew. 'Eleven years, of course,' she said. 'My God, eleven years.'

Connell stood behind, looked past her at the blackness and the jittery dance of lightning on the skyline. He silently took the miniscule content of Jane's glass, poured it in his own, drank it back. The African knew death from his crawling days, grew up with it, knew how much or how little fear it deserved and then put it aside, perhaps ended it. The whiteman caged it like a beast: the whine, the howl followed him for ever.

Lucy said, 'I don't think the staff are back, Connell. Robert, Samuel, Josiah. We'd have heard them, wouldn't we? Did you hear anything?'

Connell said, 'They haven't come.'

From the house came the sound of rhythm, the strange, as yet cacophonous blare of a music that had returned to its birthplace.

Lucy said, 'Jane playing her records. Music is different too.' She held out her still suppurating hand towards Connell. 'It's gone again. Like a nerve pain. I'm breathless and then it's gone. The relief!'

There was the sound of Freddie's car engine coming to life. 'Putting it away for the night,' Lucy said. 'Such a great monstrous machine. Extravagant, I always thought.'

'Only moving it,' Connell said. 'Making room.'

'Oh yes.'

In a few moments Freddie came. 'Listen,' he said. 'Those damn drums. Boom, boom, boom! Enough torches down there to burn the village.' He raised his glass to Connell, drained it. 'You went to the gaolhouse, Connell old man? Failing a bit, is he?'

Connell said, 'He's dying.'

'Dying?' Freddie said. 'Dying? Impossible!'

'Yes, dying,' Connell said.

'Dying already?'

'He hasn't taken food for six weeks.'

'Does Connell exist?' Freddie suddenly remembered. Damn fools!

He gestured despair. 'This political hocus-pocus upsets every damn thing. It turns their heads, you see?' He went to the sideboard for whisky. 'You get your gardener out to pitch a ball at you. You know, over-back, over-back, not very demanding, you'll agree. And what happens? You turn round, let him off the leash for a split second, and he's gone for bush. Gone!'

Connell thought of the gaol and the awful smell of a body consuming itself, the sweaty meat of the gaoler, the urine drum, the thunderbox. But somehow Freddie's ingenuous politics endeared him. Freddie, without malice, had learned only to bluster. Connell smiled and in an instant Freddie saw the humour too.

'Yes,' Freddie said, 'I know it's not so simple.' He paced about. 'Six weeks, you said? I didn't think it was so long. What do these johnnies want anyway?' He drank a little. 'Dying, you said? Where is he? They haven't moved him?'

'His cell. They've put a bed in his cell.' When Freddie was still again, Connell said, 'He wants to rebel for all of us. Yes, all of us. An offering, a beginning. Death is the down payment. I rebel therefore we exist.'

'Damn fellow could be right.'

'You've heard it all before.' Connell went on to the verandah:

forked lightning on the horizon now, momentary dazzling cracks in the firmament. 'It's always someone's turn to call the tune. "This is my own my native land."'

Freddie shook off his moment of solemnity. 'Ha! Native land, damn right. Natives everywhere, drumming, shuffling about. Thousands of them. How long have I known you, Connell? Eleven years?'

'Nearer thirteen.'

'I've always said it. At heart you're a colonial, you know. Law and order is the thing. Lucy?' She turned to face him. 'Connell will stay to dinner.' Lucy fumbled for an explanation; Connell might have spoken. 'You'll stay to dinner, Connell.' Freddie silenced him. 'I need someone to talk to.'

Lucy said, 'Mr Lorimer is coming.'

'Bloody damnation.' It had slipped Freddie's mind.

'And the staff . . .'

'Plenty for all of us. Chivvy them up out there, my dear. Get things moving.'

Lucy went slowly, left them in the silent lounge. Freddie poured a little whisky. 'Do your own, Connell, won't you?'

'Yes.'

'Thank God for whisky. Listen!' The village's distant noise, cicadas all round. 'Drums and bloody crickets.' Freddie always said 'crickets'. He listened and smiled. 'You know, Connell. These shebangs. Not all bad, you know. Oh yes, black thunderous faces wherever I looked today. Everything at a standstill. No cleaners, no porter, no watchman, no papers. Fellow in the telephone exchange said he couldn't hear me! Gardener gone to ground. Car abandoned. But it passes, shakes them up for a while.' Freddie pointed. 'Your drink, Connell?'

Connell raised his glass. 'Here,' he said. He thought of the sealed Secretariat letter in the sideboard beside him.

Freddie said, 'This fellow starving himself to death down there because he wants to be . . . what does he want to be?'

Connell drank, walked about a while, pondered on Freddie,

84

decent, generous, wearing superiority unobtrusively as possible.

Connell said, 'When I first awoke out of fever in the bush and saw African eyes and hands giving me life, I thought I'd be a saint.'

'You've failed miserably.'

'Yes.' Connell smiled. 'I had a school down there when you came, remember. I taught him.'

'This fellow? This dying fellow?'

'Yes. A good pupil, respectful, wild as the wind.'

'Clever as a sackful of monkeys, I'll bet.'

'Well, clever at any rate,' Connell said; he nodded to Freddie. 'I thought he'd be a good priest. A bishop one day perhaps.'

'That's another failure.'

Lucy returned.

Freddie said, 'Connell needs a drink, my dear. Life hasn't been kind to him. The place is littered with failures.' Lucy's sudden discomposure was puzzling for a moment. 'Something up, old girl?'

She said eventually, 'They've gone.'

'Gone what, my dear?'

'There isn't anyone out there. They've all gone. Robert, Samuel, Josiah, even the small-boy. They've left. Gone.'

Freddie stood gazing at her, at Connell, but the silence was unbroken; from a cigarette box on the table he took a cigarette, left plumes of smoke paling in the stillness.

'They've gone?'

'Yes.'

'Trappings and all.'

'Yes.'

'And the nightwatch?'

'He hasn't come.'

Freddie paused. 'They're getting a bit snotty for my taste, by God!' He went out on the verandah and looked away at the village. 'All the fun of the fair. Drums, protests, Commie wheeler-dealers up from the coast. At death's door is a good place to hawk their gospel.' He came back exhaling the remnants of his little anger. 'It'll have blown over in a day or two, you'll see.'

Lucy said, 'Will it?'

'They should never have arrested that fellow, Connell.' Freddie looked in wisdom at his whisky. 'Let him off into the bush to starve himself without a gallery and he'd have been back on his paw-paw in forty-eight hours. Colonial Office has never been very bright about the Coast. Colonial Office. Confounded oafs!' He was silent, looked back at the village. 'A bit livelier in there at least. Torches, accursed drums, wailing.' Freddie stood looking at the filament of horizon and then at the ceiling of cloud that was seeping down through the darkness to lie close to them. There was the first faraway rumble of thunder. 'Damn rains,' he said. 'Not far off now. Almost on top of us. I was bogged down in a deluge once, Connell. Little Standard 8 up to its axles. Two days before I got back to base.'

Connell passed him on the verandah. 'Won't be long,' he said. 'I'll inspect my outpost.' He was looking down at the faint presence of his hospice. 'Bolt my doors and shutters. Batten down.' He paced out across the compound and vanished. His voice came back. 'A few minutes, no longer.'

'Your bike's down there,' Freddie shouted at the darkness. 'Have a scout round, Connell.'

But there was silence. Lucy seemed to move slowly, aimlessly, as if the deep-smoked glasses impeded her.

'He's gone. Disappeared like that gardener fellow or whats-isname, the steward. Knows every track.' Freddie clicked his fingers for magic. 'Like one of themselves. An African. Well, he says he's an African. A damn witch doctor, I tell him from time to time.'

Freddie smiled. Somehow he had more in common with the heterodoxy of Connell than with poor players and a daily charade of mastery. In the war years there had been so little. Except perhaps on the coast, an official sop to Secretariat and REME wallahs. The army mobs down there were mechanics or damn writing assistants; and you didn't trust black rankers on their own ground.

But Connell had his traceless route: food or fags or booze, whatever was short, Connell came up with it. 'Not patriotic,' Lucy used to say, but she twirled the ice in her gin, blew out clouds of smoke, smelt food from the kitchen.

Christ, Freddie thought, what was this game on the coast now? Commie-bashing, God save King and Empire? Well, good luck to them. Thousands of these shifty johnnies to be rounded up. But Connell! Secretariat bloody humbug!

'Connell. A damn good fellow,' he said aloud.

'He hasn't been home for twenty-eight years,' Lucy said. 'That's 1922. My God, twenty-eight years.' She kept herself in motion. 'I'll try to arrange some kind of meal, see what's there.' The vision of drink and food was unbearable. 'Jane will do it. I'll take a breath of air.' At the door she remembered. 'There's a letter for you. The sideboard. Some black person brought it. A soldier.'

Freddie turned but she had gone. He took his letter, looked at the rubber stamp and seal. More Bulldog Drummond fodder, he thought. He poured and drank some whisky before he opened it. A single flimsy sheet this time and only a few words.

'C known to you. Delay. Murder. Crown Forces. Ulster. 1922. Await warrant, escort. No reply.'

He folded the letter and envelope and put them in his pocket. He stiffened the whisky a little and went on the verandah. They were setting the village on fire. Three great columns of smoke and flame peaked into the darkness. Even across the distance Freddie could pinpoint them: the Asian store, the railway platform and canopy, Hooker's palace of joy. There might have been gunfire too. He paused a moment to sip his drink, saw Lucy in the compound.

'Get indoors, my dear,' he shouted. 'And stay put.'

He hurried away into the house and his bedroom. Connell, a murderer. His Majesty's Ulster Forces 1922. This whole thing was tumbling into farce. 1922. Twenty-eight years. That piece could fit, Freddie thought suddenly. And Connell was hard. Connell could kill. Connell was a good man but he could kill an enemy. God damn them, Freddie thought, they could do their own tarring and feathering. He paced about with pale torn loyalties. They would hang Connell in Ulster. Christ, Connell, manacled, cowled, standing on a trapdoor. Silence could be one way. Opt out. Connell would be here when they came and they would take him. A show of disbelief, of speechless shock, and he was gone. Only guilt would remain. Freddie, in his bedroom, sat in darkness, confused.

The descent from Freddie's bungalow was a slow careful plod, each step probing out and downwards to find the next sloping foothold. Out of the blind darkness vision was returning: Connell could see Josiah's grass verges, trimmed, and beyond them the black escarpments of bush. He reached his bicycle, used it until he was hindered, then walked with it along his track, a jungle tunnel, two hundred yards of darker darkness, to his clearing. The glimmer of storm lanterns reached him first and then he was in open space. It was a great circle that he and his families had cleared over the years. Only the clusters of palms were left and, beyond dwellings and plots of vegetation, a screen of shrubs had been left to hide, to shelter, the cabins of the dying. Deeper in the scrub was his cemetery of wooden crosses. The luxury of private graves had long since gone and now Connell arranged pits for them: the dead were sewn in gunny from the mines, buried in rows and tiers, quicklimed, covered with enough earth against stench and disease. Connell had to lay them with poison too, to fight vermin and predators.

A line of a dozen cabins was his refuge for the dying, tended by the dying themselves: the walking tottering cases ministering, feeding, burying, until there was nothing left except pain, weakness, disfigurement. The refuge, the hospice, sat on the rim of the circle and at the diameter's other extremity was the commune of Connell's wives and progeny. A noisy talkative place of unhurried women, children, infants; a place of industry where garments were made, crops raised, palm wine brewed; and from where children went out to beg at the railway halt, or the older women to sit at Connell's market stall. There was peace, altercation, what happiness could be expected. They survived.

Connell was greeted with placid unexaggerated sentiment: welcome called out, raised hands, smiles; children ran to him. He had arrived and in moments a little pool of life had settled again. This was a cluster of dwellings; but substantial, wooden-clad, with doors, windows, asbestos roofs. To each a family.

Connell's bicycle was wheeled away to security.

'This evening there is a flag, Connell,' he was told.

He looked across the great circle towards the hospice: a white sheet, 'the flag', was spread on the screen of shrubs.

'How long?' he asked.

'Not long, not long.'

'Everything is ready?'

'Yes.'

The white sheet was death.

Connell lived apart. A dwelling like the others, bigger, but apart, a single space: shelves of books, a battery wireless, a cabinet of medicines, dressings, salves, cases of whisky, a kerosene fridge, a desk, chair, bed, brown and white goatskins spread on the floor, a shaded pressure lamp, glasses, delph. An amount of comfort in desolation. Everything had been shaped by Connell's own hands; or stolen for him.

He stood at the door, looked across at his families, the work, the tillage; and then again at the white death flag on his hospice. Freddie Freeman's bungalow, up there on its height, was hidden by the bush but an aura of light showed. And Lucy. He thought: Ulster, 1922 ... delay Connell ... murder ... murder. He thought of the shattered sibling skeletons deep under Passchendaele pasture now, forgotten, the gutted Antrim house, the death-wailing, the freak grotesque clinkered mass still in his study. The arrogant hierarchy, he thought, tight-lipped, back there ensconced in immemorial green fields with their own accommodating god and royal police and soldiery...

And Freddie Freeman would remember Indian hills and lakes and wonder what piece of ground covered the beloved parental skeletons that he would always see in laughter and evening splendour.

Freddie would come to him and talk, Connell knew. If there was loyalty, it should be to themselves or each other. Flags hung limp, faded in isolation, diurnal survival, final oblivion.

Each day, or when death came, Connell went to walk the paths of his leprosarium. On his bed now had been laid out the clothing for his visit: a hooded alb of gunny sacking from head to ground, loose hanging sleeves that covered arms and hands, knee-length mosquito boots of fine leather, filched from some sleepy afternoon bedroom, and canvas stockings to pull over them and tie below the knee.

Leprosy, old as time, without provenance, was feared on the coast. The incest of Egypt had bred it, the Letter Writer said, and the Hebrews and Roman legions had carried it with them. But its germ was universal, on the four winds, in heat and cold, dormant or awakened. It could steal upon the anchorite in his cleft, benignly rub shoulders with a million others, pass them by. Unannounced, it came to visit the chosen one – a single ant in a monster colony – by some perverse serendipity.

Connell's patients tended each other to death or remission and he walked among them without fear. But he stripped and clothed himself in gunny, pulled the cowl over his head. The African kept his distance from the infected, and Connell wore this insulation of canvas only for the reassurance of his commune. He poured and drank a measure of whisky now and stepped out into the darkness. Even on level ground he could see, over the miles, the flare of the burning village. He skirted the long screen of protective shrubs where the white flag was resting and arrived out of the darkness like some ghostly medieval penitent. There was a line of twelve cabins, distanced from each other, not more than five feet tall. The floors were bedded with dried brush and fodder. Beside one, a lantern burned and three figures seemed to kneel on the ground in its well of light.

Connell's leper village was a village for the dying: a year, more or less, sometimes a single season, and they were ready for the pit. Before they were brought to Connell, in darkness, borne on litters, covered, the disease had crept over them for ten, even twenty years perhaps. In the bush, Connell had seen it at every progress from a harmless insidious weakness, remissions, recurrences, until the first dread blotching of trunk and limbs and the redness of hands and feet and face. They were cast out from villages then for the wandering beggarly years of erosion, found and brought to Connell only for death. The ministering ones, the walking dead, had monstrous noduled faces, great ulcerating lumps on brow and eyelids and lips and nose and ears, creeping to the body's other parts; but they were mobile still, before blindness and deformation of hands and feet; or they were brought with limbs rotted away to stumps, throats swollen and in pain. And if there were a more evil one, it was the body unmarked, without nodules or pus, the skin anaesthetized, without feeling; but, trapped inside, great paroxysmal agonies of neural pain.

A disease of overpowering depression, weakness, exhaustion, an inexorable desire for solitude. Connell walked the spread of his cabins, bent to peer into the darkness at each monstrosity. Then he returned to the lantern. The three kneeling suppurating gargoyles had sewn the dead one into his shroud: little more than a shrunken head and trunk. They placed him on a handcart and slid him to his pit. Then quicklime, parched earth and poison.

Connell walked slowly as a beadsman beyond the screen of shrubs, out of sight. A narrow booth stood beside it, roofless, that had housed a dry thunderbox once. Now it sheltered a large oil drum and wooden cover. He stripped off his canvas robe and stockings, doused, submerged them in strong piercing disinfectant. In a day or two he would wash them and store them in his cabin. At death, about the corpse, disease raged, the African believed. Connell's was an act of reassurance. Naked now, in his knee-length leather boots, he paced the trip to his house. The light from the door showed a galvanized iron bath, steam rising from the tepid water. Beside it, smiling a little because the end of pain was a time also of only a little grief, was a young woman. He could see fresh clothes for the evening laid on his bed. He sat and she pulled off his leather boots, let her own loose mammy-cloth fall away, and came with him into the bath. Her beautiful soft flesh, he thought; and then the quicklime consuming the ugliness across the way; or a body devouring itself in a filthy gaol...

When she had dried and dressed him, she said, 'We are sorry too because of your son, Connell. The son of all of us.'

He was looking towards the glare of the village. 'Another death soon,' he said.

'Soon?'

'A few hours. Maybe less. And then fire and killing.'

'Here?'

'Everywhere.'

'Your son, Connell. African, Connell. You African man, Connell.'

'Whiteman.'

'We must leave?'

'Everyone.' He pointed through the darkness at the flatlands and the hill–bush beyond. 'Live there for a while.'

'Why, Connell?'

'Whose women are you?' Connell said. 'Whiteman's women. The children, the children of whiteman's blood.'

'Your blood in the gaol too.'

'But useful now.'

'And you?' she asked him.

'I stay. This is my ground,' Connell said.

'To be killed.'

'Who can tell?'

She was crying for him. Black flat faces that had once seemed ugly had a strange beauty for him now; tears ran down the coal-black skin, the eyes were distracted with sadness and compassion. Connell held her close to him.

'There isn't time to waste,' he said; he watched her walk away into the darkness, tall, still slender, fine swaying hips.

He sat on the verandah. This had been his school of twenty years ago: seven-thirty till midday, when the sun was overhead on the line of the Equator and it was time for shade and rest. His own progeny and a few strays from the bush had been his complement. But he taught them to be literate, numerate; and when they were older, the value of what grew or lay beneath the soil. It was theirs to plant; or dig and expose. The coast was not the country, he said, only where the foreign man had settled and the black brought him what he valued. The whiteman paid the black army and police to protect the whiteman; to punish, torture, kill his 'brother'. He built gaols and gallows.

They could change that.

He sent them in pairs to the village to see men beaten and in flight. Pride, he told them; they were men of iron. When they were older they would scatter, take truth with them to other villages and towns; wherever people gathered.

They would be remembered. He didn't talk about death; death was with them from infancy. He had taught them to burn and pillage and vanish into the bush. That was life.

It had been a single class: they arrived, spent their days, their years, moved on. He had watched his last disciple move away through the tracks. Five years now. This roofed verandah was his rostrum, pupils squatted in the dust. In the rains they crowded and took shelter with him...

And now death in the gaol would be the signal. How many,

93

he wondered, would rise, how many would fall? He thought of his own flight from Ulster. Should he have remained? Who could he preach to? He might have lasted a month. They would have hanged him. Was killing and flight only revenge and cowardice? He drank a little. He had even lied to Freddie.

He left his house untouched, took two medium-sized wooden boxes with leather grips and walked the bush-tunnel and rolled dirt-road towards Freddie Freeman's bungalow.

Tonight would not be a victory; but defeat would be a beginning.

Freddie had come to the bedroom for his guns, and sat thinking of his years with Connell, the whisky they had drunk, even dangers faced. The village turmoil, fear, strikes, agitators, he had seen them all in various mixes before, in the war years and the aftermath. Connell had been the mentor then: 'Ten-minute storms come and go. You forget when the last one was.' Connell always careful. But today, Freddie thought, there might have been caution too. Christ – he saw himself – lugging a case of money from his bank to stick it in a sideboard; spring-rattling a pedigree car out to that poisoned creek to round up Jane. And this Lorimer fellow? He saw Lorimer's boot lodge between crotch and rectum to send the water-carrier rolling, squirming, to the edge of the scum. Not done, in Freddie's book. Lets the side down. Scots of course had a short fuse, you knew. But there *was* a rule book. Pot-bellied minders too, with staves, thrashing these poor primitive bastards to hell. Freddie didn't care for Lorimer.

And now, down on the coast, some shower of Secretariat time-servers bumbling over twenty-eight-year-old whodunits. Christ, warrants, escorts. It was a damn good bet they wouldn't be risking their skins on the road with these johnnies on the warpath. Freddie wondered.

94

Like the lounge, the bedroom had a steel-framed window running the length of one side, polished woodblock floor, wardrobe, easy chair, bedside rugs and lockers. There was a single bed and, suspended from the ceiling above it, a wooden frame letting its mosquito net drop down. The net hung limp, unfastened, Freddie noticed. These damn half-day insurgents had hared off, left their chores undone. He would have to make a little speech for them. He tucked the linen skirts of the net beneath the mattress, making a neat secure cage where one could sleep locked away from whatever flew and crawled in the darkness.

There was a slim metal cabinet in one corner and he crossed and unlocked it: his shotgun was there, a service revolver in its holster, a box of cartridges, bullets.

He stuck the holstered revolver in his belt, shouldered the shotgun and carried the boxes of ammunition. He met Lucy in the corridor. By God, she was failing, he thought: moody, seeming to drag herself with a kind of silent stoicism through the hours.

'Probably safe as houses out there, my dear. But better indoors. Always the off-chance, you see.'

Lucy studied him. 'My God,' she said, almost a whisper. 'You look like some kind of desperado. Don't fire any shots without asking me. I couldn't bear it. I couldn't bear the noise.'

'Of course, of course,' Freddie said.

'I'm going to rest a while.'

'Good idea.'

'Jane will prepare something.'

'Yes, she'll manage.'

Lucy moved slowly past to her own bedroom. Freddie watched, went back to the empty lounge. He was with the crickets and drums again; he had forgotten them for a while and now they crept back. A drink. He poured a little whisky and carefully let the soda mingle with it. He drank and smoked a while, looked across the miles at the flickering village. He had loaded his weapons: the revolver, in its holster, hung on the folding doors, the shotgun he propped in the nearest corner; ammunition was on a drinks-stool.

Connell, he thought.

Murder, those boneheads said. He would have to tell Connell, he decided. Connell was a friend. Some damn cock-up, you could be sure, with their Secretariat sealing wax and ramparts of bumph. Connell wouldn't be pleased. He wasn't without friends either. It could be a good old hornet's nest. Freddie suddenly was not displeased about the whole thing. Connell could handle it.

Jane had entered, unseen, unheard. She stood smiling for a moment at Freddie's armoury and went to the sideboard. She picked up and examined her glass which Connell had drained.

Freddie turned. 'Ah, there you are, girl.'

Jane said, 'That Connell donkey. He pinched my drink. Why do we have him scrounging about the place? Every afternoon for a week he's been pickling himself with our whisky, damn him! And his menagerie down there for the poxed and infirm!'

Freddie was amused but appeasing: Connell brought more liquor than he drank. And inside Jane some anger was spending itself. Freddie said, 'Well, he's just down the road, our neighbour for years. Generous too. Whisky doesn't improve standing about.' He paused and said, 'He's white. One of us.'

'If black tarts were wet paint you wouldn't see him in the dark,' she said.

He laughed: her father's daughter. Connell would have laughed too.

'All that unspeakable disease and death. Some day he'll bring it up the hill with him.'

'It isn't like that. Funny damn thing. Down in the coast hospitals, my girl, whites do the dirty work. Doctors, nurses, the rest. And we ask them out to tea and drinks. Connell knows his business.' Freddie was placid, stating, not pleading, the case. 'They come there to die. He lets them flop. He's not a bad fellow, really. Kept a good school down there once, frightened hell out of those little golliwogs. A good thing.' Freddie paused, wandered about. 'Your mother feels sorry for him, of course.'

'Sorry for Connell?'

'Well, he might be a lame duck missionary or something like that, twenty-eight years sweating it out here and not a tribal mark to show for it. He doesn't talk much about times past, does he?'

'Has good reason, maybe. Though he's a shade young for Jack the Ripper.'

Freddie laughed again; pondered a moment. Twenty-eight years. Ulster 1922. The whole thing was a sweat of confusion. Drums and dying patriots and goddamn crickets didn't help.

'I like Connell,' he said.

Dear Papa, Jane thought. She said, 'Connell is a ravishing soak with all his black women down there. How many would you say?' Jane paused but Freddie was silent. And then, suddenly, a hilariously wicked notion from Jane. 'A groping quack, by jiminy, that's what he is. 1922 he's just let loose from books and scalpels and bang! Struck off for some unmentionable bawdry or worse. On the run.' She waited. 'Well?'

A murderer, a fugitive. Freddie was pondering absurdity.

'Well?'

Freddie said gently, 'I've never asked him. It never seemed important. Oh, people whisper, I know. "What are you?" some passing-through Red Cross bigwig said in the war years. "Come and ask my patients," Connell invited him. And that was the end of that for some reason.' Freddie laughed. 'He tried to teach you Latin once or twice, poor fellow.'

'Several times,' Jane said. 'He smelt of fu-fu and stale whisky and God knows what else. Black women, ugh!'

Black women, Freddie thought. He went on the verandah and looked at the distant burning village. Hookers was a small flicker now. Freddie could locate it between the burning stores and the railway halt. He wondered about Hooker, broad, honest enough, and when there was the crinkle of notes, a stout fellow of discretion. Had they burned him in the grease of his last-chance whorehouse, nailed his genitals to the door? You wanted a lively piece, clean as a whistle with a bagful of tricks? Hooker had the royal seal. Freddie did business with Hooker on gold shipment days. A special room, naked girls, lassies not out of school. One, two, three if you wanted, to work you over for an hour. By God, it was good. Then a scrub, a shower, a couple of Tuborgs from the fridge and you were ten years younger.

He hadn't coupled with Lucy for twenty-three years. There had been a wedding night consummation; and in a bleak honeymoon two faint sallies of partial invasion. That was all. In a few weeks she was pregnant, she came and told him, kissed his cheek, a kind of consolation prize. No more, she told him: the whole thing disgusted her, the panting, pushing, the sweat and its smell. She was 'extraordinarily' fond of him of course, 'extraordinarily', and if he went away she would miss him.

He didn't want to leave her: that was love, he supposed. But the London married years, ten, eleven of them, had been hollow. London whores were a gamble and the clean trade was out of reach. Tommy Atkins had taken his pox to Europe to mix and bring it back invigorated. There were occasional clumsy encounters with caps and condoms in strange beds; and — somehow always degrading — the act of self-relief. And then, the Hun and the coming battle had rescued him.

He looked again at the flicker that might be the end of Hookers and smiled a little wryly. Everything was changing.

'Black females, how can anyone touch them?' Jane made a show of airing her nausea and smiled. 'I'm just being rotten. Some black people are very nice.'

She was at once assured and ingenuous, Freddie thought. She was coming across to him now and put her arms about his shoulders; she said, 'Mother looks haggard. She doesn't need Connell hanging about.' She pointed at the empty bottles. 'All that booze.'

'No, no,' Freddie said. He smiled and kissed her forehead. She deserved better than Lorimer, he thought. 'No,' he said again. 'Connell brings his own booze, keeps his end up.'

'Once in a month.'

'Whenever he comes. Never fails.' Freddie explained it simply. 'He doesn't like swigging it all alone down at that death camp of his.'

Jane was amused. 'Oh, dear, dear, such delicacy.' Freddie was gazing out still at the end of Hookers. 'What's wrong?' she asked. 'All these weapons at the ready and you keep peering out there like a gundog. We've had all this before.'

Freddie turned, smiling. 'It's good to have you back.' He nodded towards Connell's spectral territory down below. 'Connell,' he said. 'He came across a leper place far up the river, years ago, wandering about tsetse country, a kind of end-of-the-road camp. Just a field, I think, mud huts on three sides and all these cadavers waiting for lights out. American gospel wallahs, you know. Good people, I suppose, with some brand of god up their sleeves. Whiteman's job, they told Connell, to bring the Word and peace to these "aboriginals". That's what they called them, "aboriginals".' Freddie thought about it. 'Annoyed him, I think. Must have sparked him off too, I suppose.' He smiled. 'Then two dumped on his doorstep.'

'He's a stallion.'

'Virile,' Freddie agreed and thought of his own tom-cat life. 'And he's an African.'

'An African?' Jane had to laugh at that.

Freddie came back in from the verandah, broke and examined the shotgun, put it in its corner again. The night was black as pitch now and you could smell the rain.

'He wouldn't agree, of course,' Freddie said, 'but he's a bird of passage like ourselves. A good fellow. Can play on my side any day. There's nothing shifty there.'

'Not a club member,' Jane said with a little glint of wickedness.

Freddie wasn't happy about it. 'A lot of johnnie-come-latelys about these days, tell you he's a Mick mucking in with his mammies, snout in the savage's trough, all that rubbish.'

'Hardly a secret, is it?' Jane said.

'An African, I tell them. They shouldn't worry. A generation makes Americans of wops, gyppos and jerries. After twenty-eight years he's an African.'

'He lives like one.'

'Yes.'

She remembered, for an instant, London: a pervasive dullness soaking into Victorian brick and masonry, into minds and skins. 1945. Peace: the expectancy of times that would never come again. Flags would have been flying back in Muswell Hill, Mother said, bells ringing for the living and the dead. The dead in Finchley. And it was time for Jane Freeman to go. She had been packed off across three and a half thousand miles to a genteel Highgate enclave of knowledge-cramming that might 'civilize' her before University days. 'I've spent five hours a day on you for six years. Even Connell. I hope we've saved you. I hope. A year in Highgate, you might be literate enough for London Entrance.' Mother, of course, Cantab. Hons., tolerated redbrick only in Muswell Hill residences.

Mother dreamed thirties dreams when there had been servants and grocers, milkmen, bakers, busmen, haberdashers, how many more, who would tip their hats to the doctor's young lady: decent people, salt of the earth, they had their place.

'London,' she said aloud to Freddie.

'You didn't like it back there, did you?' Freddie waited.

'No.'

'Maybe you're an African.' That made her laugh.

College had had an unsavoury pong with the closeness of grinning accented huckster and tradesman progeny. Once, before a week-end dance, she had been accosted. 'Goin' to drop 'em tonight, eh girl?' Some shiny little counter-jumper out of his depth. Maybe Africa was home.

She glanced at Freddie; he was right. The club was awash

with humbug too. Connell, at least, she supposed, had some kind of honesty. She sipped her drink.

'Connell should be back,' Freddie said. 'He went to lock up his doors and windows, have a scout round.' He raised his glass. 'Plenty big palaver in village, I'm afraid, girl. Johnnie politics, everyone talking, no one listening.' He looked into the darkness. 'Rains on top of us too.'

'Aren't they sending troops? Those idiots on the coast.'

'On their way, I imagine,' Freddie said. He held up his hands, closed his eyes: the sound of drums and crickets. 'A storm hanging up there. The rains, you see. Could block that puffing-billy railway for a couple of days.' He thought for a moment of Connell.

Jane looked at the shotgun, the revolver and then at Freddie.

Freddie said, 'Some fellow starving himself to death for the past month or so. Funny, I had no idea he was at it so long. Six weeks, I think, Connell says.'

'Yes, I know,' Jane said without much interest. 'A car greaser or something. Everyone knows. He's in the gaol.' She drank a little. 'Alec Lorimer will be here soon,' she said. 'He lays it on a bit heavy, doesn't he?'

Freddie let it pass, paused, gently laid down the rules. 'Connell will be back. We'll put him in charge, I think. He knows the ropes.'

Jane accepted it in silence. Eventually she said, 'This fellow in the gaol?'

'Dying.'

'Lighting a damn touch-paper.'

'Well, yes.'

'We're being kind to him?'

'He has a bed, of course.' Freddie felt some atavistic need to defend imperial propriety. 'Every possible comfort, I'm told. They've seen to that.'

'But he's dying?'

'Oh absolutely. Any time now.'

London had hardened her, he thought. He remembered the drabness, himself, and the weight of despondency that blessedly had dropped away at his reprieve even to this sweat and pestilence. And now they had retired him. Don't come back, old boy. As if ever he would set foot on that miserable postage stamp again. He felt the head office redundancy in his pocket. He must wait; the right moment would come to tell Lucy. She would go home of course, he knew, and expect him to be at her side. But it would be South Africa for Freddie. Beyond his relief was the arrival now of a sadness that their journey together, even dry and celibate, had reached its parting of the ways.

They loved each other, cared for each other, that was the trouble. He took up the shotgun again, held it at the slope and stood guard on the verandah. But for the village and the skyline flares it was a black universe. Freddie Freeman, retired, he thought. And then, John Connell, Ulster 1922.

When he turned back to the lounge Jane was smiling her approval of him. 'Horatio,' she said.

Freddie put the gun back in its place. 'Rabble-rousers up from the coast, Commie wallahs, you know. Spouting, gobbling. The usual claptrap, keep the mob shuffling. Keep the blighters awake, more like it! All that chanting, drum-walloping, stirs it up too.' Freddie laughed suddenly, pushed it aside. 'In a few days we'll be plodding along as usual, don't you know, girl. Slower than ever, I wouldn't mind betting. Damn country.'

'Better than Land of Hope and Glory.'

'Yes,' Freddie said. 'Yes, better than that.'

'I wanted to go out this evening.'

'Not this evening, I'd say. It could be tricky out there.' Freddie suddenly remembered. 'Your Mother's resting. You're i/c commissary this evening, my girl. That chap of yours, remember?'

'I'll open tins,' Jane told him. 'Soup, meatballs, peas, home-baked bread and get on with it!'

'Thank God for drink,' Freddie said.

'Do you want a drink?' Jane said.

'Later.'

'Damn their palavering ju-ju! Black politics,' she said. 'Isn't it a scream.' She was decked out in expensive cotton, everything of the moment: flared skirt, fitted waist, cuffed sleeves to the elbow, shaped neckline. It was a pale aquarelle blue.

Freddie studied her, the brown shoulder-length hair catching the lamplight. It might have been Lucy, all those years ago. 'You look a picture,' he said.

She came across, took his arm and they stood on the verandah. 'When this fellow dies,' she said, 'will they all go back to sleep again? The whole thing is so boring.'

Freddie shrugged. 'The trouble is you can't biff them any more, you see. That is, not officially. It costs you a tenner if you biff one now. Court appearance, pay up, grin and bear it. All this human rights thing, dignity, that piffle.'

'I'm shocked,' Jane said. 'Bank people don't go about biffing.'

Freddie was amused, happy again. 'When I came out in '37 it was no holds barred, I can tell you. But you had to be fast. They've got this built-in thing, an instinct, picking up a scent or whatever. And they vanish!' Freddie enacted: feinted with a left, threw a right. 'Nothing, you see! You swing round to deliver and they've gone.' He was silent for a while and said, 'The damn war was salvation of course, but it changed everything. Things are slipshod now. Ask Connell. They want to know why is God white and shouldn't hell be cold and rubbish like that.' Freddie laughed. 'He still biffs them of course.'

'Connell?'

'Well, nowadays,' Freddie said, 'not personally. Not often at any rate. He's getting a bit settled. But, if he's upset, he can whistle up a kind of bodyguard. Not very pleasant. For pence they can be downright savage.' Freddie lowered his voice, amusement bubbling through it. 'For a pound, he told me, he could have the Governor removed.' Freddie pondered it. 'All his people scattered, up in arms now, I suppose.'

Jane was pleased. 'I'm getting you a drink,' she said; she brought it.

He raised his glass to her.

'I'm glad you're out *here*,' she told him.

'The coast?'

'I'm glad you're out here.'

It was burning hostile country, he knew, impoverished, a battle ground of disease, but it had restored for him some little importance, a vestige that had perished in London streets and terraces. He had come down from boarding school to the City to be tutored in the style of colonial banking. And behaviour. You could see London Bridge from the staff manager's office; and, in the old thriving fish market, the Monument to London's great medieval fire rose up two hundred feet ...

The staff manager, a decent fellow, said, 'Two years with us now, Freeman. Another year and you're for posting. We'll miss you on the rugger. Cricket too.'

Freddie smiled.

Freddie, skipper and stand-off half, and they had blazed through two seasons without a shadow of vanquishment. 'Sahib' Freeman they had dubbed him when the pint pots were raised. He was with a senior squad too and could go to the top.

Freddie thanked him.

'You'll be turned twenty then.'

'Yes.'

'We've pencilled you in for the Med. Alexandria. A couple of years there. Alex is good. You'll like Alex, learn the ropes, learn the patois. Then Beirut, Jaffa, Tripoli, Benghazi ... You can make a nice life, Freeman. There shouldn't be any difficulties. But we'll miss you on the rugger.'

Like storm clouds and rains the difficulties were blowing up then. Disaster even. A memo on his desk only hours later invited his rugger XV to meet the MD's selection. The memo writer's identity, typed beneath a sweeping underlined signature, was *Major R. F. K. Sunderland, MC, Assistant Director (Exec.)*.

Christ, Freddie thought. Managing Director's Selection.

'Old Spike is going to cut you down to size, Freddie boy,' someone said.

'Spike?'

'Sunderland. The Galloping Major. Thirty-eight, still going strong. Says he'll hang up his boots at forty. Stupid bastard, of course. Spike's XV, *he* likes to call it. Pick of the City. Steam-rollers.'

It was an end-of-season February Saturday, 1921, when they lined up. At the interval Major Spike's 'barbarians' were ten points down. Freddie, peeing in the shrubbery, overheard the prescript for his demise.

The Major, a little strutting fellow, of battles to be won, smiling sang-froid. 'The big fellow. I want him fixed. Understood. I want him taken out.'

Freddie hardly noticed: half-time councils of war were common as sweat and liniment. But the Major's MC, with tenuous claims to gallantry on the field, had steely bonds only with victory. The Major led from behind, a strategist, took no prisoners. Within minutes, when a ruck had cleared, Freddie was kneeling, head to the grass, a bizarre Islamic figure giving praise to his prophets. He seemed to haul himself erect, pushing assistance away, falling and rising again, staggering. Blood ran down from his nostrils, dripping from his chin or smeared with muck across his face. He could feel a dislodged tooth hanging by a shred of gum and spat it out. His ribs ached, might be cracked. He fell on his knees again.

'Get the fellow a stretcher.' The Major was snapping out commands. 'The light's going. Dark in half an hour. Get a bloody move on!'

It had all happened near the sideline where a few dozen people stood. Lucy, without interest in conflict or muscle, chattered with a little fashionable coterie. It was her first glimpse of Freddie Freeman: one moment, an almost handsome rugged thunderbolt; the next, a blood and muck addle-face, spitting out a tooth.

The stretcher men came.

'Come on, get him away!' the Major was still commanding. 'Get on with it, ref!'

Freddie took a wet sponge to clear the bloody war-paint.

'Cotton wool,' he said; he stuffed his nostrils with it, rolled a tight wad of it to grip in his bleeding gums.

'Come on!' the Major shouted. But the first-aiders, empty-handed, were already moving to the pavilion.

Freddie had surrendered the key role of fly-half and gone to a flank position where he could rest a little and study the Major's footwork. Lucy looked at him again: his nose bulged a little and there was a faint trickle of blood too. He was handsome, she thought, and brave.

The Major, at full back, was a flash operator, Freddie saw: always a kind of bodyguard at hand to give and take the flak. The Major fielded the safe ones, kicked with style to the touch-line. Flutters of applause.

He had to be isolated, Freddie knew, and the moment had to be right. He dropped back a little – resting, he would call it – and took a stand behind his centres. Then suddenly everything was in place! Freddie, in full flight, intercepted his own thundering line, fly-kicked to the Major an unavoidable 'gift'. The bodyguard was wrong-footed, the Major suddenly agape as the ball dropped in his arms.

Freddie crash-tackled him at hip level. The first-aiders came again and took him away. It was the Major's last game; thereafter he walked with an almost imperceptible limp ...

Spring, summer, autumn came, went, like crawling buses; and his days in London, Freddie thought with deep gratitude, were drawing to a close. Now he had been dispatched across the City for that final assessment, interview, posting. A September day when he could reach out for the whole world.

Marble, brass, ironwork, polish. A hall porter said, 'Staff? Sixth floor, sir.'

He found the great panelled door and read the legend. Oh Christ! Oh Christ! he thought, what a turn-up!

It said, 'Major R. F. K. Sunderland, MC. Director Overseas Staff.' He knocked and entered.

In a large office an elegant desk and, behind it, phone in hand, the Major in pleasant conversation of exclamation and laughter. Some 'priceless idiot', it seemed, had bashed his second off the first green, left a twelve-inch divot. Absolute peasant. Public house keeper or something.

He hadn't turned to look at Freddie but stretched out a hand with a drooping pencil that pointed to a chair. Freddie sat and waited.

Eventually to business; no hint of recognition. 'Freeman. Alexandria, I see.'

'Yes, sir.'

'Prime territory, the Med, you know?'

'Yes, sir.'

'Feel you're up to it, do you?'

'Oh yes.'

'Father. Indian Army.'

'Died 1918, sir.'

'France?'

'India, sir. Influenza. My mother too.'

'Influenza.'

The Major made a slow desultory progress through the CV, snapped the folder shut and replaced it in his cabinet.

'Well, thank you for coming ... eh ...'

'Freeman, sir.'

'Freeman. Call to see your staff manager when you get back to your post. I'll have been in touch with him.'

Freddie took the premonition of doom with him across the City. The staff manager said, 'Well, not bad news really, Freeman. A delay, that's all. Six months, a year at most. Egyptians getting a bit shirty about letting our fellows in. Want to place their own bods. A few months. Time flies. You haven't forgotten the rugger, have you?'

'No,' Freddie said.

Neither had the Major.

The staff manager said, 'Well, get in training then.' He watched the well-made figure of Freddie smiling from the doorway and thought of the poisonous bastard, Sunderland. 'Freeman?' the Major had telephoned the staff manager. 'Not fit for overseas duties, I've decided. Perhaps you'll find something for him at base ...'

'Yes, I'm glad you're out here,' Jane was saying.

The bungalow lounge took shape around him again, the glow of the pressure lamps, the sideboard, the liquor, the guns, the village drums, the storm of crickets; Jane in her party dress, smiling, was for a moment Lucy of long ago. He looked out beyond the verandah at the blackness.

'I would have preferred the Med,' he said. 'Alex, Benghazi, Jaffa. Somewhere on the Med, you know. Your mother too. I promised her.' He wandered about, remembering City canyons, head office porters and lifts. The Major.

'I tried a few times but didn't make it. The Coast is bottom of the pile. Lucky to get it, I suppose.'

Jane crossed to him, put him sitting in Lucy's chair. 'It's not bad out here!' She was laughing.

'Not good,' he said. 'But I am a bit of an ass. I never seemed to hit it off with the planner wallahs, couldn't even bother to split a drink with them.' He smiled. 'Born in India, you see. Twelve years in the hills. Something of an Indian, I suppose.'

Jane faced him. 'I'm glad you're out here. Not marching twice a day along London Bridge, planning cream buns and coffee breaks. You're Freddie Freeman, in tropical kit, whisky and guns at the ready, and when you shout even the pans in the kitchen rattle. And I'm very proud of you.'

'I should have been on the road years ago,' he said, 'but they're a shifty pack in London, you know. Watch your back, is the thing. I wasn't ready for it. I never was. Not even now.'

'You're the best,' Jane said; she paused and studied him, spoke very softly. 'You're not going to retire back there, are you?'

Freddie felt the crumpled letter in his pocket; Lucy must know first.

Jane chased him. 'Down some little fading Surrey side street, convenient for the shops, where Mother can smile and smile and cherish her very own doorstep? God!'

Freddie showed frustration for a moment, stood, poured a drink. 'She isn't happy here, girl. Not in all these years. She tolerated it, just about tolerated it. And I promised her the Med, didn't I? Before you were born,' Freddie said quietly. 'She wants to go home.'

'You'd die.'

'I could manage it, maybe. They'd find something for me.'

'You weren't planned for hand-me-down houses, little rooms, little windows, little grass patches, adjacent to buses and trains in their godawful metroland.' She pointed to his drink, the display of liquor behind them. 'You'd keep a bottle in the sideboard. Maybe even two bottles. For Christmas and, of course, for emergencies.' Out of her own memory she looked sadly at him. 'It was mean back there. Mean.'

'Yes,' Freddie said; they stood together on the verandah. The village flames were distant fireflies.

'Mean,' she said again.

Freddie nodded. 'Since the war it's even grubbier, I imagine. I haven't seen it since '37. You and your mother came out in '38. I was waiting on the jetty. Together again. All three of us. Marvellous. You wouldn't remember.'

'Of course I remember. I was ten. Coming down from Las Palmas to Freetown, my birthday. A cake and petits fours from the Captain's table and the dining-room sang like a lot of toneless old frogs. Of course I remember.'

Freddie laughed for a little while, drank. 'I was thirty-six.

That I remember. Grounded all those years in London. Twenties gone for ever. Forty coming up like a thundercloud.'

'You were a handsome devil,' Jane said, 'standing down there waving to us.' She kissed him. 'It was heaven. I've always been happy out here.'

'Have you?'

It was important, she knew. 'Yes.'

'Retirement,' Freddie said vaguely. 'It creeps on. I'd settle for SA. The Cape, you know.' She was smiling to him, nodding her encouragement. 'London, ageing home counties, couldn't stand it. I can't change spots, that's the trouble. Houses are forwarding addresses, nothing else I can remember.' He walked about, remembering, uneasy. 'SA. Good, wasn't it?'

'It was good.'

'We've spent every break since '38 down there, never once been home, as your mother calls it. Till '45 there was the war, of course. Head office diktat: keep out of Europe. Cape Town, marvellous, I thought, but she only endured it.' Freddie smiled, remembering it again. 'It was good. A good forwarding address.'

Jane watched him, waited.

'Since '45?' He knew she was asking.

'Yes,' she said.

'I was afraid,' he told her. 'If they got me back, they might find a cubby-hole for me. Send out some young fellow, full of bounce. Afraid! Keep out, I said. Head office letters too. Dreaded the damn things. Every one might be a recall, I thought. Five years of bloody torture.'

'And now?'

Freddie didn't explain. 'It doesn't matter any more.'

Jane poured herself her usual tiny drink. 'To SA!' she said. 'For all of us.'

They drank.

Freddie nodded towards the house, towards the bedroom where Lucy was resting. 'We don't belong in Africa, your mother thinks.'

Jane smiled, raised her glass again. 'We've had great times together. You've given us great times.' She could sense his guilt and the fear that had prompted it. She said, 'The war still drags its feet back there, I told her. Queues, ration books, peeling paint, headscarves, bombed sites, odious people. She'd like all that? A month in the swill-pool and blackman's sweat would be balsam and rosewater.'

There was the sound of an approaching car down on the dirt road; and then the whine of low gear and the shooting headlights as it climbed the gradient to Freddie's.

Jane said, 'It's our Mr Lorimer.'

Freddie thought; a toneless voice. 'Mr Lorimer. Yes, yes, of course.'

Jane unhurried, unexcited, from the verandah looked down into the darkness of the compound to watch him park.

In '23, a year since Connell had fled Ulster, offshore British Ireland, twenty miles from the gutted Connell home, Lorimer was born. The Lorimers were people of property, wealth, Presbyterian.

There had been a struggling Lorimer, of course, Scottish crofter of two centuries past, enrolled militia man, crossing the few miles of water to Ireland, at hand to protect vast endowments of land bestowed on soldiers of rank and fortune, created nobility by England's grateful royal houses. An arable freehold of ten acres was adequate payment for honest footsoldiers. With God and austerity Lorimer, honest footsoldier, prospered.

The Lorimer estate was more than six hundred acres now, with tenanted labour, flax mills, Friesian and Jersey herds, water, woodland, a presbytery and church, a brotherhood lodge, within its confines. Lorimers had been elders of the church for more than a century.

Twenty miles away, in recent times, they had built on the

razed site of a papish house, a holiday home, sheltered on a hill, looking across the water at Scotland, beloved provenance of the clan. Alec Lorimer was a civil engineer of promise, 'giving' his time willingly, a year, eighteen months' work to the colonial Empire that had embraced them; and, in withering heat, he thought not infrequently, determined, tight-lipped, of looking down again on the rocky shore into the fresh sharpness of wind and sea.

Nearer the family homestead was the timeless village cluster, a little market entrepôt of a thousand fellow churchmen, where 'Lorimer and Son' practised at law. The Lorimer scions had been sent to Scotland before their teens, to be imbued with the discipline, the rigours of boarding school, a fear of God; and ruthless vigilance against popery and peasant Irish. It was a boast – if true humility permitted – that God's only righteous people stood unscathed in the shadow of the Antichrist ...

Lorimer parked his car on the circular drive of Freddie's bungalow. A burning unhappiness and guilt came and went. Jane: he had espied her first on the harbour gangwalk, he remembered, a face and shaped body of innocence and beauty. And they would meet, it was decided. He had decided. Reserved perhaps he was, but he had always hidden his confidence. And he had pedigree.

And now she had stripped before him, down to the very skin ... to the very ... Oh God! he thought. The beauty and the awfulness of it. He saw Freeman escort her from the site, had vowed it was the end of it. Could he taint the seed of progeny with *that*? Could that stand beside him in church to sing God's praises? It was the end!

And now he was at her doorstep, remembering. He could feel his body ready, trembling. Damn her, dear Christ, he thought. He should leave. He wouldn't be dragged down!

And suddenly there she was on her verandah, gazing into the glare of headlights. She was beautiful. He found himself on the gravel path, moving towards her.

She was in high humour; he limped a little, she could see. 'You're welcome, Mr Lorimer. Welcome to our site.'

'The village,' he said, gesturing, diffident. 'Not just fires in there, you know. Firearms too.' He saw her smiling and said quietly, 'There should be troops in there, shotguns and buckshot to scatter groaning wogs.'

'You're staying to dinner,' she said. 'If there is one. And we'll find a bed for you in the guest room.'

'The week-end,' he told her with certainty: it would be over and punishments could begin.

'I'm cooking dinner, Alec, opening the cans.' She took his hand, led him to the lounge. He was remote as martyred piety; and then suddenly stirring, faithless to his faith, gripping her fingers.

'See, it took only twenty seconds,' she whispered. 'And I'm growing weaker moment by moment, dear Alec.'

She had an arm about his waist and walked close to him. It was damnation, he thought, eternal damnation.

'We're here,' she announced for Freddie.

Freddie greeted him with all the enthusiasm he could hardly have hoped for. 'Lorimer, my boy. Come in, come in.'

Lorimer nodded.

'Felt a bit guilty leaving you out there today.'

'One day is like another.'

'Sit down, won't you. Jane will get you something.'

'Malt,' Jane said. 'Highland malt.'

'A tall glass,' he told her. 'What will damp the bottom, no more. Soda to the top.'

Freddie's generosity was endangered. 'Have a decent shot, Lorimer.'

'Alec.'

'Yes, Alec, of course. Long night. Keeps the mosquitoes off, the old coasters tell you. Have a stiffener.'

'I don't need it.'

'Ah.'

Miserable dogsbody, Freddie thought. He tried to visualize him in rugby kit: hardy, good shoulders, but he wouldn't have given Freddie any trouble. And in the bar, Freddie thought. A disaster!

Lorimer sat in silence, seemed at ease. He wore a palm beach suit, shirt, tie. Smart. He hung his coat on a window clasp. The drums crept back, the crickets.

Freddie was a calm smiling host; but patience was eroding. 'Airless everywhere,' he said. 'Always like this before the rains. Not many on the roads, I'd say. Everyone moaning and droning back in the village.'

Jane, aware too of Freddie's uneasiness, brought Lorimer his drink. He tasted it. It passed.

'Your good health,' Freddie said. Cocky bastard.

Lorimer tasted his drink again, in silence, looked from the hanging revolver to the shotgun to ammunition on a drinks table.

Jane's sudden laughter was a peal of joy. 'We're mobilized here, ready to take them at the bat of an eyelid.'

Freddie smiled relief. 'Oh, nonsense. Nothing like that. A bit of fire-raising and vandalism. Heavier than usual, I suppose. Little explosions of resentment, part of the colonial package. You get used to it, Lorimer.'

'Alec.'

'You get used to it, Alec.' Christ! Freddie thought. He said, 'I grew up in India. Always resentful, shifty, smouldering, that kind of thing.'

'You get used to it?' Lorimer said, expressionless, tongue in cheek perhaps.

Freddie didn't miss it, didn't pause. 'Give it a few months, Alec, that's all.' He thought of the vicious boot planted in the African's crotch. 'You've got what it takes. You'll be all right. I can tell.'

Lorimer smiled. 'Good. I'll get used to it.'

'You have the makings or you haven't.' You had to talk down

114

a send-up. Freddie knew the tricks, he could handle it. In the absence of Jane he might have bum-rushed Lorimer down the hill to the dirt road; but he babbled on. 'It's a trick, you know, that's all. Get your face right and ask the questions. Never answer them, don't wait for them. Attack! If they spot you're a soft mark they can whip up a yarn quick as candyfloss; mother, brother, sister, dying somewhere out in the wilds. You part with two pounds and never see his blubbering coconut again. Sympathy, of course. A pat on the shoulder. An hour later you'll find him snoozing, feet up, in the kitchen and shout in his ear. Send him flying.'

Lorimer nodded in silence, seemed to consider it all; he said, 'India style?'

Freddie looked at him. 'Well, I was born there,' he said again. 'First word you learn is "jildi". Jildi, jildi! Quick, quick! Get a bloody move on.'

'That's good.'

Jane felt the arrival of anger, discomfort; there was just the wicked shadow of ridicule in this deadpan distance of Lorimer. On site, he would give her all he had, wouldn't that be nice, she remembered. Bastard. And she had brought him here to punish him. She passed them and stood on the verandah; she said, 'Alec has been here almost a year, Father. Building his bridge on that awful creek. 'Forty, fifty, sleepy slugs to chase every day. Marvellous, isn't he? He has minders, of course.'

'Yes.'

Lorimer raised his glass but didn't drink. 'You get used to it.'

'Yes,' Freddie said; he was gently bowing out.

Suddenly Lorimer said, 'But we shouldn't.' He was studying Freddie. 'Should we?' He paused again to accommodate what might be slow-wittedness. 'We shouldn't get used to it. A few broken heads and well-placed boots in their buttocks, is how you build bridges. First steps in construction. Bring the class to attention.'

'Yes, I suppose.' Freddie assessed him without pleasure,

remembered the name on his ledgers, but had no recollection of the face. There was a chess club at the Mines; probably drank soda water and cashed his cheques there. Funny, you grew a little old and these now were the arbiters of behaviour. 'They tend to soft-pedal down at the coast,' he told Lorimer. 'The Secretariat, you know. Not a uniform in sight if they can help it. Sensible, maybe. Freedom, brotherhood, seeming to blow around like waste paper. A fresh approach or something, they call it. The end, maybe.' Freddie paused. 'I'm a troops man, myself, old boy. When the chips are down, that's it. Show the flag.'

Lorimer gave a token bleak smile of acceptance.

'Good, good. Bread, liquor, whatever tins we can find out there.' Freddie paused, hurried on with his excuses. 'Staff bother, I'm afraid. Jane will see to it.'

Jane said, 'The staff has defected.'

'Ah.'

'But Mother will persevere, sleeves up, show them how.'

Soft mark. The needle went deep. He could still take Lorimer and thrash him, by Christ! Freddie felt a healing need to remind him of a propriety even in chastisement: the chasm between fist and boot. 'Before the war we'd have biffed them of course,' he said. 'Picked up the leading johnnies and biffed them.' He was pandering to this oaf and it angered him. He went in silence to the verandah, studied the night; he mellowed. 'It'll be murky as hell out there now,' he said. 'The sky a bellyful of rain. Miles of mud roads in the making.' He came back in, smiling. 'You'll stay put of course, won't you? Plenty of space.'

Lorimer gave a token bleak smile of acceptance.

'Good, good. Bread, liquor, whatever tins we can find out there.' Freddie paused, hurried on with his excuses. 'Staff bother, I'm afraid. Jane will see to it.'

Jane said, 'The staff has defected.'

'Ah.'

'But Mother will persevere, sleeves up, show them how.'

'Resting,' Freddie said. 'A bit off colour this past week.'

Jane made a hopeless gesture towards the darkness. 'They just vanished. She's too easy with them, Alec. You'd skin them alive if they let you down. Yes, skin them alive. Josiah wants a bicycle. A bicycle! She's considering it, she said. We're in the wilderness and poor Josiah is getting old.' She moved to the rear of the lounge, towards the kitchen. 'I'll find my tin opener, gentlemen. And easy on the whisky, Alec.'

'Yes, yes,' Freddie said.

She was gone; all the mutable absent sounds of the night returned and stayed a while.

'Your boys, Lorimer?' Freddie asked, forgot the 'Alec'. 'Staff? Cook, steward?' He waited. 'Gone, are they?'

'Yes.'

'They'll be sneaking back tomorrow.'

'Good. I'll spare half an hour to break a pick handle on their damn cast-iron coconuts.'

Freddie said, 'Be careful, old man. They can get you for ten or twenty pounds, you know. Ten pounds a biff is the going rate now.'

'For twenty pounds,' Lorimer gave his rare bleak smile, 'they'll have something to show for it.'

Freddie felt anger but stowed it away behind his pleasantness; at the sideboard he poured himself a drink, looked at Lorimer's tinted soda water. 'Fellow I knew in the Mines,' he said, 'used to earmark twenty a month for biffing. It kept him sane, he told me.' He looked at Lorimer. 'After a year he was quite mad of course. They had to send him back.'

Lorimer nodded.

Christ, these silences, Freddie thought; and this insufferable jack-in-office. 'I'm glad you're staying put,' he said. 'Uneasy out there tonight. I don't waste a lot of time on these rumblings, take them as they come. But this fellow starving himself down at the gaol.'

Lorimer waited. 'Yes?'

Freddie said, 'He's likely to pop off any time now.'

'Well, then!' Lorimer said: here suddenly was a charge of venom, profanity, gutter-talk too. 'For Christ's sake, pump it into him! Ram it down his throat or up his arse!'

Lorimer, like a committee man who had jumped up to make his point of order, seated himself again; he drank a little of his wash of whisky.

Freddie, dishevelled in the sudden storm, was returning with special calmness: he used moments of silence first, then rambled on. 'Yes, they used to dump them out in the bush once. That soon put them on their feet.' He explained it in detail to Lorimer. 'Force-feeding? Well, local padres of all camps were against it. Red Cross wallahs too. A couple of these johnnies choked in the war years, you see.' Freddie's was a simple earnestness. 'The bush was the thing. Bung them in the Land Rover. Two hundred miles up country turf them out. It never failed.'

Freddie had finished but Lorimer nodded, waited, nodded. 'Yes?'

'Oh, nothing to worry about really,' Freddie said. 'We'll have the old hit and run business, bongo bongo on the drums, cars burned, a few buildings this time of course for good measure, windows broken kind of thing until the palm wine runs out. Bolshies up from the coast, hopping about, you know. They're creeping in all the time. We're too soft. The war finished law and order.' Freddie tilted his glass, let the whisky flow. 'You've done most of a year out here, Jane says?'

'Yes.'

'I've had thirteen. A lot of it good. Not now. You get tired of this rubbish. Go south, that's the thing.' Freddie sized him up and down. 'A fit young fellow should be looking that way, make a name for himself. Civilized, I can tell you. Keeps these fellows in harness too; heads down all round and get on with it. Down the Cape of Good Hope or north to Saldanha, beaches, breakers, golf, cricket, rugger. And the "Table" looking down on it all. Marvellous country . . .'

Suddenly Connell was on the verandah; he had crossed the gravel and burnt grass of the compound, muffled in night sound. He wore white cotton slacks, a black shirt buttoned outside it; his shoes were light, soled with rubber from the walls of discarded tyres. He looked fresh and agile as Lorimer.

It caught Freddie unawares, in mid-speech; a phantom materialization! 'By God, Connell, you startled me. You flit about like a shadow. Anything stirring out there? Get yourself a drink.'

Connell said, 'Nothing you can see.'

'This is Alec Lorimer,' Freddie said. 'Bridge builder out on the creeks, Jane's guest. He likes *Alec*, I keep on with *Lorimer*.' Freddie laughed; Connell's arrival was a cool breeze in this dry world. 'I never get it right.'

Lorimer's boredom had vanished.

'John Connell, our neighbour.' Freddie presented him.

Lorimer said, 'Commissar Connell!' It was a vicious spike. 'The wogs call him Commissar Connell, didn't you know?' he told Freddie. Some quiet secret excitement seemed to have been born in Lorimer.

Freddie groped, was at a loss; he said, 'Well, they find a name for everyone eventually. I'm "Carrots", I think. Carats, gold, diamonds, I suppose. It doesn't matter a lot, does it?'

Connell stilled it. 'We've met,' he reminded Freddie. 'Mr Lorimer and I.' He rested his laden boxes and crossed to the sideboard for whisky.

'Yes,' Lorimer said to Freddie, 'I've met the Commissar.' And 'shopped' the bastard too, he thought with satisfaction. Lifted the lid off something rotten ...

He remembered the oven-hot weather, when baked air was like a torch by mid-morning. It was four, five weeks past now, he remembered. Cement, stone, sand, to fill the hoppers; the black bodies bleeding sweat; the tumbling mixer drums, loaded and watered, had four minutes to spin and discharge. Then load, spin, discharge again until fatigue struck like a hammer: a limp staggering body pushed out, a fresh one in. The minders rested on their staves. At a hundred degrees plus, the concrete steamed in the mixers, ready to dry and set like granite. The wogs had to keep their fingers out or they bloody paid the price.

And Connell had stopped his bridge.

He came up on a bicycle! Miles travelled in red bone-dry dust. An albino wog, Lorimer thought. But it was Connell, Commissar Connell. He came out of the heat waves like a ghost.

'Who are you?'

'I'm visiting.'

'A Mick, aren't you?' Lorimer was listening. 'What do you want?'

'I'm an African. I want nothing.'

Lorimer nodded to unleash his minders but they remained motionless, looking past the red image of Connell.

'You came for something?'

'For the navvies, more pence per day, time to rest, a mouthful of wine for your bridge-builders.'

'I could pay you to forget about it?' Lorimer tried. 'Call it insurance.'

'I can take minders too,' Connell said. He looked at them.

'How much?'

'You,' Connell said. 'You squeeze twenty a week for expenses. Twenty a week. A thousand a year. A nice little stash.'

'Yes?' Lorimer said.

'I'm not interested in you,' Connell told him. 'Only the men.'

'How much?'

'Five shillings more a week.'

'Move off,' Lorimer said. 'You're wasting my time.'

Then Connell had held up a hand.

The site stood still. Figures were motionless, glistening images; the mixers ground to a halt, vibrators on the pier spluttered and died.

Connell said, 'In ten minutes your mixers will have pots full of solid rock. A write-off.'

Lorimer said, 'No machinery, no shillings. Fifty little nigger boys sleeping in the shade.'

'For a while,' Connell agreed. 'But they'll send machinery, Mr Lorimer. From the coast, the UK, wherever it is. Two, three weeks, would you say? The rains coming up. Money, money, money. They'd be careful. Put someone in charge who could handle it.' Connell looked at his watch.

'Game, set and match,' Lorimer said.

The site came to life once more.

'Don't bring me out again,' Connell had said; and to the minders, 'Be careful, brothers ...'

'Yes, I met Commissar Connell not long ago,' Lorimer told Freddie.

'Well,' Freddie said, 'Be comfortable.' This would be a bad evening, he knew. 'Jane's doing something about the food. If you want drinks, help yourselves. This damnable heat.' Christ, he thought, Secretariat witch-hunts, pumped-up engineers, Connell the Commissar! In his pocket, crumpled, a little damp, the generous terms of his redundancy.

Lorimer viewed Connell with strange interest. 'A good brew this week, Commissar?'

'Yes,' Connell said.

'Commissar Connell sells palm wine,' Lorimer explained to Freddie. 'He brews palm wine. Very good, the wogs say. Jungle juice but very good.'

Freddie eyed him: a glint of rugby battle days came and went. 'We call him Connell,' he said. 'Just Connell. And we don't say "wogs". Get yourself a drink, won't you? A decent drink.' He turned to Connell. 'Everything shuttered and bolted?'

'Yes.'

'And quiet out there?'

'It seems quiet.'

Lorimer hadn't stirred, was even at ease. But there was malice there, Freddie knew. Pull out the old colonial ace of smile and compromise, that was the ticket. 'We've known Connell for years,' he said; he smiled, was on Lorimer's side for an instant. 'I must confess, old boy, I can't stand that jungle juice of his either. Brain-rotting. Not for Whites.'

Lorimer said, 'Do you sup the home brew, Commissar?'

'Official taster. But my preference is for malt.'

'The wogs say you put God in it. God in a bottle. God in a jam-jar. Whiteman's ju-ju?'

'It might be.'

Freddie said, 'Get yourself a drink, there's a good fellow.'

Lorimer pointed. 'This *is* a drink.'

Freddie took his glass, tipped the contents over the verandah rail: it was all in good humour. He poured a fair measure of whisky on ice, a careful amount of soda.

'Your dram. You're a Scot, Lorimer. Alec? Somehow Lorimer sounds better.' Freddie's anger was gone; Lorimer was to be borne like the heat and sweat.

'I had my schooling there.'

'In Scotland?'

'In Scotland.'

'A rugger man?'

Lorimer didn't reply.

'Got myself to Edinburgh for the "Calcutta" in '34, I remember. Awful winter. Ground like iron.' Freddie turned to Connell, smiled, grimaced his predicament. 'Rugby football, Connell. Calcutta Cup. England–Scotland annual blood-letting. You get a bloody game north of the border.'

Lorimer said, 'Wrong border, Mr Freeman.'

Freddie was puzzled.

'I should say *Freddie*, shouldn't I?' Lorimer could give it some special nuance of unimportance. 'The wrong border, Freddie. *Ulster*. British, of course.'

Freddie was wrong-footed. He was angry, smiling. 'Ah, well done!' he said. 'Ulster, of course. Ireland, isn't it?'

'British.'

'Of course. Silly of me. I keep forgetting we still dabble about in so many little backyards after all these years. There are *some* Irish still scraping along? Eh?'

Lorimer considered it for moments, looked at Connell's unruffled – and vanishing – peace. 'We don't see much of them,' he said. 'They have their alleys and dung-pits.' The tone was only mildly, gently disparaging for something of minor importance. 'Closing ranks, you'd call it, Freddie.'

Freddie was suddenly aware, overcome with embarrassment; he hurried into the breach. 'Hold hard, Lorimer! Hold hard. Connell is Irish, you know?'

'Yes.'

'Well, he used to be. He's African now, he says. Twenty-eight years, isn't it, Connell? You can't squat in a man's field for ever, he says. You must join up.'

Lorimer said, 'We're in Ulster a long time, you know. We brought the Message to Ulster. The Word.'

'Ha!' Freddie took a deep drink. 'We brought these johnnies the message and the word and they're firing bullets up our arses!'

Connell laughed. His wooden boxes on the verandah were painted black, had a neat red cross on the covers. He brought them into the lounge. From one he took two bottles of whisky and put them on the sideboard, poured a neat measure and drank it back. He nodded to Freddie.

From the other he took a long-barrelled .38 revolver, loaded it and lodged it in his belt.

Freddie watched and went on the verandah. He had never seen Connell with a gun. The darkness was more overpowering than he could remember. Lorimer drank a little; there might be a trace of diffidence creeping into his isolation.

'The bank's gone up,' Freddie said.

Connell nodded; he saw the flare of it.

Lorimer stood to look across the miles of steaming night. 'The bank?'

'Yes,' Freddie said.

'Burning?'

123

'Yes.'

'Looted?'

Connell said, 'I wouldn't burn down a bank until I'd looted it first, would you?' He saw a moment of appraisal in Lorimer's eyes.

Behind them, at the rear of the lounge, the house door opened and Jane came walking towards them.

It was a village theatre, Jane thought from where she stood, a little proscenium. The folded doors were hidden, the drawn-back curtains and pelmet framed it; even the banistered verandah, painted white, needed only a passing pale flannelled figure vanishing to the tennis courts to recall a small suburban girl, West End bats in belfries and sport of kings. The guns and ammunition had been set for some silly Woosterish wheeze, you knew. The performance was over, the trio took their curtain call. Only the inky backdrop behind them was reality.

And Connell wore a gun!

She said to Freddie, 'She isn't well, I think.' And explained to Lorimer. 'Mother isn't very well. Just resting a while.'

'Resting? Restless?' Connell asked.

'It isn't anything serious and she doesn't want a fuss,' he was told.

Freddie was nodding. 'Quite right. Sensible. She knows the drill, Connell.'

They waited.

Jane said, 'There isn't any food.'

'No food!'

'Nothing.'

'They've made off with it, have they?' Freddie's astonishment was a silent glazed wonderment.

'Yes.'

'Left the place skint?'

'Even pots and pans.'

'Christ!'

There was a faint sound. From the house? Someone calling out, perhaps. Perhaps nothing. Connell heard it. Jane.

Connell said, 'You found her restless, didn't you?'

'She doesn't want fuss!'

'Fever,' Freddie said.

'She was angry, trembling, pacing about and then, just once, rigid like a post. Staring at me.'

'Weather sprouts every damn thing.' Freddie showed a moment's compassion and swung to impatience. 'Fever comes in all kinds of parcels. Headache, trembling, rigor, you get them all.'

Jane said, 'I wanted her to drink something. You need to drink and sweat, I told her.'

'I'd leave her for a little while. Alone,' Connell said.

Lorimer looked at him with awe. Lorimer had had his information from the coast too, delivered on site after Freddie's departure. He knew Connell's 'form' now. He looked at the hanging revolver, the shotgun. Too easy, too good for a murderer. His awe was to look at the coolness of a killer's face.

Connell stood there, glass, cigarette in hand, spare, tight-skinned face, deep-tanned as if the filth of his life had rubbed off on it; Lorimer looked at the hands that had murdered God-fearing men of Ulster. He felt funk and loathing. And then a throbbing satisfaction that Connell would sweat the journey home, shackled in the brig, to pay the price. Pay a fair share of it too before the lever was snapped and he dropped into damnation.

How long, Lorimer thought, for his escort to grind over the miles of rail, cut through rock, skirting swamp and volcanic barrier, in times like these? Midnight, later, first light? And if the rains broke? Christ, if the rains came...

Freddie was saying, 'Get him in the bloodstream and the bug makes his appearance from time to time, keeps cropping up.

Old timers walk it off in a day or two. Part of the business. The first shiver is like palsy...'

Lorimer interrupted him. 'What troops in the village?'

'Ten this morning.'

'Now?'

Freddie laughed.

Lorimer appraised him. 'How many on the way, Mr Free-man?'

'They don't tell me these things,' Freddie said. 'I'm a bank manager. Two, three companies. A hundred, two hundred. Enough to nail this bloody thing down, I suppose.'

'How long?'

'When it gets here,' Freddie told him. 'Three days if it rains. Drink your whisky, my boy. Give it a rest.'

In the lounge there was an enclave of silence, seemingly distanced from the crickets and pulsing drums; lightning on the skyline guttered like dying candles or forked down beyond the end of the world. It was silent in the house too.

In a little while Jane said, 'It didn't seem like fever.'

Connell went to stand on the verandah: death was in the house already.

Freddie called out to him. 'That fellow in the gaol's hanging on, isn't he, Connell? Damn charivari, fireworks and shake-your-arse dance when he goes, I suppose.'

But Connell stared, in doubt, towards his hospice.

'Wog fireworks?' Lorimer said.

You couldn't help this hard-head, Freddie thought; but he smiled and was pleasant. 'Infernal things, their damn fireworks. Dangerous as hell.'

Connell, his back to them, was holding up a hand in signal. Drums and crickets had become part of the silence now. They listened to it. Suddenly Connell had gone from the verandah. Freddie called after him into the darkness. He had vanished.

Lorimer was on his feet, almost alarmed, Freddie thought. Strange reaction.

'He'll be back, he'll be back, he has a gun,' Freddie said. 'Told me once he wouldn't know a gun from a gatepost. You just pull the trigger, dammit, I told him. But Connell can shoot, I'll bet.' He laughed. 'He's not a bad fellow, Lorimer, remember that.'

'The wogs will protect him?'

'I wonder,' Freddie said. Lorimer was an arrogant bastard, he thought again.

From the house came the faint sound of someone exclaiming. Then silence.

'Yes, she's restless,' Jane said.

'Restless.' Freddie pondered it. 'And it's not fever, you think?'

Jane said, 'I'll go to her.'

'No,' Freddie said. 'Let me. I'll see to it . . .'

They were alone: it should have been the time to chip away wickedly at Lorimer's pose and prudery, sit facing him with outstretched legs, let him hear the creep of her palm along the flimsy cotton on her thighs. He was a tethered, untried savage, to be cut loose and punished, that was all. Bed-battles should be great exhausting moments of joy; but life with a Lorimer would be death in a cage, with moments of hebdomadal release perhaps for holy congress. And then remorse, even in sacred matrimony. A catharsis of hymnals and bibles.

She glanced and saw that he lay back, eyes closed, resting, gathering strength for tomorrow's chase with wogs and minders. But there was a tenseness there too, a sense of waiting. Tomorrow, she thought. His drink was warming beside him. Desire, something of laughter and tussle and drowsy happiness, would never come for his surrender. She had felt the sly disparagement of Freddie, hardly a veiled contempt, and been suddenly aware of integrity, a fairness, generosity, beside a young buck's withering dogmatism. Freddie was a man. She thought about Connell too for a moment: a strange calmness.

'You're Irish,' she said to Lorimer.

'British.'

'In Ireland?'

'In Ulster.'

'Ulster's in Ireland.'

'Yes.'

'Well?'

'We made it British.'

'A colony.'

'Not a colony.'

'I give up, dear boy,' she said. 'It all sounds like a wagon train fighting off the Indians.'

There was noise in the house, distant, a shrillness; and then the drone of Freddie's voice restoring peace. They listened.

Jane said, 'Mother. It was odd. Not like fever. We've all had fever. For a moment I thought she was mad. Rigid! Tension, I suppose. She loathes it out here.'

Lorimer was patient. 'After all the years?'

Jane nodded. 'Twelve, thirteen.' She thought about it. 'Every fifteen months, three months down on the Cape. Incredible holidays. Parties, sun, sea, servants, every damn wonderful thing. Incredible.' She stood up and paced about. 'England! Back to that bloody godawful dustbin. God, she is mad.'

'She loathes it here?'

'Yes.'

'Twelve, thirteen years?'

'Every minute.'

Lorimer said, 'She should take herself home.'

Jane studied him, hid her annoyance, went to the sideboard and poured a drink. 'How long have you been in that colony of yours? Ireland, you said.'

'Ulster. Not a colony.'

'Whatever you call it.'

He smiled. 'The Lorimers? Two hundred years, give or take.'

'Why don't you take yourselves home. Britain waits.'

'We don't loathe Ulster,' Lorimer said. 'Only the Micks wanting to meddle, that's all.' He found that amusing.

'Some day they'll pull it asunder, maybe, like this piece of Empire.'

'We're not a soft mark,' Lorimer said. 'That's the difference, you see.' And then suddenly, 'Are you afraid?'

'Sometimes.'

'Wogs make me spit,' he said. 'Fifty years on they'll still be squatting out there like frogs in the bush.'

Jane remembered earlier days. She had been ten when Freddie had driven them up the steep hill and along the circular gravel drive. She had grown up – six years – with Connell's children, climbed palms with them, learned where to walk, where to step aside, was alert as a hunter. And she had almost forgotten it in the years of exile.

'I spent the war years here,' she said. 'Had Mother and Connell for teachers.'

Lorimer laughed.

'They were good. I was the dunce. Or didn't give a damn,' she said. 'A year of cramming in Highgate, then ready for greatness.' Jane's amusement had a trace of regret. 'Four years to a groggy BA.'

'Students are as good as their teachers.'

'They were good teachers. I tried to rebel when they parcelled me for the UK and Highgate, screamed out there in the compound until Connell struck me dumb with his open hand.'

'Connell?'

'Connell was right.'

'You wanted to stay?'

'Yes.'

'Be a savage?'

She thought about it. 'For a while.'

'And then in charge?'

'Just to live.' Jane looked at the black world beyond the verandah. 'You dislike them out there, don't you?'

'Wogs? They haven't arrived yet,' he said. 'Still up in the trees.'

'You won't ever be in charge,' she told him. 'It only means making the rules, drawing lines to you.' She smiled at him. 'I was in love with Connell's son once. Pale yellow skin, a smiler, tall, very special. We'd meet in the bush, commit little sins. I gave him a ring I bought in the market. I was *living*, Mr Lorimer. *He* could be in charge.'

Lorimer was motionless in his chair. 'You let him touch you?'

'James was his name. James Connell. The name of an Irish grandfather. He was proud of it. I saw him crying when they drove me away. I waved to him. But three days on the ship and I'd forgotten. Heartless, you see. All those young gods at the swimming pool bringing ice-cream and cold drinks.'

'Where is he now?'

'James Connell?'

'James Connell.'

Jane paused, was silent for moments. 'He's twenty-four,' she calculated. 'Has a woman and children somewhere, I suppose. At the mines, maybe. Or the whiteman's kitchen, making whiteman's chop-chop. On your bridge, maybe. I didn't look.'

'He touched you, you said?'

'Everywhere. And I touched him. That's the fun of it, Alec.'

'You were *living*?'

'Poor Alec,' she said and dismissed it. 'People like Mother spoil them of course. When the time comes you talk *at* them. Father talks at them. They move!'

'And now?'

'Strange, I don't notice them very much any more.'

'When your kitchen is empty?'

'Oh yes. I'll be angry about that.'

There was movement from outside, Connell announcing himself: footfalls on the verandah steps. He said, 'I'll get myself a drink.' He poured malt and drank it back.

Connell was angry.

'You heard something out there, did you?' Jane asked.

'A dozen things,' Connell said. 'Under that crust of bush

130

down there are tracks to everywhere. Darkness that doesn't dissolve. Sounds. Hearing is like seeing.' Connell looked at her. 'You remember it, don't you?'

She could see Lorimer's hovering amusement; and Connell aware of it and its unimportance.

'Yes.'

'You could sit here, remember, listen to the small sounds of lizards in dust powder, know there was danger when birds panicked or something scampered for cover. You could smell rain and storms.'

'James could,' she said.

'I used to watch him,' Connell said. 'Watch you both.' He paused, remembering. 'You were ...'

'Thirteen,' she said. 'He was fifteen. Same birthday.'

'Twenty-four now.'

'Has a woman and children?' she asked.

Connell was silent.

'Women and children?'

'Children here and there, you can bet,' Connell said. 'Had his school too, behind Hookers. They closed it.'

'He was always gone, travelling, preaching, when I came from London.'

'Yes.'

'You made him a schoolmaster.' She suddenly smiled.

Lorimer said, 'Wog politics, Commissar?'

'Yes,' Connell said.

Jane watched them. 'Where is he?' she asked. 'James. Where is he now, Connell?'

Lorimer was silent, waited in vain for some careful Connell response; eventually he said, 'I hope he's not burning down the village, Commissar.'

'I'm certain he isn't,' Connell said.

'Or the gaol or his forbidden academy of politics?'

Freddie was arriving.

'Or the bank,' Connell said.

Jane said to Lorimer, 'What's this damn "Commissar" thing?'

'Some infantile joke Lorimer keeps harping on. Give it a rest, there's a good chap. It's worn a bit thin, you know.'

Freddie had arrived, almost in silence, from the house and Lucy's bedroom; he had closed the door with infinite care behind him and now came to join them. Connell brought him a drink. Freddie's was a brave face, Connell thought, looking towards the village.

Lightning struck closer now, an instant flare to strip darkness from bush and hills and flatland.

'Still a fair old blaze in there, Connell.'

Jane studied the calmness, the incongruity of missing servants, ammunition, firearms. Lorimer was within his impregnable self.

Connell said to Freddie, 'Lucy?'

But Freddie brushed it aside in reassurance. 'She's got herself in a fine old tizz. Not fever, she says. Nerves, I told her. Fever too. She knows I'm right. Everything is unpredictable in this damn country.' He said to Jane, 'I'll book her a flight tomorrow. If there's a flight. If there's a damn telephone line standing between here and the coast. If there's a train on the rails. Christ, what a balls-up! Let her have a couple of months back there. London, Muswell Hill, all that.'

Jane said, 'She was calm for a little while, it came and went. She remembered her select church bazaars, afternoon tea dances, messenger boys on their bikes delivering groceries, daddy's golf clubs, mummy's sheet music. Smiling but sadness in everything.'

Freddie sighed, raised his glass to Connell. 'All quiet out there?'

'All quiet.'

'Lucy. She's a bit low, that's all. She'll have a month or two back in Muswell Hill or Hornsey or wherever it is.' Freddie was thoughtful. 'Parents gone since '41 of course. But she'd like to walk all the old ground, I know. Kneel at their graves, pray a little. She'd like to be there, Connell. A good person, you see. Connections in Worthing too, I think. Or is it Worcester? I can never remember. She'll be upset about dinner, Lorimer. Bad enough, idiots deserting, but looting the larder is no holds barred. My apologies too. Have a drink. It'll keep us going.'

Lorimer stood. 'They hide food, you know.' He smiled at Freddie. 'Easier than carrying it. Tins rattle too.'

'Good thinking,' Freddie said.

Jane said, 'I'll poke about their huts. Under beds and bushes. Come on, Mr Lorimer,' she led him. 'Young ladies need knight errants on black days such as this.' They went down the verandah steps, out of sight, Jane's voice and laughter diminishing as they moved away to the lee of the house, crept quietly to the periphery where the huts were.

Freddie and Connell stood alone in the lounge. There was noise from the house. Footsteps? 'By God,' Freddie said. 'It's Lucy. She's up and about. Damn fever comes and goes, you see?'

'Yes.'

Freddie looked at Connell. 'There's nothing wrong, is there?'

'Your gardener's out there.'

'Josiah?'

'Out there,' Connell repeated.

'Dead?' Freddie asked.

'Yes.'

Lucy's footsteps in the house were closer now.

'Murdered?'

Connell said, 'I'll wrap him up, shove him in the bush. They'll come for him.'

'They?'

'His brothers.'

Freddie nodded. 'Dustsheets, ropes in the garage,' he said. Lucy's footsteps were close. 'Should I come?'

'You should be here. With Lucy.'

'Lucy?'

'Yes.'

'Is she ill, Connell?'

'Yes.'

Freddie watched him move away into the night.

Lucy walked the corridor, slowly, in darkness, pausing for moments at the lounge door: the almost total absence of pain and convulsion brought now a fear of its recurrence. Only a faint dullness of headache remained and weak shooting stabs from the tiny inflamed 'boil' on her hand; she could still feel the skin of mucus in her throat and the almost audible friction of humid air sucked in, pushed away. She tidied her hair and clothing, arranged an untroubled face for Freddie.

'I'm fine,' she said as she entered and Freddie turned from the verandah. 'It blotted me out for a while in there. But it's passed.'

'Gone?' Freddie said.

'Almost clear,' she said. 'Wonderful.'

Ill, Connell had said; and he didn't whip up storms for nothing. Freddie said, 'Come, sit, rest a while.' He could see her illness.

'Don't fuss,' she said.

Freddie smiled, composed himself for the disclosure of Josiah's murder that might trigger off this rigor of illness. He felt the head office letter in his pocket, damp, and put it in the sideboard to dry. He saw the crocodile bag stuffed with the bank's money. The village drums, crickets, were suddenly thunderous, it seemed: he saw Lucy flinch when lightning flared and vanished. A grip of dread held him for a moment.

'Where's Connell?' she asked.

'He just popped out.'

'That boy Lorimer is coming to see Jane. Dinner.'

'He's here. Everything is being taken care of.'

Freddie pulled across a large leather pouffe, coloured, panelled, fringed: passing Hausa traders could sell all kinds of rubbish to Lucy. He squatted on it, facing her.

'That's bad news,' he said.

'Yes, yes,' she said patiently. 'The village is in uproar, servants missing, guns, bullets in the lounge. We're like outlaws.'

'It's Josiah,' Freddie said.

Lucy waited, eyes closed. He could see the tightening muscles of her neck. Christ, had he blundered into this thing? The adhesive dressing was on one hand, the other clamped on top.

'What about Josiah?'

'He's dead.'

There was no movement; eyes closed, she seemed to sit and rest. 'Murdered?' she asked.

'We don't know. Connell is wrapping him up. Dustsheets, ropes from the garage. What he can find. His family, or whatever they are, brothers or something, will come for him.'

'Connell said?'

'Yes.'

She sat for minutes in silence; but there was no expected movement of shock or deep grief. Now calmness seemed to be a strange manifestation of her illness.

'If you use the sideboard,' she said. 'Don't make noise. My head aches a little.'

With almost horizontal bottle and glass he poured a little measure of whisky and drank it. He slid the glass back on the sideboard.

'Are you there?' she asked.

She was sitting up close to the verandah. 'Yes,' he said.

'Connell shouldn't be out there without help,' she said. 'You should have gone with him. Poor Josiah dead. He loved his garden. I used to watch him sitting for hours out there.'

Sitting, Freddie thought.

'We didn't want to leave you alone,' he said. 'Do your eyes hurt? I could bring your glasses.'

She raised her lids for a moment, closed them again. 'Darkness is more restful,' she said.

'I could turn the lamps down.'

'No.'

135

He took the redundancy letter from the sideboard, put it in his tunic pocket.

She said, 'I don't suppose they liked him going down to the club playing at cricket with you. Pandering, they might call it. He wasn't paid to do it. A gardener. They have rules too, I suppose, haven't they?'

Freddie felt the prod of irritation; he sidetracked. 'We heard you on the move in there,' he said, 'Connell and I. We thought it best you had company.'

Silence again. Then suddenly she said, 'I'm sorry, darling.' She smiled at him. 'You did what was best. You always do.'

Years had scarcely changed him, she thought: a little more weight, hardly noticeable; and the past decade of alcohol was showing its colours of late. He had been the victor ludorum of the sportsgrounds, man for all seasons, when she had seen him all those years ago. And seen him in so many other eyes too. But he had asked her to dance with such courtesy, held her so properly apart, and so gently, as they foxtrotted and waltzed in a kind of gossamer courtship. He was bound for Alexandria and the Med zone at any time: staff directors had seen him. A little delay, that was all. It was a time of dreams. Blue water, sunshine, towns with fairytale names. And he had lived in India. She held him in awe, was almost afraid that she loved him. They were married, a joyous day for everyone, even a Freeman grand-aunt who had materialized from Harrogate and departed again for her uncharted vacuum with smiles: 'Do write to me, child. His parents would be so proud, dear departed things.' She was gone. Write where?

A joyous day but the end of joy too. There had been no blissful consummation of a wedding night. Freddie had drawn the curtains, making a new tiny world without familiar voice or sound or reassurance. She looked away from its intimacy when he opened a travelling trunk and beneath its tray saw the exposed nether garments that would lie against his skin. She had asked to be alone for a little while and even his compliance tightened the grip of fear. In the wardrobe she hung her outdoor garments but the delicate hidden ones remained locked in her trunk. When Freddie returned she lay in bed, almost terrified in the darkness of the room. She could smell whisky, hear him undressing. When he lay beside her she knew he was naked. It was a night of degradation, tears: it was the end of her heroic Freddie.

And he had been passed over of course, left office-clerking year in, year out, down by the fish market until, in wartime shortage, they had offered him this great vast airless midden.

From the kitchen she heard Jane's voice and for moments remembered the hours of confinement and delivery. Freddie had come from his rugger, shining, polished, childish almost in his joy. She had always loved him; but the game of groping, grinding, coition was impossible. She had told him. 'Yes, my dear,' he had agreed.

She looked up to find him standing there: the smell of whisky. Throat muscles contracted for a moment and she was hoarse, breathless, growing old.

'All right, old girl?'

'Of course,' she said.

Freddie said again, 'We didn't want to leave you here alone, that was the idea. Connell and I. You'd be better sitting up a while, I thought.' He was holding out the crumpled white envelope to her. He stood on the verandah while she read it. It took a long time. The darkness was a jet crêpe veil within reach. Only the village flares and embers, the skyline flickers, pierced it.

'Of course there'll be a place for you!' she said.

He turned to look at her face, pulled tighter now, the illness sitting there. 'They've superannuated me. Pension, gratuity, all that.' He paused. 'But finished. Nothing back there.'

'Nonsense.'

'Nothing in London.' He remembered to say, 'At home. Nothing at home.'

'Of course there is.'

He remained silent.

She stared at him. 'We're going home, Freddie. Away from this dirt and disease. There'll be Twickers and Dublin and Edinburgh for you again. All your friends, remember?' She closed her eyes to see it all. 'Regent Street at Christmas ... Dear God, let it happen.'

'Muswell Hill,' Freddie said.

'Home.'

'London Bridge. The Monument.'

She was breathless, groping in a moment of discomfort. He came and held her shoulders. 'Everything will be all right,' he said. Laughter came from the kitchen, not loud but discordant. Lorimer's laughter, a kind of ridicule. He said, 'Jane and that fellow in the kitchen. We can tell Jane later. I'm not sure I care very much for *him*. Could be troublesome, a bit flinty for my taste.'

Lucy was recovering: breath was coming a little easier, the shooting pains from her hand lessening, a momentary paralysis ebbing fast. 'Scots are flinty,' she said. 'That's why they get on.'

'He's Irish,' Freddie explained. 'Well, he says he's British but I'm always confused with that Ulster thing. I thought we'd finished with the damn place years ago.' He paced about in restlessness. 'Connell should be finished out there soon.' He stood before her. 'I'll book you a flight tomorrow. You're not well. This climate is getting to you. It's hard on women. You'll be back in a couple of days maybe. London.'

'And you?'

'I'll see the tour out. That's the drill.'

'Alone?'

'Jane might stay.'

She pondered it. 'Yes, Jane will stay.' She was smiling.

He felt relief at her happiness. 'Will you be all right? In London, you know? It'll have changed. Jane was unhappy there, felt everything was dirty. Even the people.'

'Jane mightn't fit there,' she said.

Freddie said eventually, 'You see, I never wanted to go back. You knew that, didn't you? I didn't ever belong there.' He was standing beside her but talking at the darkness beyond the verandah. 'I was twelve when I left India. Home, whatever that is, was out there. Naiani Tal, Udaipur, the lakes, the palace, the Irish Brothers in Rajahputana.' He was groping about for irrelevances. 'The finest teachers in the world, my father used to say. Law and order, heads down, no rubbish.'

'Yes,' she said.

'They're buried at Udaipur. My father and mother. Well, near it, at any rate. Goganda. A few miles. Sometimes Connell reminds me of India.'

'Yes.'

He moved on to the verandah, turned to face her. 'I haven't amounted to much out here. I'm just a stop-gap really. If the war hadn't happened I'd still have a desk looking out at Billings-gate and the traffic crawling into London Bridge. I've always been afraid of that, kept out of the way.'

'Yes, I know.'

'You go back, my dear. There's money enough.'

She held out her undamaged hand to him and he took it, kissed it, kissed her on the forehead: it was burning and dry.

'And you?'

'The Cape, I suppose.'

'I understand,' she said.

He went to the sideboard, wanted to drink, and steeled himself against it.

Lucy was saying, 'Twelve years in this steamy decaying place and not one glimpse of home. Oh yes, I know. The war, the war. Three thousand miles to London and Jerry subs out off Freetown and only raids and ration books if we got there.' She might have been wickedly echoing him, remembering. 'It wasn't on. Cape Town was the place. Cape Town. All the flotsam of dead empires showing Bantu houseboys how it's done. Jildi,

jildi!' She paused a little while and said. 'The war's been over for five years.'

'Yes.'

Silence settled gently on them now. He remembered London years, morning and evening, the stations at Highgate or Winchmore Hill, the 'semi' with everything in its precise place, the flower-beds with Lucy and toddling Jane always in her wake.

'I can't believe Josiah's dead.' She might have been 'rambling', speaking aloud her thoughts. 'That was his name. Josiah. The gardener's name was Josiah. I should feel sad for him but I feel nothing. Feelings waste away out here.'

Freddie said, 'Connell is wrapping him up. Dustsheets, tarpaulin stuff from the garage. No question of bringing him in. Bodies pong in no time out here. And insects flock round.'

'Helping you at your cricket. They'd call it fratting or something, wouldn't they? But it seems such a little thing. For that would they kill him?'

Freddie decided to tolerate it. 'I suppose it's possible. They are bloody savages when you boil it down. The jungle doesn't wash out in a rinse of baptism, Guinness, and whiteman's soap powder.'

She was silent. Sounds came from the compound, voices perhaps, a door shutting.

'Connell?' she asked.

'Jane and that Lorimer fellow more like it.' He hadn't told her about the food. So many things had been told: Josiah, redundancy, Muswell Hill, the Cape. He wouldn't mention Connell. 'The staff. They cleaned the kitchen out when they left,' he said. 'Jane and Lorimer are poking about. They might have hidden it, you see?'

In a little while she said, 'No food.'

'None.'

She was looking at his guns. 'If there's a prowler will you shoot him?'

Freddie was stung. 'Of course I'll shoot him! I'm not interested in whether he's Jumbo, Jomo or Jeremiah, if he wants buckshot in his buttocks he'll get it. A whole Milky Way of johnnies out there. We try to put the place together, give them law and order, and they want to run before they can bloody crawl. We're too damned easy on them. The German up in Togo had it right years ago. Fence them off. No fratting. Catch them speaking your lingo and lash them for it. And they loved it! Used to cry when their masters went on leave. Blubbering away on the jetty like old mammies.' Freddie paused for breath. 'Someone said they're even flying a swastika up there now. Longing to have the Hun back. By God, I'll shoot them all right!'

Suddenly Connell was on the verandah, would seem instantly to have materialized out of the darkness.

Freddie said, 'I'll get you a drink. Everything all right?'

'Yes.' Connell was looking at Lucy. 'How do you feel?' he asked.

'Go and tidy up, won't you,' she said.

'Yes.' Connell moved towards Freddie and the sideboard.

'A bit messy?' Freddie said. 'I should have come with you.' He held the drink to Connell's lips, looked at Connell's hands smeared with dirt and blood.

Lucy said, 'You'll find soap, towels ... You know your way about.' She hunched forward a little, peeling back the small stick-on dressing on her hand.

Freddie moved forward to peer at it. 'That thing's upsetting you. Your *hand*.' He paused, looked back at Connell. 'Iodine. Pour it on, never fails. No use until it burns hell out of you, of course.' It was a suppurating angry pustule.

Lucy was silent.

'A scratch was it?'

'A sting, a bite.'

'Sure you won't have a whisky, my dear? Better than gin. A good deadener for everything out here.'

Connell watched the tautness take its grip on her again: hands clasped, upright, staring into darkness; throat muscles in motion, then tight, rigid. Battling with a monster, Connell thought. Battles would be more frequent now, take longer to repel, until in the end there was nothing. He listened to her breathing.

'Days ago, a sting, a bite,' she told Freddie; a weakening voice. 'I'll have it seen to in the morning. It's painful, that's all.' She had recovered a little, waved Freddie away.

He looked at Connell, puzzled, perhaps irritated. 'Some venomous little flying speck, the air is full of them.' He dismissed it. 'Before the rains all kinds of things are let loose. Looks harmless enough, I'd say.' He stood on the verandah and looked back at her. 'How long? Days ago, did you say? I'm hopeless. You should have waved it about. You know how "blind" I am!' Freddie's anger was turned upon himself; he would make amends. 'We'll drive up to the mines in the morning. Early. They've got a good quack there now. Polish fellow. Unpronounceable oski boski something.'

Jane and Lorimer were arriving. Lorimer had dredged up humour from somewhere; he said almost joyfully, 'Nothing.'

Jane said, 'Not a crumb. Bare as a cell.'

Lucy stood to greet Lorimer, thanked him, motioned him to a chair. Connell could see the faint trembling of her fingers.

'It's unforgivable,' she said; she sat carefully down and arranged herself. 'And poor Josiah.'

'Josiah?' Jane said. 'What about him?' But Lucy had lapsed into silence again, fighting her own silent battle with sudden floods of pain.

Freddie said, 'Josiah is dead.'

'Dead?'

'Yes.'

'Where?'

'At the edge of the compound. Connell has seen to it.'

Lorimer said, 'A burial service, Commissar?'

'No,' Connell said. 'I've parcelled him up, that's all.'

'Everthing that walks and crawls will be boring at it all night.' Jane said, 'It'll stink by morning. That's the coast, dear Alec.'

'He won't be there very long,' Connell told her. 'A little while into the darkness they'll come for him.'

Lorimer said, looking at Freddie's armoury, at Connell, gun in belt. 'If anything moves out there we shoot it, don't we?'

Freddie's exasperation leaked a little. 'Give it a rest, there's a good fellow. A couple of bangs in the air would scare the bloody lot of us.'

Lucy said, kindly she thought, to Lorimer. 'Didn't you hear Connell? They'll come for Josiah's body.'

'Who comes?'

'His brothers.'

Jane said, 'They all have brothers. Same father, different mother. Same mother, different father. But brothers, dozens of them. Brothers everywhere. A great celebration of palm wine.' She looked at Connell. 'You need to wash,' she said.

Lorimer's humour continued to improve. 'On the bridge,' he explained, 'my wogs say, Commissar Connell. Same father, sons galore and the holy spirit of palm wine, amen. Do you have sons, Commissar?'

Lucy was confused, in pain, but she said, 'Yes, he has sons. They used to climb our palms out there. They used to bring me fruit. Pineapples, mangoes ... limes...' She tapered off into silence.

Freddie said quietly, 'Oh, drop this damn thing, Lorimer. You've stretched it a bit fine. We've known Connell for years. We call him "Connell".'

'Alec. Call me Alec.'

'Alec,' Connell said. 'Come and have a drink with us one day. Malt whisky. Meet my wives.'

'The handmaids of the Lord.'

'They'll appreciate that,' Connell said. He looked at his hands, held them out. 'I'll wash,' he said. 'They hacked old Josiah a bit. Storms are times to settle old scores.' He walked back through the lounge to the house door and said as he went, 'Revolutions always need bandits in the end.'

Jane watched him close the door quietly and leave them in silence. She would punish Lorimer, she decided again.

Freddie and Jane stood side by side on the verandah. In the lounge Lucy and Lorimer were seated. But Lucy was alone, sitting, eyes closed with her pain: it shot like a thread of current to fingertip extremities and along forearm muscles to biceps and shoulders. For moments her whole body was in seizure; and then moments of blessed relief. Only her head ached without cease.

Lorimer glanced at her, paused momentarily to watch the clutched hands, and slightly parted lips sucking and blowing the burden of air. On the verandah, Jane and Freddie were motionless, backs towards him. He looked at the bare arms and legs of Jane and remembered her lying naked in his riverside hut. Without shame, he thought; but felt a stirring down in his injured genitals that even pain could not suppress.

They turned back from the verandah to face him.

Freddie said, 'He's still holding out.'

'The hunger-striker,' Jane explained it.

Lorimer said, 'Connell,' and pondered it. 'He visits the jail every day, did you know? Never misses.'

Freddie said, 'He visits the dying.' He seemed pleased about it all. 'He's an African, you see. He tells you he's an African.'

Lorimer said, 'That's crap. Sometimes I feel grimy just looking at him. Can't help it. Creepy all over. Imagine living with them, smelling them, watching them put what fingers they have left of revolting mess in their mouths. The stench of their sickness.' He looked towards the house where Connell had made his exit. 'And bedding down with black women.'

'You don't talk like that before my wife,' Freddie said. 'Or about Connell in his absence.' He was remembering years of joyous surprise and pleasure at Hookers.

Lucy was aware again, wide-eyed, almost free of dreaded spasm; only her head would burst with pain. 'Connell's a good man,' she said.

'A matter of taste,' Lorimer said. 'I wouldn't have him here.'

Jane said, 'No?'

'He's a wog.'

Freddie looked at Lorimer, seemed to run out of patience at last. 'Now, look here, Lorimer!' he said. 'You're talking to my wife. You're talking about Connell.'

Lorimer raised a hand in what might be an apology.

In silence, Freddie viewed him with distaste; but when he spoke it was without edge or rancour. 'Connell doesn't rush about setting up altars, peddling bibles and brands from the burning. We've half a dozen assorted missions out there putting on their shows, confusing whatever puddle-brains these johnnies have. But, make no mistake, Connell's a law and order man. When they needed schooling they got it. And the odd biff along the way to keep them straight. The old ones come for lint and boric on their weeping sores. Sometimes they move on, sometimes they come to die. By God, I wouldn't stick it long. Or you, Lorimer.'

Lorimer said, 'I often wonder why he stays.'

Lucy's voice slipped away to weakness; little pauses too as if words and breath had to be gathered before she spoke. 'We know all about Connell,' she said and paused again.

'Of course you do,' Lorimer said. They waited.

'My God,' Lucy said suddenly, 'Josiah out there in that awful darkness.'

Freddie watched her. She was ill of course. Connell was right. He would take her to the mines in the morning, put that Polish fellow to work. He said with undue kindliness, 'My dear, of course that cricket practice didn't land Josiah in it. Absolute nonsense. Like Connell said, someone settling old scores. That's about it.' He paused, waited for her to look at him. 'He enjoyed bowling at me, you know, could launch a sudden attack, I can tell you, almost got me low a couple of times last week.' Freddie needed a drink. On his way to the sideboard he said to everyone, 'Today? He was there, large as life, God is my judge. I turned and he was gone.' He poured a drink for Connell and left it. 'He was afraid, you understand? He'd got the scent of someone creeping up for him. They can do that kind of thing, you know.'

Lucy said, 'You were never really cruel to him.'

'I shouted a bit,' Freddie said. 'I shout at them all.' Freddie gave it up. 'Oh, to hell with it, it works, that's the thing.' He paced about in silence; Jane watched him; the crickets and drums crept back. 'Funny,' Freddie said. 'You don't hear those damn crickets until you listen for them. Millions of them out there. Millions. They can signal each other, stop and go in a split second. Difficult to understand. Difficult. Probably told you all this before, Lorimer.'

Lorimer stood and stretched, felt the soreness at his groin; he passed by Freddie, stood on the verandah, gazing at the darkness.

'You get used to it, old man.' Freddie needed to talk, repeated himself. 'You get used to everything, take people as you find them.' He was silent for a moment. 'We are intruders, I suppose,' he concluded. 'Intruders.'

Lorimer on the verandah, his back to them, held out his hands, a great crucified figure against the darkness. 'This is *ours*, Freddie. All of it out there. A couple of hundred thousand square miles of it. British!' Lorimer raised his voice to send words booming into the stillness.

He was an idiot, Freddie decided; an arrogant incurable idiot. 'Yes, yes, of course,' he said. 'And keep your bloody voice down, won't you?'

Lorimer's speech had ended. Hands in pockets, he surveyed his property. Jane looked at Freddie's face, the hard gentleness of it seemingly drawn tight. She felt a sudden immense compassion for him.

Lucy said, 'Is Ulster so very big, Mr Lorimer?'

146

Lorimer turned and studied her for a moment. 'Not very,' he said.

'That little piece near Scotland, isn't it?'

'Yes.'

Freddie said, 'Ireland really. You see it on the map.' He turned quietly, inoffensively, to Lorimer. 'Don't you find it a bit of a quibble sometimes? Being British when we're all kinds of things? I feel nothing, very little at any rate, when they come swinging along with the old rousing tunes, banners flying, heads erect, straight backs for the King.' Freddie thought about it for a moment. 'Courtesy, respect, of course. All that. But we're colonials, carpet-baggers, journeymen, part of the mob and not very important.' He looked at Lorimer. 'Mercenaries, really. They bury us where we drop.'

'You wouldn't build a lot of bridges, Freddie,' Lorimer said.

'We built a lot of bridges in India and hardly knew why.'

Lorimer said, 'Law and order to the blackman, Freddie. Jildi, jildi!'

'Yes,' Freddie said.

The whole impending weight of rain and storm seemed to press down on them, driving out the air, bringing a clammy film of sweat. Not a leaf stirred, or a shrub; the sound of crickets came and went; lightning flickered on the horizon where the world curved and dropped away. The thread of paralysing pain rested a while and only the throb of head and wounded hand was a pulse and a reality for Lucy. She looked at the dry skin of her arms, felt the dryness of her body. A moment of peace.

Freddie's retirement, she thought in sadness. The end. He was a good man, always lonely of course.

Jane said, 'Do you know how many labourers Alec has on his bridge, Mother? Fifty, sixty. He makes a deal: good work palm wine, bad work skin flying! Isn't he a scream?'

Lorimer looked at her smiling appraisal.

Lucy had shut herself away from the babble, looked into the darkness to forget noise and the small sounds of liquor in glasses.

She tried to release the tightness of muscle, to cling to these moments of remission.

'I think he's an absolute howl,' Jane said in the silence.

Freddie nodded. 'Absolutely,' he said.

'And double measures and big sticks for his minders,' she said.

Words were pebbles in a pond, plopping their entries, making soundless rings of concentricity that spread out to reach and destroy each other. The Freeman faces all looked out at the darkness. Lorimer watched them.

'Double measures,' Lorimer said, just faintly aware that he was being ridiculed and striking back. 'A bonus system, Freddie. You have bonuses and promotions in the bank, don't you? Big manager, big branch?'

Freddie nodded.

'Every good boy deserves favour.'

'And punishments,' Freddie said. 'Bonuses and punishments in the bank.' He felt the sudden anger of Jane. Lucy was almost cocooned in her illness. He thought: redundancy with pension and gratuity, the Cape, its clubs, rugger to watch, cricket to watch, to practise, to play; all he wanted. But Lorimer had winged him. Redundancy had hurt.

Jane hadn't missed Freddie's moment of bleakness or Lorimer's expressionless calm. She stared at Lorimer for a long time without response. She moved towards the verandah. 'I need a change of air,' she announced.

Lorimer said, 'It's just as hot out there.'

'I need a change of hot air.'

Freddie said, 'Listen.' The village cacophony was without end. 'It's not a game they're playing, you know, Lorimer. And that body is still there, remember. You'll be sitting ducks for some johnnies prowling about.'

'Waiting for its brothers?' Lorimer asked. 'That body?'

Lucy raised her unblemished hand: it was trembling. Lorimer watched it. 'That body,' she said, 'is Josiah. Deserving your respect, Mr Lorimer.'

'Oh, I respect him,' Lorimer said. 'All dead johnnies have my respect.'

'Air,' Jane said; she crossed the lounge and went out into the darkness, looked at Lorimer as she went. He followed. Only as he moved out of sight, a slight limp, did Freddie see the glint of the shotgun barrel.

Lucy said, 'He's taken your gun. Should he do that?'

Freddie paced about for moments.

Lorimer was calling back. 'Don't come scouting, Freddie. Might take you for a wog. Blast off at shadows, you know.' His laughter seemed thunderous in the stillness. 'Pity you can't send the Commissar.' It tapered away.

Lucy said again, 'He's taken your gun. Should he do that?'

Freddie said quietly, 'He's a bit gutless. Can't take his liquor either. Bad marks out here.' Freddie looked at the illness shaping Lucy's face now. 'Jane's taped him, I think. She'll tumble him all right.' He was silent for a little while. 'Funny, Scots get mean in their cups,' he said.

'Irish, isn't he?'

Freddie thought about it and smiled. 'Yes, it was Ulster,' he said. 'British, of course!'

Lucy's voice was slow, quiet, with hardly a modulation. 'British? *We're* not so rude, are we? Scots were always rude.'

Freddie shrugged.

'Connell, Irish,' she said.

'The Scots are British,' Freddie remembered aloud. 'Even the damn johnnies are British.'

Lucy was holding her damaged hand again, her head a little inclined: vague ghostly pain hovered, dissolved, hovered. Eventually she said, 'Well, at any rate, it's nonsense. Being British when it's perfectly obvious he's nothing of kind.'

It was upsetting her. Freddie could see the illness tightening its grip. Her face changed, her eyes; restless hands. 'It doesn't matter, my dear,' he said gently, smiling to her. 'We'll put him up for auction.'

She nodded, might not even have heard his feeble joke.

'The gun,' Freddie said. 'I'd feel easier if he'd left the damn thing. He's a braggart, of course. Jane won't miss that either.' Freddie poured a drink, almost in silence, and drank it back. 'This infernal heat. No air. Connell is right. The climate is a hired assassin.' He moved about, paused, looked into the darkness, listened. 'This tour has dragged its feet, hasn't it?' he said.

But Lucy was sitting, asleep or hiding her pain. Her fingers twitched, her throat tightened as if she swallowed, even saliva, with difficulty. This damn poisonous bug that had bitten her. Not fever, now Freddie knew. He stood on the verandah and listened. The cracking sound of dry brittle undergrowth, Lorimer's voice, faint: they were out there somewhere.

Africans were out there too, shadows, silent.

From behind him Lucy called, 'Freddie?'

He turned. 'Yes.'

'Jane will be all right.'

'Yes.'

He came in and stood facing her, looked at the pain in her eyes.

She said, 'I'm ill, you know. I think I know how very ill I am. My head aches until I can hardly see. So strange.'

Freddie glanced at her. Yes, she was ill. But illnesses came and went. You suffered them. 'Oh nonsense,' he said. 'That gardener thing has upset you. And the fellow starving himself down at the village. I wish he'd get it over with, let them have their damn war dances.'

She sat, perhaps not even listening.

Connell would know. Twenty-five years with blackman's sickness. He would ask Connell. Twenty-five years with blackman's death, he thought for a moment.

Lucy seemed to revive.

'Are you all right?' he asked.

'For a little while I felt like death,' she told him.

'Nerves, nerves. Shot to pieces. I'm none too bright myself. End-of-tourish. A couple of months back there and you'll be right as the mail.' He knew she was looking at him and turned to her, smiling. 'Forty-eight hours and you'll be home, you know. London after all these years.'

'You will take care of yourself?' she said.

'Yes, yes.'

'You'll take care of yourself when I go?'

Freddie nodded his reassurance, wanted to escape.

'When I'm gone?'

It had a ring of death about it, and a trace of anger distracted him for a moment. His words meant nothing. 'Well, of course. You mustn't go on about it, my dear.'

She was nodding, agreeing with him. 'I must pull myself together.'

In a little while Freddie said, 'I'm out of humour with this idiot Jane has foisted on us. He's jumpy. Needs a bottle of malt in his gut to loosen him. He'll want to cut a dash, shotgun at the ready, wogs beware.' Freddie looked out and down at the great mat of bush and palm with infinite movement and life beneath it. 'Afraid. They know when you're afraid, they can smell it.'

'Jane will be all right,' she said again. He was thinking of Jane, she knew. 'She's hard,' she told him. 'You were never hard enough, and I'm glad really. I was angry of course. You were punished, Freddie. The Major punished you. A little man. Chained you first to a London desk. Pawned you off with this stinking place in '37. Closed the file.' She looked at him. 'I haven't been much help, have I?'

'The White Man's Grave,' Freddie said; he went to the sideboard and spent time trickling whisky into his glass. 'A pity we didn't make the Med,' he said. 'Alex, Tobruk, Jaffa, Beirut ... Good places. A pity.' He put his glass down gently and moved about, listened. He said, 'You mustn't worry about retirement, redundancy. Back to the UK makes sense. Of course it does. I'll have to think about it again.'

Lucy rested back in her chair, closing her eyes to shut out even a glimmer of light that seemed to fuel the creeping pain and the tightening of her body. 'Yes, yes,' she said softly, 'I know you'll think about it.'

The door from the house, behind them, opened and shut and Connell, cleansed, fresh, came up the lounge to join them.

Without looking at him, Lucy said, 'You found everything?'

'Yes.' He stood behind her chair. Freddie brought him a drink. Freddie said, 'Bad, was it? Butchered him, I suppose. Poor fellow.'

'Yes,' Connell said.

Freddie's uneasiness kept him in motion. 'Made him my ball boy down at the club four, five years ago. All of that. They used to be quite proud of it once. Big job, a few extra shillings to jingle.'

Connell said, 'Yes, they used to be quite proud of it. Once.'

It was all beyond Freddie. 'A bit bothered of late, I thought. Not in the spirit of things, you know.'

Connell nodded.

'A conscript, I thought once or twice, every inch of him.'

'Warned,' Lucy said in a whisper.

'I'll miss him,' Freddie said without sentiment. 'Very fast. Kept me on my toes.'

Lucy looked so ill, Connell thought; she was saying to him, 'They wouldn't chop him up on that account, would they?'

'Of course not!' Freddie said. 'Times are changing. Old times gone. That's about the sum of it.'

Behind Lucy's chair Connell drank in silence.

She said, 'Poor dear Josiah.'

'Yes, a good fellow.' Freddie dismissed it.

In a little while Connell said, 'They chopped his hands off, put a cricket ball in his face like a boar's head with an apple.'

'Christ,' Freddie said, almost inaudible; he was at the window, looking across his plateau at the fringe of bush where Josiah's body waited.

Lucy broke the tension of a long silence. Connell knew the pain and sudden rigidity of muscles that could grip her; her hair was brown and youthful still. She had been a sparkling girl when Freddie Freeman had preciously wooed her, Connell thought.

She said, 'We wanted to tell you, Connell: we're sorry for the person in jail too. You visit him, watch him die from day to day. It's a Christian thing. Good of you.'

'He's my son,' Connell said; he walked round to where he could face them both.

'Oh my God!' Freddie said.

Lucy looked out through her pain with deep compassion for him. 'It's James, isn't it?' she said. 'Dear Connell. You're an African, you say, close to them, and we understand now.'

'Your son.' Freddie blundered over it. 'Weeks of wasting away. We're sorry, Connell.'

'Yes, we're sorry,' Lucy repeated it, so weak now, Connell thought. 'I remember him, you see. Pale skin, running up our palms to tap for wine. Jane too. She could climb like a monkey. It seems another time. She was twelve...'

'He was fourteen,' Connell said. 'Twenty-four in a week or so now. But he'll die tonight.'

Lucy closed her eyes, bowed her head: pain or prayer.

Freddie poured drinks, noisily now, without care. 'Have a drink, my dear,' he pleaded. 'Things will seem better.'

Connell watched her clamped in a moment of awful paralysis and then huddled in pain as the grip loosened.

'She doesn't need a drink,' Connell said quietly. Freddie's eyes were signalling puzzlement but Connell had turned away towards the verandah.

Freddie raised his glass, said eventually, 'Your son.'

'We don't have to feel sorry for him,' Connell said. 'The secret of dying in peace is to have a good reason for dying. He told me weeks ago.' Connell stood on the verandah.

'We'd know if it had happened, of course?' Freddie asked. 'If he had died?'

'Yes.' Connell was listening to the gradual rising tempo of the drums and a faint monotonous chant filling the voids.

'You should be with him,' Lucy said.

'In daylight only,' Connell explained. 'There are rules, you see.'

'Rules?' Freddie said: one had to keep talking at moments like these.

'For Africans. Police rules.'

'Johnnie police rules.'

'His Majesty's police,' Connell said.

Freddie drank his whisky, was angry for a little while. 'His Majesty's police. His Majesty's army!'

'It's a good job for Africans,' Connell said simply. 'Fed and found, they can rise to three stripes.'

'White officers,' Freddie said.

Connell nodded. 'Down at the coast, of course, dug in since the war years. Spit and polish, all the rest. Garrisons up at the mines to guard the ingots.'

Freddie thought about it. 'If there's a bust-up,' he said, 'I wouldn't trust johnnies in or out of uniform.'

'Nor I,' Connell said.

Freddie looked at him for a long time; he said, 'Careful on that verandah, Connell. That Scottish fellow has a gun out there. He just whisked it away. A bit jiggy, I'd say. Jane is with him.' He stared at Connell. 'Is it safe, do you think? Wandering about out there . . .'

Connell leant on the rail of the verandah. How many dawns and sunsets in twenty-eight years? He had seen them all; and the scattered irruptions of disobedience with punishment hangings until the war was looming. You needed troops to stop holes and bullets then. And, when it was over and you had hanged tyrants in Europe, you were homo sapiens, you were circumspect. You punished and hanged discreetly. There was a finality about that

154

tiny burning village. For better or for worse, tomorrow was a new world. He thought about James Connell in that stinking jail and closed his eyes to remember him when he used to walk free. If they had hanged him, he would be forgotten now. If he had starved for a week and surrendered they would have shut him up until he rotted. But he had won: he had died second by second for forty-one days and a whole country was growing moment by moment. How many seconds in forty-one days?

Connell remembered the gutted house in Antrim and his father's black cindered body. That had been the dominie's victory. And two of His Majesty's police with bone and shreds of flesh for faces. White merciless policemen. That had been Connell's revenge. In remembrance no shred of compassion softened him.

Freddie was repeating, 'Is it safe out there, Connell?'

Connell turned. 'They don't like him,' he said. 'Lorimer. His *wogs* don't like him.'

Freddie said, 'They don't like being kicked.'

'They don't like being hated.'

'Hated.' Freddie understood.

'I went to see him on his bridge once, talked to him for a little while, didn't leave him in doubt, put him on my list. A little punishment. I explained I was an African.'

'Good,' Freddie said. 'Good. He needs to be softened up. And his minders. Today he booted some poor skin and bone bastard down a thirty-foot batter into the creek. Bad blood there.' Freddie moved beside Connell on the verandah. 'I'm worried for Jane,' he said, 'if he's waving that gun about. I wonder if he'd shoot?'

Connell said, 'It needs a good reason, like dying, like starving.'

Freddie pondered it. 'You're an African, Connell. That's what you say. I'm an Indian, I suppose. Born and raised there, never anywhere long enough to settle. Didn't want to. That idiot out there with Jane doesn't know what he is and the bloody wogs have us all under siege . . .'

The sound of a shotgun, very close in the bush, had the roar of an exploding landmine. Freddie was silenced. Lucy, drifting for a moment from consciousness, was suddenly in rigor, trembling, in convulsion again.

'Christ!' Freddie said and moved. But Connell had gripped his arm: Connell's fingers, tightening, held him still.

'I'll see to it,' Connell said. 'You're in charge here, Freddie.'

Lucy was mouthing, 'What is it? ... something's happened...' But total rigor gripped and released; her fingers moved then, a strange atactic rhythm; her head, full of awful pain, rested back, stretching the locked muscles of her throat.

Connell had gone, was lost in the darkness.

Freddie knelt at Lucy's chair, held her dry hands, could see the ugly small suppurating blot where the dressing had moved. Christ, he thought, drowning in helplessness. He could get her in the car, now perhaps, push through the up and down miles to that Polish quack at the mines. He saw the twisted road through bush and desert. He had a shotgun. Lorimer had his shotgun. If there was bother you needed the scatter of a shotgun. He could feel Lucy's hand softening in his; her body loosened. Before she spoke she looked at him for a long time, kneeling at her feet. 'The noise,' she whispered. 'It was terrifying.'

'You're better?'

'I don't think so.'

He peered out into the darkness. 'It was that ass, Lorimer,' he said, 'firing at shadows. Shouldn't be let loose with a spud-gun, damn him. There's nothing out there, my dear. Nothing we need worry about. Connell will round him up.' He looked at her weariness. She needed help, rest.

She said, 'You're worried for me.'

'Yes,' he said.

'You asked Connell to stay, didn't you? I'm glad.'

Freddie nodded. 'He kept watch all week. I won't forget it.'

'We should all be Africans,' she said.

Freddie thought about that, looked at the amber bottles on

his sideboard. 'We're all white,' he said. 'Connell's white.'

Lorimer's voice sounded out in the bush, a kind of surprised roar straggling unevenly away.

Freddie listened to the silence. 'Christ, that fellow whinnying and braying out there, needs to be smashed.'

When he turned Lucy was standing; she seemed unsteady, older, shrunken. 'Jane will be all right,' she told him. 'Don't worry for her too.' She stayed a moment to clasp his hand, looked at him with more tenderness than he could ever remember.

'You need to rest,' he told her.

'Yes, I'm going to rest a while. No, I don't need help. But you will take care? When I'm gone?'

Freddie anchored himself to his patience, watched her move across to the house door. She turned and smiled to him.

'Yes, yes,' he said as she closed the door. 'Good idea, my dear. Get your feet up.' She had gone. 'I'll take care of myself,' he said aloud. He had always taken care of himself.

He poured whisky and waited for the reassurance of Connell.

From the balcony, Connell had rounded the house, away from the light, and stood motionless among the tall shrubs. He waited for the darkness to dissolve a little, listened. The sudden shattering discharge of Lorimer's buckshot, skywards, or blindly into the bush, had silenced the jungle: the crickets were mute. Whatever slept was awake and in hiding; whatever crawled, slithered or scampered, held its ground and waited.

Jane's voice, faintly, came to him and Lorimer's humourless laughter. They were at the distant end of the compound, among palms and shrubs. Life had begun to move everywhere again, teeming minute life with its almost silent signals; a cricket gave a castanet rattle, and another, until the air was crowded with them.

Connell, in the lee of bush and shrubs, moved until he could

157

see them: Lorimer, stout sentinel, feet apart, immovable, cradling his shotgun, listening with a show of amusement. Jane upright as Freddie, speaking in soft tones. It was inaudible to Connell.

Connell found concealment in an outcrop of rock. He waited. He could see them plainly now. Jane had looks and style, could turn heads, was a winner. This was her country. It could never be Lorimer's. And she was twenty-two.

He had been twenty-two, he remembered, when he had fled, leaving love and murder behind. A mother and sisters he had loved.

They had gone westward to Derry, perhaps farther, away from the black-death of dogma, vanished from his life and he from theirs as finally as two brothers sunken in French mud or the grotesque melted corpse in his library. He remembered the church service and the burial; his mother's emptied face, eyes seeing nothing: in five, six years, a family decimated. Police at the church door, a handful of friends in an almost empty church, defiant or foolhardy. The funeral prayers softly, quickly intoned, no eulogy for a pillar of society. Police at the cemetery too, and only the memory of women's tears and a half-dozen still granite masks to hover above the fistful of earth thrown on the coffin lid. He had loved his father with admiration and sorrow. The rain fell without cease.

He remembered the beautiful chased fowling-piece that lay somewhere now in Belfast Lough, how many fathoms deep, beneath twenty-eight years of settlement. He had dismantled it, packed it beneath salvaged clothes and books in a Gladstone bag, put cartridges to rest beside it.

The women, in the dreadful black weeds and veils of mourning, were strange amorphous woodcuts.

'Where will you go?' he asked.

'Derry,' he was told.

There was refuge in Derry and ragged armies you half despised to hide behind; murdering armies.

'You're coming?'

'No,' he said; he held up the Gladstone bag. 'Belfast. A bus, a train. I'll finish my course. He would have wanted that.'

'Money?' his mother said.

'I have money. A degree too, you know,' he said very gently. 'I can teach nights, take a Master's in a year. That was our plan.'

He embraced them all, for the last time, he knew, and dry-eyed walked out of sight to the railway station that was also his bus terminus ...

Belfast was a grimy city in '22, and in early darkness and gas-light it had the single-dimensional flatness of smudged newsprint: crowded streets, a kind of bubbling euphoria of victory. And it was raining. It had been raining since morning, on the church, the grave, and now on Belfast's black and white streets. The elders had drawn their heavy black line around all of Ulster that they needed, and His Majesty's squaddies, His Majesty's armed policemen, law and order, were everywhere to show possession.

There was a shipping office near Royal Avenue and he bought a twenty-eight-day first class return, Belfast–Liverpool; he used their telephone for a private call and moved away into the city centre. He sat for half an hour in a chain-restaurant, watching his tea grow cold, wrinkling with age.

Then he saw her coming across the floor. She was so beautiful, he thought, her eyes, even in the distance, showing her love for him. He went to meet her, took her hands. They sat looking at each other across the table, talking a little. Her face was sad for him and yet full of happiness. The clock on the distant wall behind her said it was two hours to sailing time.

'I'm going to Derry,' he said.

'Derry?'

'My family are going to Derry. I'll settle them in. I came to see you first.'

'You're coming back?'

'A couple of days,' he lied.

They went out into the evening. In a deserted alley he took her in his arms and embraced her. She knew, of course.

Everything was a last time now, he thought.

'Don't come with me,' he said. 'I have calls to make.' The rain fell heavier, great driving sweeps.

He waved to her from the corner as he moved out of sight. He could feel his tears barely held in check; and her tears.

It had been cold premeditated slaughter, he thought. No sweep of unthinking passion had submerged and beached him. In the church, in the cemetery, he had plotted step by step: he knew where his cartridges would find their mark, where bodies could be pushed out of sight. And then the night boat to Liverpool, a return ticket that would never be used. That ... or he had a spare cartridge in his pocket.

Behind Belfast's raucous centre of horse cabs and combustion engines, the tangled myriads of people, the endless clamour of voices, police, the soldiery, the armoured cars, were rotting strings of abandoned workers' dwellings, narrow streets, alleys, open spaces. He hurried into the dark and seclusion of them. The rain had settled to a steady pour. He assembled the shotgun, loaded, cocked both barrels.

All about him was scabrous weedy ground and only stubs of brick and foundation for cover; mounds of detritus had been gathered like a harvest, where the builders would be at work soon again. In the black cul-de-sac beside him, with lengths of cast iron and wood, he loosened and levered up the manhole cover of a drain. That would be their grave. Or his own. A twenty-foot drop.

He went back into the cover of brickwork and waited. A hundred yards away gas-lamps lit auras of rain; and beyond them, faintly, storehouses, loading bays, shuttered places of business. It was a desolate expanse now, only patrolling police slow-marching its length at intervals, testing a lock, stopping to light dog-ends and nick them again. He needed patience. The waiting would gather and drip like a forgotten tap.

It took forty minutes. The rain hadn't ceased. Then a constable, a sergeant, in green-black capes, slowly moving towards his ambush. As they passed he made a noise: a groan, half anger, half pain. They stopped, peering blindly at the darkness.

'Someone there? Come on, out of it. Out of it!' The sergeant: a deep unafraid voice; he had a revolver in hand now. The constable shone a torch. Connell drew back into cover, dropped a sodden piece of mortar at his feet. A small sound.

'Come on, move, you bastard! Out!'

At ten feet Connell stood and stripped their faces to the bone. The sound of the gun seemed to thunder in his ears; but he was already dragging them to the open manhole. From twenty feet he heard the dull arrival of their bodies below. Then a live cartridge, two spent ones. The manhole cover gave them the privacy of a grave. He was moving at speed now, dismantling, packing the gun, standing for seconds, listening. There was only the close-by roar of the city.

It had been as simple as that. Twenty-eight years, he thought. A long time ...

He moved behind the shelter of Freddie's scrub and bush now, passed Josiah's wrapped and bound body, went on almost without sound until he could see faces, hear each single word.

Jane was saying, tongue in cheek, Connell knew, a kind of spurious naïveté, 'I don't know if it was wise to fire blind into the bush, Alec.'

'A warning', Lorimer said. 'Clears the air and the ground. Upsets Freddie too.'

'Oh him,' she said.

Lorimer, flat and dry as a tired old magistrate. 'He never grew up,' he was saying. 'He's still back there in the faded rugger gear and cricket pads.'

'Maybe even in India?'

'Jildi, jildi!' It was Lorimer's little flat joke and her smile was full of enthusiasm. She stood facing him, resting back against a palm, hands clasped behind it, her legs slightly parted.

She was a pretty picture, Connell thought: cool, confident, leading him on, but hardly to sinfulness.

Connell wondered, waited.

Lorimer's uneasiness was in his movements, guilt with his passion, seeming to keep his distance from her. He held the shotgun at the ready and gazed at the embers of the village and listened to its untiring throb.

'How long?' he asked.

'1937,' she said. 'He came first.'

'Thirteen years.'

'Yes. Mother and I came in '38.'

'What a place to rot in.'

'Oh, I think he likes it,' Jane said. 'Don't you?'

'I came out to build a bridge,' Lorimer said. 'When it's finished, I stay or move. I'm an engineer.' He tapped his head. 'I take my nous from place to place.'

'You're not a clerk, Alec,' she said with great seriousness.

He looked at her for the slightest flicker of ridicule, but it was an earnest face. She was a cow, he thought. Freddie, a failed half-brained idiot. But he was due the respect of what he had sired. She was a whore. He remembered her stepping out of her clothes a few hours before, and facing him. And his own nakedness, a stout rod of passion to impale her. And that blimp, Freddie, had come. Looking at her, he felt the tightness at his groin like pain.

'Alec,' she said; she raised her skirt midway along her thighs and looked very beautiful. 'It's safe, Alec.'

He had dropped the shotgun and come rushing to take hold of her. A whore, a whore! Whores were for blocking, he thought. He ran his hand along her buttocks. She was naked! He unbuttoned, unzipped himself; he felt his hands and knees unsteady. He looked at her eyes. There was the faintest smile.

'This one's for the old buffer in there,' she said. 'My dear father. My mother. Connell too.' She brought her knee hard into his genitals. He might have been laughing or crying as he tumbled in the brush. She unloaded the remaining cartridge and leant the shotgun against the palm ...

162

'You're not good enough to talk about them, Mr Lorimer,' she said. 'When you're ready we can go back in the lounge and tell them how we enjoyed the hot air and how you fired a shot to heaven in thanksgiving. I wouldn't think you're very safe out here. Your little wogs from the bridge might see you.'

Times were changing, Connell thought. He moved away into the darkness.

Freddie had watched Lucy's slow deliberate progress, each measured careful step, her turning to face him and smile to him from the house door. He was in a confusion of anger, pity, love. Anger at the need of constant reassurance that he would take care of himself when she had gone. He had always taken care of himself from boarding school to bank to marriage bed, the latter however brief. Taken care of Lucy too. And Jane. The thought of intercourse and ensuing pregnancy had become a terrifying prospect, unbearable, for Lucy, and he had accepted it, slept apart and still loved her. 'When she had gone.' He thought about it. It sounded like death when, in fact, it was some venomous flying thing and her own final surrender to the heat and sweaty humidity that had dragged her down to the point of leaving it all. To find rebirth, even youth, in her beloved Muswell Hill? And parents dead, buried now in Finchley, he thought; the house, the pear tree leased. Happiness. Freddie stared back at the London years. Before W.nchmore Hill it had been a ground-floor flat and garden in the Highgate fringes, while he waited from month to month, year to year, for an overseas call-up. Rugby and cricket had filled the early days but passing time told him that the Major had consigned him to the shadows; and he had drifted into after-work drinks and liaisons and rough trade whores to loosen the black knots inside him. He could take care of himself.

But he had felt pity and love too, seeing her turn at the house door to smile to him, a faint glow of the sparkle and excitement he had married. He remembered the euphoric dream of Alexandria and branches dotted round the Med. The dream had never totally vanished but it had faded, grown distant, with the ringing in of each New Year. Eighteen times he had raised a New Year's glass in London. But Lucy needed him, he knew, and was a little afraid of him then. And Jane was growing up.

Only the blessed holy war against fascism and the gathering up of youthful fighting blood in '37, soon to be sacrificed, had set free a thirty-five-year-old from his desk where he could see the Monument and the buses turning for London Bridge.

Lucy could have opted for London then, stayed behind with Jane to keep the home fires burning but, Freddie knew, she felt she owed him something. In some strange way, she loved him, he supposed. They followed him out in '38 ...

Freddie went to the sideboard and drank his whisky. He could hear strange sounds, like stifled laughter. That would be Lorimer! Christ, he thought, what a mess. And then he saw a silent shadow and in a moment Connell was facing him from the verandah.

'That fellow's a bloody ass,' Freddie said. 'Listen to the cackling. Get yourself a drink.'

'Yes,' Connell said.

'Ignored you, did he?'

'I didn't intrude,' Connell assured him. 'He'll be along any time now.'

'And Jane?'

'Jane is in charge.'

'Good. What did he fire at? A noise, a rustle?'

'A warning, I think,' Connell said.

'A warning!' Freddie repeated. 'Christ, there's always something crawling in the bush. He's windy, Connell!'

Connell was impassive, raised his glass.

Freddie relented a little. 'We all are from time to time, I suppose.'

'Yes,' Connell said.

'When he dies. Your son, Connell, when he dies. It could be a touch-paper, could it?'

'That might be the idea,' Connell said. 'Slow dying has a purpose.'

Freddie pondered it. 'Are we safe?'

'We're white,' Connell said.

Freddie moved about, sat for a little while, stood and walked again. All restlessness. He looked to where his shotgun should be standing. 'I've never killed anyone. Anything. Never had reason, I suppose. Put the war years down potting at ducks and geese out on the creeks. I never got anything. Never wanted to, I think. Glad to be here, that was all.' Raising his drink, Freddie suddenly remembered. 'I nearly got one of these johnnies once! He had a smart little piece, fourteen, fifteen maybe. They were screwing. I heard a rustle and let blast. They took off, bare-arse, into the bush, left clothes, the lot.' Freddie was smiling. 'Taught me a lesson. I didn't mean it, you see, Connell?'

'They were afraid,' Connell said.

'Afraid?'

'The whole damn village was afraid. And what lives in the bush too, "Big master for bank he shoot everything," the black-man say.'

Freddie was laughing. 'Damn it, you've put me back in humour. I haven't laughed for weeks. Ha! Big master for bank he shoot nothing!' Freddie sobered and thought about it. 'I've never disliked them.' He looked at Connell. 'Do you think they know that, Connell?'

'Some of them,' Connell said.

'But we're white, Connell?'

'Mulattos, quadroons, octoroons, they'll all be "white" one day. Whiteman's trash.'

'Your son? Is he trash? Dying for these johnnies.'

'He's useful, that's all.'

'He's not black?'

'Black enough for now.'

165

Connell thought of him for moments. An acuteness would come before death: sight would be fading but hearing would be attuned and sharpened; he would hear the roar of the village, a great confusion of sound and destruction. But now he would have slipped from consciousness. He saw that Freddie was watching him and turned and brought a whisky bottle from the sideboard. He topped both their glasses.

'We don't need to spoil it.'

'Not tonight,' Freddie said.

They drank and Connell poured measures again. Freddie would need to feel no pain before the deep loaded sky opened and the rains were here, and choked screaming would leave them chilled in this sweatbox, Connell thought. James Connell, down in the jail, had offered his life, had made a choice. Lucy had none.

Her agony was beginning.

'Lucy's resting?' Connell said.

'She put her feet up. Nerves, Connell. Shaking all over at times.' He raised his glass; they drank. This was the moment to ask Connell. He took the revolver from its holster, examined it, put it back again. 'Wartime issue,' he said. 'No one ever came to collect it.'

Lorimer's clipped voice came through the compound to them, the edge of anger not missed by Connell. To Freddie it was 'a bloody noise'.

'Sorry about that fellow, Connell. The bastard will have us ambushed. The johnnies are out there, flitting about.' Freddie waited.

'Somewhere,' Connell said.

Freddie put his whisky glass down. 'I'll go and get him in here. By the balls, if I have to!'

'No,' Connell said. 'Jane is managing very well. Needs a little time, that's all.'

Freddie took his drink and sat uncomfortably in an easy chair. 'Kirks and hymnbooks and elders and lodges, that's what does it. He's a bloody Scot, isn't he? All their thinking done for them in the Big Book, you see. Says he's Irish, Connell. I'd pull him on that one.'

'British,' Connell said.

'Born in Ireland, isn't he?'

'British Ireland,' Connell said. 'They didn't give it all back to us in '22, you know. Kept the good bits of Ulster.'

'You were born in the Ulster place, Connell,' Freddie said.

'Yes.'

'But you're Irish.'

'Was.'

'And he's British. The whole thing's a bloody conundrum. I give it up.'

'Most people do,' Connell said, and changed direction. 'Lucy,' he said. 'You were going to ask me about her, weren't you?'

'She's ill, Connell.'

'She's very ill.'

'I'll take her up to the mines in the morning. That Polish bod will patch her up. Then a flight to London.' Freddie held out his hands towards the darkness. 'Madness driving about in this ink pot with bands of johnnies waiting to pounce. And then, the *rains!*' He gazed at the low blanket of cloud. 'Could come in five minutes, in five hours. Madness!' He stood and walked about; then faced Connell. 'It's not fever, I know that. But in twenty-eight years you've seen the whole damn calendar. What is it, Connell?'

'You're doing the right thing,' Connell said. 'She needs care. It takes time.'

It was easier to lie to him. She would never see a Polish doctor or walk the pavements of Muswell Hill again. The rains, Connell thought. Dear God!

'Is there a name for it?'

'A kind of blood poison.' Connell garbled it again.

'Sit down, Connell. Sit down.'

He sat facing Freddie.

167

'We share a house, Lucy and myself. Not a bed. We haven't done since 1927. Twenty-two years, give or take. It was Jane. She had a bad time with Jane, Connell. A murderous bloody delivery. Couldn't bear to be touched afterwards. Told me she loved me. She was sincere, of course. Wanted to stay with me, all that. But it was the end of tumbling in the hay.' Freddie thought of the London fogs, the whores, the late-night booze-ups. 'I paid to get it up, Connell. Took it for nothing if it offered. And here? You know, Connell. Hooker's best.' He paused. 'And Connell?'

'Yes.'

'I love her, you know.'

'I understand,' Connell said.

He looked out now at the forked lightning cracking the sky, distant still so that the sound hardly reached them, but moving imperceptibly towards them; looked down at his commune that was empty now except for pieces of dying men and women in their coops, lost in darkness. His women and children had gone deep into the bush to scatter and hide until the wave of anger had passed over and spent itself. And James Connell, in the gaol, was nearing the end; Lucy at the beginning of the end. The end out there too, Connell thought, looking at the vast flickering skyline. It was a moment of change.

'She cares for me now but I don't think it's love any more. A kind of duty,' Freddie was saying. 'Lonely for her, I've always known that. Not a female blob to gossip with for bloody miles, except missionaries, dry as dust. Miners' wives? Coarse people, she calls them. Lonely, Connell. My fault. She learned to drink out here too. Crept up on her, I suppose. A half-bottle of gin from sundown to bedtime. A few boosters in daytime too, I could tell. I don't think she ever felt happiness here. Was she happy, Connell?'

Connell looked at Freddie's troubled face: he wanted only confirmation. 'I don't think so,' he said.

'I could have left her in London, you know. When the war

was over spent furloughs there. Like a deep-sea skipper. Fifteen months afloat, three, four months ashore. A lot of "coasters" do it. I came out a year ahead, remember, Connell?'

'I remember,' Connell said.

'She wrote to me every day. Loved me then, I suppose. Or missed me. To have left her would have been like putting her down, I felt. I brought them out in '38.' Freddie dismissed it with a little shade of anger, Connell thought. Perhaps guilt. 'At any rate, Connell, I'm sorry about this fellow Jane has dropped on us. We'll have a drink. We drink a lot, don't we?' He looked kindly at Connell. 'You've been a help, old man. Lucy doesn't care much any more. She's kind to me, of course. And she's going home.'

Connell said, 'We've been lonely, Freddie. That's all. Lonely.'

'Funny, I'm the one who cares, you know.' Freddie poured whisky and they drank in silence. 'It would have been like killing her to tell her to stay put. Left her back there.' He faced Connell. 'You would have done it, Connell. Killing is a kind of healing too, isn't it?'

'She's ill now,' Connell said.

'Yes,' Freddie agreed. 'She's ill. Should never have brought her out here. On my own in '37 life was good. Almost took off in '37, you know. An Aussie in from Porto Novo had a truck. Christ, we used to drink. "Freddie boy, we'll drive all the way to King's Cross, Sydney, and if we don't like it we'll keep going. Come on, matie, move your ass!" Drunken talk most of it, but it was good. And women? Black women in whiteman's bed. Old hat!' Freddie looked out at the compound buried in darkness. 'That sneering jock out there wouldn't understand, of course. We used to have a rattle when the alarm went off, pressure gauges at red, you know. Hooker was setting up shop, would send us his best, school lassies who didn't need schooling. Beautiful black ebony. By God, they can work. Born to the business.' He looked at Connell's almost smiling face. 'You can pay them with kerosene tins, remember? Empty ones, of course.

And a couple of pounds for Hooker.' Drink had relaxed Freddie, brought colour back to his face. He was remembering, laughing. He turned to Connell. 'I'm sorry about your son. Why did you pitch your tent here, Connell? Never moved?'

Connell paused only for a moment. 'I was on the run.'

'Murder?'

'Yes,' Connell said. 'An eye for an eye, Freddie.'

'I'm glad you told me, Connell. They're coming for you.'

'I read your letters.'

Freddie paused. 'You have friends?'

'Yes.'

'Shouldn't you go somewhere? Get to hell out of here!'

'When James Connell dies in the gaol, soon now, and if the rains break, there won't be trains, Freddie, or troops or warrants for days. When he dies, I'll think about it. I can get lost out there in minutes.' Connell raised his glass. 'But I'm grateful.'

Freddie nodded.

'A long time ago,' Connell said, 'I came down from Liverpool, days, weeks at sea on an old Elder Dempster cargo, and started walking in from the coast. I opened my eyes out of fever down there where my huts are now and saw black faces tending to me. Getting stronger was like being born again. And then bedding down with a young girl. In love really. I stayed and built my settlement. Had a school, a hospital. Got older. Saw death every day. A mixture of sinfulness and bliss. I could feel the skin of everything. I forgot bitterness and went to work. Something like that.'

'You could have changed your name, Connell.'

Connell laughed. 'My passport. I awoke from fever and they called me Connell.'

'Do you feel bad about it?' Freddie said.

'About killing. About murder?'

'About an eye for an eye?'

'I feel nothing,' Connell said. 'They took my life too, you see. You can take a life without killing.'

Freddie thought about it. 'Calling it British doesn't make it any simpler, I suppose. Back there or here. It's changing here, Connell. Do you want it to change?'

'Everything changes.'

'We haven't much to offer.'

'We haven't,' Connell said.

'You're an African, aren't you?'

'A white one without papers.'

Connell sat in Lucy's chair, stretched his trousered legs and drank.

'We're almost finished here, aren't we?' Freddie said.

'Yes,' Connell said.

'They've made me redundant, Connell. Or did you know? The bank.'

'I know,' Connell said; he paused. 'My settlement is redundant too. I'm redundant.' Connell was remembering aloud. 'A stinking climate but it was a good place to be with good people once. It was good to have children. Making them, having them, watching them run for twigs, for water, learn to stitch, scutch a floor. Get stronger every year.' He raised his glass to Freddie. 'I have a market garden down there, tilled like a window-box, a stall in the village, beggars to meet every train, palm wine tappers like monkeys up the trees at first light, draining the gourds. An industry.'

'An industry, Connell,' Freddie said.

'Yes, a day at a time. Children pay their way. Take off when the season comes. I never remember birthdays but they bring me whisky to remind me.'

'They want to be like us, don't they, the johnnies. Like me, I suppose.' Freddie listened to the drums, the interminable rhythm of drums. 'Innocent skins, wouldn't you say, most of them, at any rate?'

'They'll fight out their battles, rob and cheat each other. They'll be good at it. Like the whitemen. We aren't different. We'll sell them guns and gods to keep them fighting.'

Freddie thought about it, drank, pondered. 'I suppose it's their turn, poor bastards. Dirty job, Connell. They can have it. Me? I can go now, pack my trunk, or finish my tour.'

'Where?'

'Oh, south, Connell, where else? The Cape. You should come. It's all that's left. Good times will last a little longer there.'

'A little longer,' Connell said.

A low tenuous sound came from the house, and garbled words. Silence. Then the faintest dying thread again.

'Lucy,' Freddie said. 'Resting, I told you. Restless. She'll be in flight in forty-eight hours if this bloody nonsense peters out. London, Muswell Hill, home. I probably won't see her again. We both know it.'

They were facing each other and Connell wondered if he should tell him or let the enormity creep up on him with Lucy's pain. Freddie was looking in Connell's eyes for some message that might be there, perhaps sensing even the finality of everything.

'I know she's ill,' he said, close to anger. 'Nerves, Connell. She's in pieces. Women don't last in the tropics. She always needed drink and now, suddenly, dammit, she shies off. Two, three days. Pale, trembling sometimes.'

Connell said, 'She's afraid.'

'Afraid?'

'Afraid of drinking.' Connell didn't say any more.

Freddie's gaze was blank, unresponsive; there was even a trace of ridicule. 'Afraid? I can't see her forever paling before a pink gin. Can you? Subdued, burnt out, I thought.' Freddie suddenly wondered. 'Drying out, maybe? That's it. A sudden resolve, she dug her heels in.' He went to the sideboard and took his careful measure of whisky. 'Drying out, that's it!' He raised up the bottle but Connell refused. 'Why the hell didn't I think of that. Drying out. Well, we'll keep the flag flying, Connell. If you see an old coaster trembling at the sound of liquor, it's excitement, for my money. It'll be a damn bad day when we're afraid of drink, you and I, Connell.'

There were sounds on the verandah and Jane stood smiling at them. Very beautiful and tough, Connell thought.

Jane said, 'Afraid of drink? What mad dog would sink a fang in two old boots like you?'

It stirred a reaction in Freddie. He stood in silence for a moment or two while he struggled with it and it was still unreachable, amorphous. Jane came to kiss him on the cheek.

'I'm going to have a little drink,' she said. 'A little private celebration. I feel very good.'

For Freddie everything was still. Even drums and crickets; and the low groaning pain from the house had passed him by.

Jane said, 'What was that?'

But Freddie, distracted again, was saying, 'A celebration? Nothing between you and that bridge-building fellow, is there?' Freddie was worried.

'Lorimer?'

'Yes.'

'Oh God,' she said; her laughter, her derision, was balm to Freddie, restored him. And he tried to remember her salutation from the verandah. But it was lost. To hell with it, he thought. It would come again. She had spotted the chinks in that bible-bound idiot, that was the important bit.

She raised her glass to them both. Connell seemed to have been forgiven, reinstated in her affection. She said, 'I thought I heard a noise from the house. Moments ago.'

'Your mother,' Freddie said. 'A bit restless, that's all.'

'I'll go to her.'

Connell said, 'She should rest while she can. It would be better, I think.'

She looked at Connell's face, wondered, nodded agreement, put the spare cartridge back in the box.

'Where is he?' Freddie said.

Lorimer's progress on the steps to the verandah seemed laboured, awkward. He appeared in view, dishevelled, limping, his face tight with anger.

Jane said, 'Poor Alec. Tripped, took a tumble.'

'Not your day, is it?' Freddie said and turned to face him. 'Did you fire at something out there?'

Lorimer sized up Freddie, would like to crush this bumbling bank clerk and his inquisition. He said, 'Nothing I could see, more's the pity.' He passed Freddie and sat carefully on the chair.

'It isn't clever to fire at the dark, at shadows.'

'A warning blast to all, Freddie old boy. A rumble of hellfire and punishment.' He paused, studied Freddie from the toes up, let his disregard lazily rest on him; he avoided Connell. 'A letter from head office, you know. Buckle down or else. Promotions and punishments kind of thing.'

Jane, unceremoniously, took the gun from him and put it standing in the corner. Freddie watched him.

'A heavy old piece, Freddie,' Lorimer said. 'Like old coasters, clapped out, bad balance. Must be fifty years old.' He turned to Connell. 'Quite a shindig they're knocking up in there for a week now. In the village, you know. And tonight, a wog dies and the village is a bonfire. Sales of palm wine up this week, Commissar?'

'And prices,' Connell said.

Freddie was in confusion. A blundering idiot, he thought; but he drained away what anger he could, pondered it. Eventually he said, 'It's Connell's son. Connell's son dying in there, you know, Lorimer?'

'It was a fair guess,' Lorimer said. 'You're out of touch, Freddie. The Commissar's half-breed son dying for forty-something days. For the wogs. They say he's not even black. And it never crossed your mind, did it, Freddie?'

'Christ!' Freddie said; but he watched the calmness of Connell's face.

'Half-caste,' Lorimer tried.

174

'Mulatto,' Connell said and went to stand on the verandah.

'And the whole village hopped-up on your jungle juice.'

'They pay for it.'

'Were converted with it in the old days, weren't they, by the paid-up members of Rome.'

'Oh yes,' Connell agreed. 'God is quite unscrupulous in crossing his bridges.'

They had forgotten Jane.

'James?' she said. 'James Connell dying in there. You didn't tell me, Connell. You didn't tell me! . . . Why?'

'It wasn't very pleasant,' Connell said.

She was almost in tears.

'He's dying,' Connell said without turning.

'I could have gone and sat with him.'

'Only I can sit with him.'

'Every day,' Lorimer said.

Connell said to Jane, 'You wouldn't recognize the stinking skeleton of James Connell. Just remember him.'

Connell was impassive as he had been down all the years. When they had arrived before the war he had been thirty-eight and twelve years had changed him only a little: broad shoulders, flat stomach, the line of jawbone tight against his skin. She had been ten, eleven, curious, unafraid, and crept down at sunset beneath the huge canopy of bush to the clearance of Connell's land. Connell sat beneath the roofed canopy of his cabin, alone, drinking. His bright eyes and damp face might have been tears. 'Alone', was how she always remembered him. Two years later when he came each day to teach her, she sat close to him, her skirts pulled higher and higher along her thighs but he hadn't noticed. She had seen him naked with his shining young women, being caressed, taking them from time to time, and felt the excitement of it. When she had met James Connell, he was fourteen, she was twelve, and he had been given the rules of the game. Only one rule. They had known each other's bodies and how to excite and exhaust them. But he had never entered her.

James Connell had loved her, she supposed, and played the game . . .

In the silence, Freddie said, 'You'll apologize, of course, Lorimer.'

'Should I?' Lorimer said. 'I don't apologize to papish scum, white wog politicians.' He turned to Connell. 'Subverting His Majesty's law and order, Commissar?'

Freddie watched the unruffled Connell and felt his own anger diminishing. 'Then I'll do it,' he said. He raised his glass to Connell.

'That pile of rags,' Lorimer said. 'That wog body out there. Insects everywhere.'

Connell said, 'They'll come for Josiah's body.'

'And they don't like being shot at!' Freddie said.

Lorimer surveyed them, moved his thighs and swollen groin on the chair. He pointed at Connell. 'Do you hire him, Freddie? This talisman to ward off wogs and witchcraft?' All his contempt for Freddie was aimed at Jane: a time would come, he thought, a month, two months, and they would find each other somewhere, somewhere remote, and he'd strip her down and block her like an animal. He could feel anger burning inside him. 'Troops at the mines, Freddie. That's where we go. The mines. Not to Commissar Paddywhack here. Troops, wog troops, to shoot wogs when they're told. For us. We pay the bastards.'

Silence followed Lorimer's attack. Jane could see Freddie in disarray and then steadying before Connell's faintest glint of humour.

'Help from a wog paddywhack,' Lorimer said. 'With a wog half-breed bastard laying down his miserable life to wake up these sun-sodden boneheads.'

'Oh, shut up!' Jane shouted. 'Or I'll bloody shoot you, by God!' She put her hand on the grip of Freddie's revolver. She looked at Connell and thought that behind the calmness there must be loneliness and isolation.

Freddie changed tack, stood by the shotgun. 'Have a drink,

for medicinal purposes,' he told Lorimer with what kindness he could find. 'You might find humanity.'

'I don't need liquor to prop me up, old man,' he was told.

Freddie said, 'It's eighteen miles over there to the mines, pitch black, and if the rains break you'll sit like a duck in a pond.' He looked down at Lorimer. 'You won't have a gun,' he said. 'What do you say, Connell?'

Connell said, 'They'll cut you to pieces,' and saw in Lorimer the shadow of uncertainty and cold.

'Let him go,' Jane said. 'He's not afraid of wogs, are you, Mr Lorimer?'

'They don't like you, Lorimer. Nor do I,' Freddie said honestly. 'They've put a marker on you. You hate their guts and they know it. They always know.'

'You should stay,' Connell said.

'You'll stand guard for us, Commissar?'

Lorimer had got up quickly, in discomfort, pain, and moved behind Freddie. He picked up the gun and weighed it in his hands. Jane's anger shot out at him.

'Listen, listen, you brainless oaf,' she said. 'Connell knows. It's his country. Listen to him. And put the damn gun down.'

Lorimer saw her as a kind of Happy Valley whore; he would nail her some day. He said to Freddie, 'You haven't read the rule book, have you, old man?' He nodded towards Connell. 'Keeping a wog in the house. We don't let paddywhacks in our houses in Ulster, you know. Unless they're clean enough to work, of course.' He put the gun standing in its corner, said to Connell, 'In my house you'd be a hostage, Commissar. A gun barrel up your rectum.'

Freddie was winded by the flow of bitterness and profanity from such a white Christian animal under his roof. He stared at Lorimer.

But Connell's smile scattered his tension like a breeze. 'You know they mightn't be grief-stricken if you shot me. I'm white, you see.'

177

Freddie's anger didn't so rapidly evaporate. 'Surprised, more likely,' he said. 'Put the gun away. And I mean now, Lorimer.'

Lorimer complied, looked ingenuously at him.

God, Freddie thought, nonconformists had moved backwards into the Dark Ages. But he wanted peace at all costs. 'We're all safer here,' he pleaded. 'We're just the caretakers and the tenants are squabbling. Let them get on with it. Come the King's birthday, all will be forgiven, the flags fluttering again. Connell even sells the damn things.' Freddie paused. 'I'm sorry,' he said to Connell. 'Keep forgetting, old man. It's your blood down there in the gaol.' He gestured the hopelessness of it. 'It's a bit absurd, the whole thing,' he said to Lorimer. 'You must see it like that. A game.'

Lorimer said, 'A game?'

'A game. A changing game.'

'Not a game, Freddie, old man,' Lorimer said. 'Not a changing game. You're a player but it's not a game.'

Freddie gave it up; he moved about, found comfort in it. Jane was standing on the verandah, looking towards the village, the gaol. He said to Connell. 'In India there were little English churchyards and graves, you know. Names mouldering on stones no one could remember. Good soldiers, clerks, workmen who put in a stint and went down. Born there. Died there. Changeless, they thought. But it had changed and slipped every day beneath their feet. Their changeless Empire.'

Lorimer observed them without respect; he poured enough whisky to wet the bottom of his glass and topped it again with soda. He toasted the black mess of darkness. 'To changeless empires,' he said; he drank. 'An empty gaolhouse in the morning,' he said to Connell. 'A tidying up. Remember him with pride. He was a motor mechanic, wasn't he? You know, a monkey, a grease monkey? A hammer and chisel mechanic.'

'A schoolmaster,' Connell said. 'But good with cars too. Very good if he liked you. Not a businessman, you see.'

'A politician?'

'Politicians are businessmen,' Connell said. 'He was a rebel. Did a little dreaming too. The early days down at the gaol we talked of all the roads to be made and pounds and politicians and petrol pumps and the blackman having time, maybe, for a Sunday drive. Humour didn't pass him by.'

Jane remembered his pale brown skin, pale brown skin of James Connell, dying in the gaol, how they had been happy and excited. She hadn't been aware of love then but remembered it in his eyes when she had left. He had been hard and strong like Connell.

'He's shrunken now?' she asked.

'Yes,' Connell said. 'A skull on a pillow. A sheet over the rest is almost flat. Weeks ago he talked of you.' Connell looked at her, at Freddie. 'I think he loved you a little once.'

'He did,' Freddie said.

'But he'll die this evening, tonight. A couple of minutes, a couple of hours. Tomorrow will seem changeless but everything will have changed. You'll look at wogs more often, remember their faces. Fear does that. Changes everything. Weeks, work-days, evenings like this, can be the beginning or the end of battles, you know.' Connell looked out past the verandah. 'It's motionless out there,' he said. 'But time only seems to stand still.'

'It hasn't far to go, young fellow,' Freddie said.

Lorimer said, 'Yes, old man.'

'It's running out. Plot your course from drink to drink, no further. It's best like that. People die out here and we push them underground before they stink.'

'Like the wrapped-up wog out there?'

'Yes,' Freddie said. 'Or you or I. Last year I drank beer with a Swiss fellow Saturday lunchtime and we buried him at sunset. It was nothing. He was absent, that's all. He might have gone on leave.'

Lorimer was amused. 'From drink to drink, I'll remember that. James Connell,' he said. 'A good paddywhack name for a dying wog. A couple of minutes, a couple of hours, that's all we have left. All he has left!' Very mildly he upbraided Connell. 'Didn't you thunder at him about self-destruction and the canons of the Almighty?'

'My God is a ghost without a name, real only to me,' Connell said. 'And self-destruction in *hope*? He might like that. There has to be a good reason for dying. Like living, or killing.'

Jane had poured herself a drink and felt all her silent tears. Freddie had his arm about her shoulders.

'Killing?' Lorimer said in the silence and then paused for what seemed a long time. 'How many have you killed, Commissar? In your hospice, out of it? With good reason, of course.'

Jane said, 'For God's sake ...'

'He's an African,' Lorimer pleaded. 'They kill each other. Savages, you see.' He turned to Connell. 'Don't you?'

Connell said, 'Somewhere, every day.'

'You see!'

There was a harsh coughing sound from the house now, a kind of fighting for breath. And then silence. It was the beginning, Connell knew. Lorimer, in pursuit of everyone, had scarcely heard it.

Jane left them, crossed the lounge towards the house door. In the darkness in there she could weep. Connell called out, 'There isn't anything we can do for her now. You mustn't touch her. Just watch.'

Jane turned and looked at him. 'Yes,' she said. Connell was afraid for her, she knew. 'Why?' she asked.

'You'll take care?' was all Connell said.

'Yes,' she promised and left.

Jane left moments of silence behind her. Unease was gradually piercing Freddie's brave front. Lorimer and Connell were seated. Freddie wandered from window to verandah, seeming only to watch and listen. But he neither saw nor heard. Connell's warning to Jane – because however brief and innocuous it had been it was a warning – had begun to draw all his doubts to a mass, a cold gathering premonition of something repugnant. Jane's footsteps sounded in the corridor of the house, and instants of escaping sound at the opening and closing of the bedroom door came in the stillness. A bite, poison, something that must run its course to a climax. Connell had said only enough to restore calm and reassurance. When the time was right the story would be told. Freddie had known and trusted Connell for a lot of years.

Connell, a murderer, he thought. If revenge was murder, Connell was a murderer. A warrant, an armed escort, travelling towards them from the coast. If the rains held off. Connell killed in anger, Freddie thought. He killed 'Lorimers'. And you were hanged for it in His Majesty's possessions. He looked at Connell and thought again of strapped arms, legs bound as he stood on the trapdoor while cowl and noose shut him in darkness. And then the drop. Eight, ten, twelve seconds from life to death. Good, Mr Hangman, ten seconds! The waiting coffin down there, hands reaching out for Connell's legs, to add weight or cut him down. Christ, Freddie thought, Connell should be moving away into impenetrable jungle.

Freddie said, 'Jane? Is she all right in there, Connell?'

'I think she can manage,' Connell said.

Freddie felt that some of the burden had been lifted; he looked at the blackness of the skyline and the flickering thread that exposed it and vanished in some cosmic whim.

'And Lucy?' Freddie asked.

'Let this night pass,' Connell said.

'Yes,' Freddie agreed; he wandered about again at his watching and listening game, talked of everything and nothing. '... I forget how many tribes out there. Hundreds ...'

Lorimer laughed.

'Don't interrupt, damn you,' Freddie told him. 'Hundreds, I

said. Lingos, gods, ju-jus, headmen's huts, mad dogs, bloody sacred crocodiles, and you name it. And the whole thing worked. The blackman had law and all the order he needed when we came. And he'll see us out.'

Lorimer nodded; it was all very amusing.

Freddie said to him, 'Do you chop them down back there ... wherever the hell it is, that territory of yours, damn it? Do they fight back?'

'They try.'

'So does the African with knives and knobkerries. But you'll teach him a few tricks, won't you?'

'I'm building bridges to get at him.'

From the house came distant muffled noise. It could be from the house or the compound. Distant muffled coughing, harsh, faint, a bark. Lorimer was looking out into the blackness of brush and undergrowth. Moments of anxiety rested on Freddie's face. He looked at Connell and saw him motionless, far away.

A few seconds and it had passed: a little unremarkable interval of silence for Freddie to jettison unpleasantness and take hold again. 'Damn country,' he said. 'You can feel it tonight, leaning on us. Sorry about all this damn sniping, Connell. We can start again. You never came in the bank, did you, Lorimer? Could have shown you round. A pokey little place, you'd have called it. That's what it is. What it was. One white Freeman, three blacks. We bought diamonds over the counter. These johnnies pan and scrape, hoard them in aspirin bottles, matchboxes, old rags. Brown pebbles, that's all they are. Gold from the mines too. A whole strongroom of it sometimes. Emptied it on the down train this morning. Got rid of it.' Freddie paused, held out a smile of truce to Lorimer. 'And I'll come out to see your bridge again and ask a lot of damn silly questions, I suppose. You might build me a new bank, Lorimer.' Freddie was thinking, no more banking for Freeman.

Lorimer said, 'Pick a good day, Freddie. The villages, you know. Unpredictable. They often have bloody tussles when it doesn't rain, or when it rains too much, or the headman has a balls-ache. Commissar Connell could tell you. Stiffs in the river, bellies of air, stink and flies.' He looked at Connell. 'The sick too, Commissar. They tip them in.'

Connell said, 'When they have to.'

'God's will?'

'It must be.'

'Help them on their way?'

'Of course,' Connell said.

Freddie, with drink, sat, anxious, tired of being angry, of peace-making.

'You see them limping in the bush,' Connell said. 'Great knobs of flesh, like dung on their faces, not looking for people, only a place to flop. It's a long death for some. The pain stays inside, trapped in a bag of dead skin. Or limbs rot away to stumps. The missions used to pray for them when I came first. Here, deep in the bush, far up the creeks. A miracle, someone would say, when a body was suddenly shriven of illness. But the stumps didn't grow again.'

Connell remembered his first 'ju-ju' patients, wasted, lost extremities, tumescent disfigurement stretching and distorting features, ulcerated. He had washed them, soothed them with oil, found what balm he could for pain, built the first of his isolated huts. The African dreaded the red skin, the rings, the first white patches of the leper, and Connell could only teach them to live within range of his hospice and grow food and leave a share for the unclean to collect. And then his numbers grew and they tended each other. Connell walked the round of his huts each day and peered into the darkness of each one and gave them humanity; stood silent at their burials, watched their withered remains wrapped in brush and foliage, returned to the clay. Like God, there had always been lepers.

He turned and said to Lorimer, 'I've killed a lot of people down there in twenty years, people weeping in pain. Let them sleep in peace. Their gratitude is silent, overpowering. Palm wine alcohol,' he said. 'And the white ooze of bush roots. A kind of ju-ju. It brings rest.'

Wogs were nothing. Lorimer thought of murder in Ulster. Connell could see his anxiety, Freddie's solitary unease.

From the verandah Freddie watched the glow and sudden flares, the deep reds and orange and yellows, like great stacks of paper burning from the outside, leaving a baked brown core awaiting a spark to give it life. Little irruptions shot in the air, lived and died. A pall of smoke had risen up from the village, sat above it, hardly dispersed, a grey canopy in the blackness. Then Freddie saw movement, almost imperceptible. Not the haphazard flash of ignition and its afterglow. This was a tiny thread of light, moving, coming to a halt, then merged into the village fires. Freddie placed it at the burnt-out railway boards. A train, by God, he thought. It had beaten the rains! Troops piling out to leave blood and carnage on the hot streets in there, to send the chanting mob into the cover of the bush. A whiteman and his warrant and troops coming for Connell. Freddie was silent.

Eventually he said, 'I wonder if their train will make it? Troops to clear the village out.'

It was a signal and Connell came and stood beside him, looking at the village, the hanging sky, the glows and flares, the stationary pinheads of light, putting it all together. 'Always a chance,' he said.

Lorimer said, 'Troops to take us out of this stinking hole.'

'An even chance,' Connell said. 'Eight miles to the village. Road blocks, trees down, ambushes. A couple of hours.'

Freddie said, 'I think the rains will win.'

'Win?' Lorimer asked.

Noise came from the house again, closer, muffled strangled sounds, for two, three seconds, a kind of snarling bark. Lorimer had grabbed the shotgun, stood at the open window, facing the vast night.

Freddie said, 'It's just noise in the house, old man. Open

184

windows back there can be confusing. And there's no light. Lucy didn't want light.'

Lorimer ignored him, pushed the barrels of the gun into the darkness. 'It was in the bush,' he said. 'Some damn wild mongrel. Or wogs. Brothers in grief. The stink of that body is pulling them in.'

Freddie's patience was ebbing. 'No light in the house, I told you!' he said. 'Jane's dropped something, in the darkness, knocked something over, swore, called out, that's all.'

Lorimer turned to face him.

'You point a gun at the ground, there's a good fellow.'

There was silence.

Connell said, 'Why don't you put it where you found it?'

Both barrels swung towards Connell now.

Freddie was outraged. 'Damn it, man, you're a guest in my house! You've been drowning us in claptrap all evening and I'm tired of it. Bloody tired of it.'

Lorimer said, 'It was a dog or a wog.' He put down the gun.

Connell said to Freddie, 'I'll bring back some medicine.' He went out by the verandah into the darkness.

Lorimer fumbled in anxiety. 'He'll be back, will he, Mr Freeman? You're sure? They won't take a shot at their Commissar, will they?' Connell had become precious for Lorimer.

Freddie wondered. 'They save their shots,' he said, moving away. 'You'll feel safe on your own for a spell, will you?' I'll send Jane to take care of you.' Freddie, at the house door, relented again. He turned. 'Pour yourself a stiff drink, Lorimer. Pour yourself a stiff drink.'

Lorimer, in silence, looked out at the gathering weight of storm and rain. He saw only fires and a pall of smoke.

'We're all a bit jumpy,' Freddie said, and waited a few moments for a reply.

But there was only silence.

★

Lorimer listened to Freddie's fading footfalls in the house. He went to the verandah, looked, listened for Connell. But like his wogs he seemed to vanish as you watched him. Lorimer wondered if down on the coast, in the polished air-conditioned Secretariat, they knew it was Connell's bastard wog who had been the long-smouldering fuse now reaching the charge. Commissar Connell: labour-fixing, politicking; palm wine brews, market gardens, beggars at the station, clothes, old and new, ageing black hags tending his stalls.

He thought of Freddie's fortuitous arrival on site when it seemed he had broken through his fear and would have pinned that screaming randy bitch against bare unyielding boards.

He remembered the creek: no visible sun, hot air consuming its fuel, humidity painting bodies in sweat; a grey ceiling of cloud encapsulated the world, the blacks like struggling scarcely surviving scarabs.

Twelve months in this dying sweating orifice. Six months before he saw the coast again, leant on the taffrail of the ship until the rim of this gross piece of God's handiwork had slipped out of sight. He damned the papish whore who had committed him here. Damned her, damned her! Ulster, Antrim, to have it under his feet again ...

The village streets of home — market town, if you were generous — where his father's law business dominated the square, were twenty miles drive from the sea, easy to reach, distant enough to escape the nine, ten months of empty houses and stagnant trade. The Lorimer home sat at the fringe, two-storeyed, ivied, spotless with a beautiful austerity. The brick walls, stone coping, hexagonal pillars with pyramids and orbs held wrought-iron gates, close-barred and secretive to guard the virginity of lawns and shrubs and raked gravel paths.

His mother, eyes averted as if to avoid any human contact, had turned fifty now but had the attractive body and soft skin that twenty-five years of celibacy might have bequeathed. At marriage, with money and land, she had brought servants and a gardener. They were older, hardly ever visible, the immaculate house and grounds proof of their industry.

Alec Lorimer remembered early years when he and an ailing brother each held one of her hands as she walked through the town to shop, to call out her lists to the proprietor only – assistants kept their distance – and on her graceful, dignified journey home she sometimes stopped at the crowded windows of millinery and drapery stores. Once he had stolen a glance and saw her perusing her own almost disguised beauty. Even in their childhood days – she was perhaps thirty – she and her spouse had taken to their separate beds. His father, a dark, square man then and now, would return from his office, hold out his hands for her to clasp. Then to the bathroom and, later, a page from the Bible was a prelude to an elaborate grace. The Bible, on a low domestic lectern at which he could sit, was a tome of tooled leather and gilt, brassbound, soberly decorated, opened and closed by two hinged brass plates. In the empty dining-room, once, he had dared to open it: 'Brown's Self-Interpreting Family Bible, containing Old and New Testaments to which are annexed an extensive introduction; marginal references and illustrations; an exact summary of the several books; a paraphrase of the most obscure or important parts; explanatory notes, evangelical reflections etc. etc., by the late Rev. John Brown, Minister of Gospel at Haddington, with many additional references, and a life of the Author.'

Over the years he had committed that opening page to memory: gilt-edged pages too, one thousand, one hundred and twenty-three pages of the prophets of God; and in addition, unnumbered, a family register of Parents, Children, Marriages, Deaths and Events. The graphics, the illustrations too, he could remember in extraordinary detail.

Grace before meals would rumble over their bowed heads, and then a pause until the paterfamilias had knife and fork in hand and the plain almost silent meal, adequate, was taken.

Norry, a kind, strangely wasted woman, put them to bed and Father, dressed for church or lodge or businessmen's club, came to pat them gently on the forehead. No more. They heard his footsteps on the stairs and the click of the hall door as he left. The maids and gardener were abed by ten o'clock ...

With his hand he pushed the sweat from his face, brought the night into focus and let it slip again; looked about at the austerity of Freddie's lounge, scattered drinks, ashtrays ...

He remembered nights creeping down to the drawing-room door, listening, peering at his mother, alone, in tears. Strange, he used to think. Strange. She had everything. Later she would come and kiss them and he would feign sleep and smell the sweetness of her body. Was it sinful, he wondered ...

They were of age, suddenly, it seemed, and the brothers Lorimer were consigned to boarding school at Edinburgh. Education, religion, plain fare, religion, religion, religion, early to bed, early to rise, education, religion. He had always remembered that John Knox had borne nineteen months as a galley slave for the glory of God and his church. But he was being shaped: fable became fact, indifference became dislike, became hatred. Rome and the Antichrist; the native Irish papist, dirty in body and mind. It all filtered into his thinking and settled.

Holidays were times of work too: for church, for the lodge and its members, household chores to give staff their annual week's rest, daily grinds in the weak spots of school reports. Summer vacations, though, incorporated free time. After dinner they could wander in the grounds or use drawing-room or library to read what had been chosen. Ten o'clock was bedtime.

Alec was growing up: he had begun to notice schoolgirls' legs and thighs, budding breasts, wondered what lay beneath skirts and blouses; his first lascivious dream was explosive ecstasy and then fear, guilt. When it happened again he went to find his mother alone in the garden.

'Your father will explain,' she said; she was blushing, almost in shock.

'Is it something bad?'

'Your father will explain.'

In a day or two his father had isolated him, pointed to a rough wooden seat in the shade.

'Here,' he said. 'Now, there was something to be discussed?'

He was dumbstruck before this unsmiling demi-god.

'While sleeping, your body discharged some tainted fluid?'

'Yes.' Oh God, the relief!

'It's a passing thing with boys, hardly even an illness. Ignore it. If it happens again, pray for strength. God will help you. And don't talk about it to anyone. Understood?'

'Yes.'

Only two evenings later, with dusk creeping on, he sat hidden in the shrubs, bored, pondering, when his father passed out on his evening duties: he wore lighter clothes and hat for summertime, but always sombre shades; he carried a light silver-headed cane.

On impulse he went to the gate and watched him turn the corner out of sight; and then he followed him. He had no motive: it might have been to savour the freedom of night air beyond the imprisoning walls, to walk, hands in pockets, through the streets, duskish streets, shop windows. Girls. His father turned off again but it was a small town and an easy job to find him. At the lower straggling end where large houses that once had grandeur were now tenements, he saw him use a key and vanish. He ran to the locked door and then down a sloping side alley to the rear. There was a door, a cellar, wooden steps to yet another door and hallway.

His father's voice up there. 'Ah, my little doll, I've been a naughty boy today.'

'Oooh. We'll have to see about that, won't we?'

His father's laughter! He had never heard him laugh; a ghostly smile seemed the limits of his humour. It was a three-storey converted dwelling of flats: a brothel, but clean and inoffensive.

He looked up the stairwell and saw the coat, the cane, heard the click of a door. Silence.

He padded almost soundlessly to the top and listened to the high brittle laughter, the tinkle of glasses. Through the keyhole he saw them: a young naked girl, hardly out of her teens, brown hair to her shoulders, firm body, nipples circled in brown. Beautiful thighs and his father's hand on them. They drank, she kissed his nose, his cheek. He was laughing.

Alec Lorimer, fourteen, was breathless; and ashamed. Breathless at such beautiful nudity and the knowledge of what lay beneath all those schoolgirl clothes: ashamed to see this dour bible-reading man, this pillar, in giggling sexual excitement. Suddenly he thought of his mother's tears . . .

But they were standing, ready to move! He hadn't expected it. He was suddenly in panic. A door opposite opened at his touch; it was a bedroom; a mirrored dressing-table sat across a corner and he slid behind it out of sight. Oh God, let him have his filth, whatever it was, in the other room. And go! Then it would be the lodge or the businessmen's club for more laughter, he thought, and whisky. The god-fearing mask was for home.

But suddenly the door was pushed open and from the darkness of his retreat he could see them plainly. She had taken his cane and paraded about, swirling her nudity, a little crossness in her beautiful face.

'You have been naughty. Remove your clothes!'

'Oh, my princess,' he pleaded.

'Remove them!' She flicked the cane; he pleaded, undressed . . .

He was naked, a square bull of a man, a great erectile rod of anticipation.

'Down!' she ordered.

He lay prone on the bed and she beat him; sharp smacks to his buttocks, and he groaned either in pain or ecstasy.

Alec Lorimer called out! The terror of shame, he thought.

Silence fell like a monster blow. The girl vanished.

'Come out!' the naked bull said. 'Come out!' With one hand he sent the dressing-table slithering across the floor.

He saw his son gazing at him. 'You?' he said.

'Yes.'

Still naked, he pulled him out of hiding and, with the cane, beat him to the floor; dragged him up and beat him down again. The cries got weaker and weaker. When he had dressed, he stood him up again, beat his face with open palms until he was broken. Then when focus had crept back into the eyes, he said, 'You left the house without permission, strayed into the papish backstreets. You were set on. A gang. Understand?'

'Yes.'

'Your mother will tell me about it later, ask for restraint. I'll find a little mercy. We might even pick up a couple of thugs. Are you listening?'

'Yes.'

'You have never been here. Never seen me here. Repeat it!'

Alec Lorimer, shivering in pain and fright, said, 'I have never been here. Never seen you here.'

'You came in the back?'

'Yes.'

'You go out the back.' He held open the door. 'Remember,' he said almost in a whisper. 'Papish whores are nothing. Remember!'

Fourteen years ago, Alec Lorimer thought; and he had never taken a woman or a man. He was celibate, twisted, dangerous.

Celibate, he had gone to college; celibate, he had joined the 'Specials'; celibate, he had qualified BE, BSc. A half-dozen doors were open for him and he had taken the best. He was still a 'Special', with pips and power now. Pips and power when he saw Ulster again.

A Lorimer on the battered embankment of a creek, prodding wogs with his boot, yelling at them. A central pier topped out before the rains! Christ, a deadline in this dead land! The rains came and went. And this smart-ass Freeman bitch in heat.

He was bitter.

He remembered the dry cool night driving a black Wolseley along an Antrim coast road. He had three men with him. Routine part-time stuff. Ulster defended itself. Call on papist houses, rough them up if they got shirty: names, addresses of family and friends; take one to the station for the night, questions, questions, leave him with sore balls. It was a way of shifting them: make their lives a bloody misery.

Coming down a hillside road, near midnight, the headlights picked out a lassie, stepping it out: good legs, good body, long hair. He had pulled up. 'ID?' It was a papish name. 'Address,' he said, as if testing her. She pointed at a lighted window, half a mile down the road.

'You live there?'

No fear, no insolence.

'Sit in,' he said.

The rear door was opened and she was suddenly on her back on the knees of these peace-keepers, a hand clamped on her mouth. He reversed the car and drove into the mountain wilderness, listening to the controlled almost silent struggle while they undressed her.

'Now!' he got the signal.

They took her out, three of them. He saw them put on condoms: that was important. Two held her, one raped her. They took their turns. He thought of his father's 'beauty', the spanking, the filthy charade; he thought of his mother's isolation. Passion rose for a moment inside him and died. He remembered the thrashing, the agony of the cane, the white explosions of light that each open palm brought. 'Remember, papish whores are nothing.'

The deed was done; they called to him. 'You want a bash, Guv?'

'No,' he said, 'Bury the rubbers.' He needed something that was his own, that he owned. Untouched. Oh God!

He watched them collect her scattered clothing and virtuously cover her from abdomen to thigh. A white beautiful body; until now perhaps clean. But she was nothing. A papish whore, he drilled himself. Again and again.

She was so still: not a movement of fingers or feet, a turn of her head. Not a sound.

His crew were back in the car. 'Wait,' he said; he got out and crossed to where she lay. She was dead: staring eyes, sagging mouth. He tried for a pulse at neck and wrist. There was nothing.

'She's dead,' he said. 'Put her in the boot. Clothes, everything. Leave nothing.'

In half an hour he had dropped them, sat in the library window, awaited the return of the great man from lodge or club or brothel.

'We killed someone,' he told him.

'Where is he?'

'A woman. In the boot of my car.'

He told him the story.

'Four of you?'

'Yes,' he lied.

'You left nothing?'

'Nothing.'

'When?'

'An hour ago.'

There was no anger, displeasure, anxiety. He rang the under-taker, a fellow lodge member. 'Alec's car. A dead woman, her clothing too, in the boot, Come and collect it. You're alone down there, aren't you? Tidy her up, dress her, neatly, you know. Put her on the back seat, under a blanket, a rug, whatever you've got. Must be quick. And ring us.' He hung up. 'Your keys,' he said to his erring boy.

'In the car.'

It took scarcely twenty minutes. Lorimer dumped her on the verge of the main road: he held her a moment in a stand-ing position and let her fall. Those had been his instructions. There was an autopsy, a coroner's court. '... Cardiac arrest ...

Embolism . . . Condolences to relatives . . .' Lodge members were friends in need.

A month later, the local weekly broadsheet, in a prominent column, said, 'Mr Alec Lorimer, BE, BSc, son of our leading citizen, will give eighteen months of his professional skills to King and our West African colonies. The loyalty of the Lorimers has come down the centuries . . . we wish him well in his selfless option for what is probably the most dangerous and infested corner of our glorious Empire . . .'

His mother had kissed him when he left and he felt he had stained her.

He banished it from his mind. At Freddie's sideboard he took a neat dram. He would blot it out with the memory of the black motionless creek soaking in the greyness from the sky.

He pondered it. For the mainland Brits, governors, administrators, honoured clerks and their ilk, colonial service was a bloody sinecure. A soft job. The wog would have it all back in a decade, to play drums and sleep standing up in doorways. Ulster Brits, men of Kirk and King, would hold their grip for ever on their Irish conquest, keep the papish workman in his place. Brits should spend a little time in contemplation of Ulster, temper the steel to weld together a crumbling Empire. He would finish this damn bridge for them, go back to his Antrim village, to real people, the Church, obedient natives . . .

The noise again! He stopped, listened, thought he could hear the faint crackle of brush. He took the gun, stood out of vision, peered at the blackness from time to time. He could feel a little trembling cold fear in his gut. He looked at the amber whisky and heard Jane's footsteps coming through the house. Even the sounds had a warm reassurance in this awful wasting place. He thought of her naked body again, her smile, the excruciating knee deep in his groin. He put the gun away.

She came in arranging her hair, a face without expression. Drunken Freddie had sent her, in peace, and he was glad of her presence.

'I'm sorry,' he said.

'Because your balls ache?'

'Because I was out of order,' he said: but stiff as a ramrod.

'You've never had a woman, have you, Lorimer?'

'No,' he admitted. 'I've never had a woman.'

'Your little Ulster lassies keep it under lock and key for the marriage bed. Then you can rape to your heart's content, give them all you've got.' He was about to defend his Ulster women but she said, 'Forget it, dear boy. For me, it's fun and games. For you it's dirty work at the crossroads. Oh, I believe in God. Freddie and Connell too, I suppose. I crib and tongue-lash. Almost without morals. Almost without charity. But I don't hate. You're a hater, Mr Lorimer.'

'Yes,' he said, stirred again. 'I hate. Connell, that shifty white nigger upsets me.'

'You hate him,' she said. 'You're sitting on his land back there, flying your flag, and you hate him.'

'Our land,' he said. 'For three hundred years.'

'And before that, his, for ever and ever. You should be Irish, Mr Lorimer.'

Jane had left the house door open and a mixture of sound and struggle was clear now, and above it a harsh drowning cough. She went and closed the door.

'We'll forget Ulster,' she said. 'Where's Connell?'

'Gone for ju-ju medicine, he tells us.'

She stood and wondered if she should drink.

'Your mother?' he said

'Yes.'

'It's a retching sound. Awful. I'm sorry she's ill.'

She nodded to accept his condolence. 'Being ill here is like death, lying in sweat or dry as paper.' She left the sideboard and the whisky. 'In the end you pay the piper, that's all. Drink. She's an alcoholic. A soak.' She listened to sounds loud and clear now even behind closed doors. 'I'm two weeks back from London,' she said. 'She was ill then. Yes,' she said, 'I'd say she's at the end of a binge. Call it what you like. Working out in a fit, heaving, grunting like a maniac, years of gin bottles clanging about in her head.'

There was a long silence. Lorimer said, 'Why does he come here? The Commissar?'

'Connell?' she said and waited.

'Yes.'

'Not for screwing if that's what you wonder. He always came. He was asked. He's a guest.' She saw Lorimer's inexplicable anger. 'He might keep the rabble off, you know.' She paused. 'Are we afraid? I think we are. I am. Josiah had his hands lopped off. Christ, he's just out there!'

'The mines are just out there.'

Jane dismissed him. 'The mines are a thousand miles away tonight. Understand?'

'Will Connell come back?' he asked.

'If he said so.'

'Down at that kip of his, passing out the soup, floating his black wog souls to paradise.' Lorimer laughed, a laugh of astonishment. 'Wogs on my bridge send their young females to do his housework. They go about naked for him. Did you know?'

Jane said, 'Of course we know.' There was so little to enjoy; everything to sneer at, nothing to laugh at. 'They like to go about naked. I was twelve. I used to walk naked down in the bush with James Connell. James Connell dying in the village. We hunted, set traps, fished on the creek, washed each other's bodies; when the mood took us we tumbled in the shade until we were slippery with sweat and the ease of passion too. He could have taken me then, any time, but he had promised Connell.'

'The Commissar?'

'He had promised Connell,' she repeated. 'You wouldn't understand, would you?'

'No.'

'Then forget it. But you are listening?'

196

'Yes.'

'Forget Connell too.' She paused. 'You can't forget him, can you? The Commissar.'

Lorimer was smiling.

'Forget him,' she said; she went and leant against the verandah rail, changed the pace, the conversation. 'The rains are a nuisance,' she said almost in soliloquy. 'The nights pitch black. And daytime? A deluge on the baking ground and the sun inhaling it like smoke.'

'Stifling,' he said.

'Oh, I like the heat,' she said. 'And lying naked on my bed.'

In the distance she could hear sounds in the bush and listened; but from the house came a moaning coughing struggling sound; and, breathless, soothing it, Freddie's anxious voice. She stood stiff on the verandah floor and waited for it to fade.

'You're not very fond of her,' he said. 'Your mother.'

'I'm fond of my mother,' she said. 'But sorry for her too.'

'Pity?'

'You could call it pity.'

'And Freddie?' he asked.

'I love my father,' she said. The sounds from the house still reached them, diminishing in intensity.

'Your mother's ill. What is it? You?' Lorimer looked at her and saw nakedness, a tramp.

'It could be,' she said. 'Or Africa. Unhappiness eating her away. Or drink. Or Muswell Hill. Sleigh bells on the Alexandra Palace snow.'

'You spent five years in London.'

'Yes.'

'She could have come to you.'

'I didn't want her. I told her.'

'Your father?'

'He understood. It was easy. I came to them. The long break. Three months in the year. I like it here. I like it in the Cape.'

'And James Connell?'

'He had gone. He had found his own women.'

'Freddie likes the Cape?'

She looked at Lorimer for a long time. 'He deserves something,' she said. 'He's in there with all his power, battling with her, lying on her, holding her down.' She poured and drank some whisky. 'Drink,' she said to Lorimer. 'There are a lot of hours until daylight.'

He went to the sideboard. 'She's very ill, isn't she?'

'Yes. Connell might know. But he's silent. That's bad.'

'And Freddie?'

'Might guess and be wrong. He doesn't understand. He's never been ill.' She remembered the great thundering crash of his rugby days, grazed skin and little dabs of blood. She had always been proud of him. 'The Freemans,' she said, 'India, the army, colonials, fighting men. Bullets not bloody bus-stops. There's a steel trunk in his room, P&O labels baked into the paintwork. "Freeman", it says, "Multan 1849". A hundred years of colonials. Freemans. Free men.' She stared at Lorimer, at his undiminished self-esteem. 'And look at him,' she said. 'Have you really looked at him?'

Lorimer thought about it. 'Yes,' he said.

'And what did you think? He's a nice poor old doddering sod? Would that sum it up? That's what she made him.' She listened to the almost constant noise from the house. 'And now, this. They knew him back in London where he sent my cash. "Freddie Freeman's daughter! Best fly-half I ever saw. Should have gone to the top. Opening bat for ten years too. Remember him, Reg? Sahib Freeman. Old Freddie."' She could feel emotion gathering but she would never expose it to Lorimer. Her words trailed away into a long silence.

It was quiet suddenly in the house. Lorimer broke the stillness. 'Well, they remembered him, I suppose.'

'Because,' Jane said, 'He's *someone*. In charge. He's a man. He doesn't belong in Muswell Hills or forgotten swamps like this. She belongs in Muswell Hill, there's the pity.' She paused, remembered. 'Local leave, once, Freddie took us up to Kano. We watched the sunset together, the three of us, on the edge of the desert. The hotel floor had all the shadows of fretted windows spaced along it, polished like glass. Outside. Rooftops, a mosque, the streets bursting with people. A fairytale!' She laughed suddenly. 'She said to him, "Everything smells so stale here." And he was apologizing! How could teeming streets and turbans and mosques and Hausa stewards pouring icy white wine smell stale, I wondered? "We should make our bungalow like home," she said. "When we get back I'll set to work." Thank God it was forgotten.' Jane paced about in silence for a while. 'I think he saw the bleakness of it then.'

Lorimer was hardly interested. They were confused, not very talented people, without God or direction, almost without occupation. 'She needs help,' he said.

Jane hadn't heard him. 'In London, suddenly,' she said, 'I used to think of him. Not doing anything was his job. Just being here. It seems easy, doesn't it?'

'Yes.'

'Not for her. She looks at their shiny skins and sees them subdued, in terror, in bondage. They aren't. They're alive, free, burning a village, dying of hunger. Civilization will be the end. Who will they colonize? Europe. England. She sees bloody slaves. You can't do that. If you buy them shoes and bikes and mumble when you should roar, you'll need the gin bottle too. Muswell Hill was so snug. She could look at white faces and see nothing.'

Connell walked into the flat humid darkness, could feel the great burden of rain stretched lower and lower, closer to bursting point. The grey cloud had soaked into the night. His face was wet with sweat.

He thought of Lucy running the gauntlet of terror and only

he, Connell, aware. Freddie never ill, brushed off the weakness of others with sympathy and a trace of impatience. But Freddie now felt doubt and a chillness, had looked at him with uncertainty, had even asked, 'What is it, Connell?' The certainty of early evening, of nerves and damn poisonous bugs, and have a drink it cures everything, had waned. Freddie hadn't seen illness like it before. But now there were doubts. In the morning, the quack at the mines, damn unpronounceable fellow, osky bosky, would look, nod, and reach for a cure. That was the hope. Everything back to normal. Then a flight to England for Lucy. And for Freddie, the end of banking, small regrets. The Cape. A dream.

Four, five hours would change all their worlds. Would he, Connell, move deep into the wire mesh of jungle, searching for a few acres of arable ground to be stripped and ploughed and tilled; build cabins for his families again, arrange dark huts and a cemetery for his dying brothers? Could there be a village and a railway and stalls? Could there be? And for how long? Could he walk abroad again with reassurance? How long could they search for him, or could he move, hiding, emerging, knowing that somewhere the lure of a few coins or pounds would buy even the faithful? The Freemans scattered. Dead? Lucy dead. Freddie had been thirty-five when he had met him, had seen him take possession of the bank, his bungalow. His predecessors – their names even forgotten for the moment – at the end of their run, going home to retirement. Failures. Freddie? Behind bluster, perhaps too much whisky, Freddie had a shrewd unemployed mind. He had been misplaced, sent to Coventry perhaps. He should have arrived twenty, twenty-five years ago, down on the coast in the cosy administrative hierarchy and be retiring now, a chief inspector, a local director. But to where? The Cape or Lucy's impressive pile of ageing brick in Muswell Hill? Lucy had dutifully followed him in '38, very beautiful, Connell remembered: tall, slender, brown cropped hair, thirty-two years old and something of unhappiness always in her eyes. Sleeping apart was hardly unusual in the deep sweats of night-time. But houseboys talked. There were never trips to each other or the musky smell of love that lingered in rooms.

Freddie found relief, discreetly of course, in Hookers. Connell liked him.

He walked noisily now around the entire perimeter of Freddie's plateau, and again, letting his sounds travel on before him. Approaching the tall scrub where Josiah's body was hidden, he stopped. An African in a cloak, splashy native colours, dignified as a toga, came out of the darkness and bowed.

'He was killed and brought here,' Connell said.

'Yes, sah.'

'There were only dirty sheets and rope to clothe him.'

'His blood is on the bush. Down on the road. Many places.'

'I'm sorry,' Connell said.

The African bowed.

'I found him,' Connell said. 'His throat is cut, his mouth stuffed, his hands cut off.'

'We are his brothers,' he was told.

'Far?' Connell asked.

'Three hours, more.'

'And you are safe?'

'Carrying death may bring us safety.' Three figures rose up behind him and bowed to Connell.

There were races and villages and tribes and clans. Somewhere always a battle, a death. Their lives wasted from day to day beyond the sphere of whiteman or his jurisprudence.

'When there is trouble it is a disease. People die for many reasons.'

'Yes,' Connell said. 'The master from the bank, his wife, his daughter, all grieve for him. They were his friends.'

The shrouded body had been lashed to a wooden stretcher now and raised on their shoulders. They moved away along their own track, out of sight, their footfalls soft, then soundless.

Connell thought of death and the undignified grave he had

given to His Majesty's policemen twenty-eight years ago. The African would bury his dead and resort to vendetta too: an eye for an eye. That was justice. He thought of the squad with fixed bayonets, and a warrant, coming to chain him, to bar him in the ship's brig to Belfast. They would hang him in Belfast, offer prayers that one less murderer lived.

He went down the steep tarmac drive of Freddie's plateau and then into the bush, towards his commune. It was a great space of darkness now. He poured whisky and sat in his doorway and remembered the chill and breaks of sunshine on Belfast's Cave Hill, squalls coming up from the water to comb and flatten the grass, looking down on the smoke stacks, the shipyards, the Lough, the football arena, how many sticks of paralleled houses for workers . . .

He had asked Elizabeth Orr to marry him. Elizabeth Orr, a fine nonconformist name. She had broken the rules, thrown her arms round an Ulster papist and loved him. They had come to college the same autumn, rented their caps and gowns together, been conferred apart. Papishes were unclean in Presbyterian purity. Her father, a quality grocer and importer of tea, a member of his vestry who walked sashed and hard-hatted each twelfth of July beside a revered lodge banner, would have been driven to violence. Or died of shame.

When Connell had told his schoolmaster parent, he had been taken aside, it had been explained to him, gently, even with sympathy. 'It doesn't work, my boy. It ends in grief, always.'

He told Elizabeth, that unreal evening, full of strange light, when the waters of the Lough glistened and even city smoke was whisked away, pale and light as steam. 'I'll give tuition and grinds for the summer, night classes when term starts, take a Master's in a year. Then I'll need a beautiful wife.'

'You have it all arranged.'

'Must be an Ulster Brit,' he told her. 'Auburn hair, beautiful, kind eyes.'

'You're in love,' she said.

'Yes.'

'And I'm in love.'

'You'll marry me?'

'No one else . . .'

Sitting, drinking his whisky now, he looked across the empty gloom of his black kingdom and remembered all the laughter. He thought of five African wives he had taken, their offspring, their chattels, pushing their way now into obscure safety; or his grown-up sons setting the village aflame, the eldest in death throes. But his whiteman's blood would always be in them, a stigma, a stain. Like Ulster Brit and Irish, it would always be remembered by the few. 'No one else,' she had said.

He hoped she had married one of her own, a gentle one, like herself, and found some happiness. Was her love-making, like his, always vicarious? Connell felt only regret. And he hadn't wept even when he had identified the charred loyal paternal cinder by its dissolving ring and watchchain. Or wept in the awful sadness of the graveside.

He poured more whisky and drank it back and walked with sureness into the darkness of the hut.

His medical store was adequate, primitive, sufficient for the dying, to soothe them, ease pain, send them wherever the dead went when final pain convulsed them. But to ease Lucy Freeman's pain there was nothing. The hypodermic overdose he had never owned, could never afford. He took the remnants of his ether, a couple of measures in a bottle and a square of lint. He took a packing needle and string.

He finished his drink, walked out along the pathways between his parterres of tillage, past the houses of his families, empty of everything that could be carried. He saw the crushed brush and esparto of their escaping file and its entry into the full cover of jungle. He walked into the dark shadows and could almost smell death. His first wife, thickened, gone to flesh, who had tended his fever, and who had had what love there was left, was brutalized and hacked. At forty she was too old for rape. He stood silent and listened. There were only crickets and drums; or someone silent as himself in watch perhaps. There would be other bodies farther on, the younger ones ravished. This was bait. That could be the price of living with the whiteman. He moved, backed slowly away from it, watchful as an animal, into the open.

Christ, he thought, a mob and its freedom was without pity, compassion. He thought of his scattered family, dead, mutilated, in the bush; he thought of the Freemans; he thought of Lorimer; he thought of home. And there would never be another Connell commune of wives and children, of tillage and begging and palm wine making. A commissar. Christ, he thought, a commissar. Revolution was the snatching of territory from hand to hand, nurtured by the honourable, possessed by the rabble.

For a moment, for a fleeting instant, he saw youth and familiar places again, and the blackness of night drifted across it like a cloud shadow: a mother perhaps dead, perhaps long dead or waiting for death; greying sisters somewhere; a stunted cinder in his coffin; two skeletons in Passchendaele mud. A page was turned. It was the end.

He walked back and sat in his doorway and watched the fringe of the jungle that framed his territory: a black wall shutting in blackness.

From somewhere very close a voice said, 'Mister Commissar, sah.'

'Come where I can see you,' he said.

A boy, hardly in his teens, wet with sweat, dust-soiled, respectful, came out of hiding and stood before him. He was tall, a powerful frame in the making. 'The Letter Writer,' he said. 'He send me to bring you this.' He handed Connell a folded sheet.

'From the village?' Connell asked.

'From the village.'

'You ran from the village. A long journey.'

'Yes, sah.'

Connell smiled; he opened the sheet. It was the misaligned

typeface of the Letter Writer. 'Friend Connell,' it said. 'There is danger. Here in the village, in other places too. Sometimes the King's army joins with the people. Many battles. Army fights army, fights people, people fight people. The King's army, two hundred men, in train from coast. Only rain and flood from hills can hold them for a little while. Go with your people away. The sick are beyond danger. They fear them. A few weeks, days, rebels everywhere in many villages, on the coast, will be dead, in jail. We will have lost. But won too. It is the beginning. Your son will die at any time. He is a man of honour. Go, Connell. There are rebels but murderers and thieves too. I walk with you, my Friend.'

Connell said to the messenger, 'Take my bicycle.'

'Yes, sah.'

'My bicycle is there. It is yours. I give it to you.'

'Thank you, sah.'

Connell took a fresh sheet of paper, for moments only lit a storm lantern. He wrote a few lines and sealed them in an envelope. 'This is for the Letter Writer,' he said. 'Pedal hard. Time is important.'

He scarcely heard the messenger hurrying through the tunnel of jungle with the bicycle. He sat for five, ten minutes and drank, listened to every sound. Only drums and crickets. He walked the rows of his lepers' huts and bade them good night, as was custom, placed them in the care of the walking ones.

Then he turned towards Freddie Freeman's bungalow on the hill.

Connell arrived, almost without sound, at the verandah and Lorimer, suddenly aware of his presence, startled, swung towards him with the shotgun. Connell waved him away.

'By God,' Lorimer said, exposed for a moment; he watched Connell put something wrapped in lint in an empty first-aid box. 'Count yourself lucky, Commissar,' he said. 'I could have put a hole in you then, couldn't I? Creeping round like a bloody lizard.'

'I'm lucky,' Connell said.

'Maybe not always.'

'Oh, shut up, Lorimer,' Jane pleaded. 'You're a damn bore.'

'Freddie?' Connell asked her.

'Still back there in the house, in the bedroom.'

'And it's quiet?'

'At times. It's quiet now.'

Connell nodded.

Lorimer said, 'What were you doing out there, Commissar? Where were you?'

Connell looked at him, a colder stare now. 'Freddie was right,' he said. 'You shouldn't point guns at people.'

'Where were you?'

'Down there looking after my sick,' Connell said. 'No lights burning, you see. It's ju-ju time. They'll be sleeping now. The best kind of living is sleeping. A kind of death.' Connell looked at the gun barrels. 'Are you going to kill someone, Mr Lorimer?'

'If I have to.'

'Good,' Connell said. 'That's the very best reason.'

He went to the sideboard and poured two drinks, brought one to Jane. 'You look tired,' he said. 'Whisky is for evenings like this. Every evening.'

Jane took her drink and sat, watched Connell, mellowed in his whisky, but alert, glancing again at the gun.

'Put it away,' Jane told Lorimer.

Connell said to him, 'My father raised killers, you know. He was a loyal Ulster schoolmaster, a papist of course, who sent his sons to fight and die in 1915. For King and Country. Two sons deep down there, mouths blocked with French mud, Mr Lorimer. It was deemed prudent, you see, for papists, to have loyal family service engraved on staff records. A kind of armour. Papists but. I saw my brothers in 1916. Khaki, huge polished boots and puttees. They brought their photographs. "Have you killed Germans?" I asked. "Haven't seen 'em yet." "How many will you kill? Ten, fifty, a hundred?" They gave me sixpence each. A shilling was a lot of money then. "In two years I can join too," I said. We never saw them again.' He looked at Lorimer, at the gun, watched him stand it in its corner; he said, 'Afterwards, I thought it was a bad reason anyway for killing people. Files and records and military service.' He paused. 'I think they knew it too. They didn't *have* to kill, you see?'

Lorimer said, 'In Ulster we have to.'

'Oh, yes,' Connell agreed.

Lorimer said to him, 'Have you killed in Ulster, Commissar?' The idea had suddenly come, with dazzling clarity, that Connell should be exposed, lessened. Exposed before this little whore and her breed. Connell living with greasy women and disease. 'Of course,' he said. 'A bloody Fenian papist! Have you murdered in Ulster, Commissar?' he asked. 'Murdered?'

'Killed when there was reason,' Connell said, remembering the faceless police and the thump of their landings at the foot of the manhole.

Lorimer was triumphant, stricken, powerless.

'The colonial servant,' Connell told him, 'brings his flag and his gun. To Ulster, the Coast, wherever. A weary life, lonely too, isn't it? Forever under siege.' He paused for a moment. 'My father was an Irishman, you see. A native you'd call him, I suppose. He was a good man.'

'You're a murderer, aren't you?' Lorimer said.

He looked at Jane and could see only humility, respect for Connell!

Connell said very calmly, 'If you raise that gun and turn to me, Mr Lorimer, you're dead. Why don't you get yourself a drink?'

Connell's hand was on the butt of his revolver. At that moment he was a man without conscience, without God. Lorimer went and poured a whisky and soda.

'More whisky,' Connell told him. 'More. Now sit and drink it. You're a bit jiggy for a night like this.' He took the gun from him.

Lorimer sat.

Jane stood in silence; there was nothing to say. Connell's power had barely surfaced. She raised her glass to Connell and drank.

'What are you?' she asked him.

'Before I was a murderer?'

'Are you a murderer?'

'I killed without pity,' Connell said. 'Hardly honourable, is it?'

'And before that?'

'A schoolmaster, a graduate, I was young, in love too,' he told her.

She had compassion he didn't need; he was thinking of the hacked, violated bodies of his commune scattered about the bush. Silence settled on them. The bush, he thought, was a battlefield for survival: survival of insects, reptiles, animals, homo sapiens. You walked the hidden beaten tracks and reptiles and animals avoided them; insects crawling, flying, devoured each other or brought you disease; before you passed underneath, you looked hard at the overhanging branch, perhaps for something coiled, that might drop on you, crush you down to the span of its jaws, envelop you. There was beauty and ugliness and danger. At night-time clusters of fireflies that must be the work of God, a magician.

Connell looked out at the end of his world with sadness. He heard noise from the bush, beyond the edge of the plateau, creeping intermittent noise of prowlers, perhaps the blood of his families still on their long knives.

Lorimer stood, looked with wonder at Connell's smile: Jane too, motionless, watched him.

'Don't turn towards the window, Mr Lorimer,' he said. 'Don't make a movement for that gun.'

The smiling urgency held Lorimer. 'What is it, Commissar?' he said.

'People,' Connell told him. 'Just off the compound. Four, five, maybe more. I can hear them.' He said to Jane, 'You could get us a drink and smile if you can.'

Jane hardly paused, went uncertainly about the business of juggling with bottles and glasses and soda.

'Good,' Connell said. 'Make noise. It's good.' Apropos of nothing, he said, 'They burnt my father's house, the bastards, my father with it. We were papists, Antichrists, I suppose, before the wrath of the elders. I shot their policemen.' He saw Lorimer glance at him with a kind of frightened anger; and then towards the gun. 'Don't even look at it,' Connell said. 'Stay still and drink. Drink! I wouldn't have to shoot you, Lorimer. From out there they could blow half your head away. They don't waste cartridges.' He watched Lorimer drink the whisky; he needed it now. 'If they have a gun,' Connell said.

Jane said, 'Your drink.' She handed it to him.

Connell nodded. 'You'll give us a little speech, couldn't you? Very normal, earnest, friendly, not afraid.' Connell paused. 'You could tell us about London and Muswell Hill. Home. Your mother's home. And tell Mr Lorimer too, remember. And you'll be listening, Mr Lorimer. You could start now.'

Jane looked at him: there was an unsteadiness of fear in her eyes but she battled against it.

'You didn't like London, did you?'

'I didn't like it,' she said.

Connell nodded; his glance ranged the fringes of the bush through the windows and beyond the verandah rail.

'Yes?' he said.

'I didn't like it. The house next door had Indians or Pakistanis, I think. Double-breasted suits and saris. And it needed paint. I counted six doorbells ... our pear tree was still there ...'

Connell, hardly listening, prompted, 'Yes, yes, go on. You hated London.'

'Washing my own clothes, cleaning shoes, ration books, queuing for scraps of bony meat, standing in the rain, being left at bus-stops.'

'Good,' Connell said.

'No servants.'

'Rest now. Have a drink,' he said.

He turned to Lorimer. 'A few loyal service medals back in the family cabinet, in the Antrim hills, I suppose, Mr Lorimer? The Russian, the Boer, two shots at the Hun. A hundred years of Empire wars.'

'Yes,' Lorimer said.

'No medals for shooting paddywhacks?'

Lorimer drank, listened; he wouldn't stand pressure-cooking too long. He said eventually, 'Who's out there? That wog beginning to stink? His brothers? They've come for him?'

'Don't move,' Connell said. 'They came and went a long time ago. It isn't like Ulster. Us and them. Everything moves out here. Against us, against each other. They're children really, Maybe some thieves and blackguards. Maybe it *is* like Ulster. Your wogs from the bridge, Mr Lorimer? Unhappy? A lot of eyes out there, maybe. They can be patient, they can wait. It's a long night.'

In the silence, thunder was rolling nearer to them, loud flat claps, and lightning forking into the ground bringing instants of daylight. An hour, not much longer, and the belly of rain would burst on them. Lucy, he thought. Oh Christ! The rain! He listened to the stillness. Freddie was with her. She had slipped into deep enfeebled sleep, perhaps her last, before the final terrible pincers of illness gripped her, and pain was a locked-in scream.

Lorimer suddenly cracked. All his fear was in a deafening shout of battle. He snatched the gun and pushed the barrels through the open window.

Jane called to him.

'Bastard wogs,' he was shouting. 'Bastards, bastards!' His

fingers slid along the triggers and tightened. There were only clicking sounds.

'It's not loaded, you blithering ass!' Jane's fear reduced her to breathlessness, to a whisper. 'You fired at nothing in the bush. I took the other one. Do you think Connell would let you point a loaded gun at him? Or Freddie?'

Lorimer, without warning, moved for the box of cartridges but Jane snatched it out of his reach. They stood facing each other.

She said, 'You're being watched, damn you, damn you. Don't you know there are grinning faces out there watching the white-man sweat. It goes with the job, Freddie would say. We don't show fear, ever.'

'The cartridges,' Lorimer said.

She stood motionless, the table between them. Lorimer glanced at Freddie's revolver hanging from the curtain rail.

But Connell's gun was pointed at Lorimer, at his knees.

'I don't want to shoot you, Lorimer,' he said.

'Another murder, Commissar?'

'That would hardly be necessary,' Connell said. 'I could pitch you out in the compound with my bare hands. Plenty of shooting then.'

He took the gun from Lorimer; Jane handed him the cartridges. He put them out of reach.

His family tragedy of bloody death down in the escape from the commune – wives, children, grandchildren – had left him without feeling: those he had loved, in a fashion, who had loved him and tended him, had been shamed, demeaned, mutilated, allowed to bleed slowly to death. Thieves, murderers? Not so, Connell knew. These were the zealots, the diehards, the purists, the fascists. They would kill the dying blood in his white son too, but he was on a glowing altar of sacrifice for the nation. There was a lot of killing to be done yet; villages to be razed, the genocide of tribes, famine, starvation, polarization, compromise, until a pale cast of hopelessness brought the beginnings of sanity. Freedom, if it existed, had a dreadful price. They had fought for twenty-eight years now in Ulster, had reached the mid-century. 1950. They might fight another fifty.

Jane was facing him; and Lorimer, beginning to gather himself, waiting for courage and confidence again, feeling humiliation and the limping soreness at his groin.

'A bad reason for killing, Commissar?'

'Yes,' Connell said.

As they stood immobile, total silence enveloped them: a hundred thousand crickets ceased as if God's hand had switched them off; and then the distant chorus of the village, ten days of drumming and clamour and chanting, was no longer there. The silence smote them like an open palm. It was a sudden ictus, or death itself. Connell raised his glass an inch or two, as if to study it, then drank it back.

Lorimer said, 'The crickets have stopped.'

Jane said, 'Everything has stopped. And out there in the bush they know we're windy. You and I, Lorimer.' Unceremoniously she dried her wet palms on the cotton fabric at her thighs. 'Damn you, Lorimer,' she said. 'Are *you* afraid, Connell?'

'I'm too old to think about it,' he said; he went to refill his glass.

Suddenly the crickets were back again, thunderous for a moment; and the distant drums crept back: a new tempo, slower, deeper. Lightning crackled out in the bush and the thunderclap was close on its heels.

Lorimer said, almost shouted at Connell, 'It's the wog bastard in jail, isn't it? He's dead!'

'Yes,' Connell said. 'Everything stopped. And he stopped for ever.'

Jane sat, looked at Connell, remembered the days of nakedness and wonder: the rising flood of excitement breaking over both of them. Beautiful vanished days. She knew her eyes were moist and Connell wouldn't miss it.

Lorimer said, 'If the wog comes, out there in the compound, Commissar, will you kill him?'

Connell studied him in silence.

'If the wog comes for *us*, will you kill him?'

Connell said, 'If he comes he'll come for *you*.' He paused and drank. 'But diehards and drunks settling old scores? Rabbles with banners and drums, Mr Lorimer, I wouldn't like that. I'd have to scatter them. For *me*.'

'Kill them?'

'If I have to.'

Lorimer said, 'For me?'

'They're not changing all this, Lorimer,' Connell said. 'You are. My kind of tyranny could last for ever. Yours makes rebels.'

'They'll learn to live with it.'

'They'll change it, Mr Lorimer. One tyranny for another.'

The house door behind them opened and Freddie entered. He closed it very softly. They turned towards him, tired dishevelled Freddie who went to the sideboard and drank. They waited for him to speak.

Freddie poured a stiff drink to swallow back; and a smaller one to carry about; he seemed only gradually to become aware of his audience. He tidied himself, mopped his face, ran his fingers through damp hair, raised his glass, smiled at them.

'A drink, Connell?'

'Not now. Is everything all right?'

'It's all right,' Freddie said. 'The damn thing has me worried.' He listened, looked at his watch. 'Asleep for minutes now. Not a sound. It might be over, who can tell? Illnesses run a course, have a crisis. Fever can wind you up like that and when it lets go you shake yourself half to death. I was in there an hour, more, wasn't it? Battling her, holding her down. She was fighting for breath, her throat blocked with bloody gunge. It could be pneumonia, Connell, couldn't it? Pneumonia closes down the tubes. All that glue in her throat?'

Connell said, 'You wiped it away, did you?'

'Yes.'

'You're not cut or scratched?'

'Me?'

Connell was anxious. 'She didn't cut or scratch you, did she?'

'No, no, old man,' Freddie assured him. 'Didn't even know me.'

'You're sure?' Connell asked. 'It's important.'

Freddie looked at him; he had a strange sensation of fear like emptiness inside him. 'Certain. I held her down. Listened to her wheezing. Sometimes she coughed, a dry barking cough. Stiff as an iron bar one minute, frantic the next. Then, a split second, and it was over. I thought she was dead.'

'She's asleep?' Jane asked.

Freddie said, 'Oh yes, yes. Exhausted. So am I.' He listened to the slow clangour of the night, the village, the bush, and remembered. 'Everything stopped, you know. Drums, crickets, the whole damn crawling Coast. You could hear a pin drop. Did you notice?'

Lorimer was staring towards the village, looking at the lowering ceiling of rain.

'Yes,' Jane said. 'There was silence.'

'That was the end of it,' Freddie said. 'She slept. Weak, spent, yes, like the end of a fever. When the crickets came back, the drums, she didn't wake.'

He stared at Connell.

Lorimer said, 'The crickets stopped. The village. There wasn't a sound. Our wog patriot, you know, has passed on. You can hear it, a new rhythm now. A slow march for the dead.'

Freddie looked at him and wondered if he should strike him, beat whatever arrogance and bitterness he had out of him.

'No,' Jane anticipated.

Freddie calmed. 'Dead?' he asked Connell.

'Yes.'

'We're sorry.'

'Yes.'

Freddie gazed at the intransigence of Lorimer, a colonial like himself, a colonial at home or abroad, giving his service to a once great, now diminishing Empire. When the time came for justice, equality, the rigmarole of restoration, then the blood would be spilt. African, Irish, Indian, Ulster Brit: decades of hate expiated. Expiated? Freddie could only guess at history. Little people always fought the battles, that much he knew. When they learn not to want us, it's time to go, he thought. What had Lorimer said? They'd learn to live with it. He felt sorry for him, as always. The colonial left hardly a trace, only vanished.

'Crickets,' indefatigable Freddie the peacemaker said. 'I told you about that, Lorimer, didn't I? Tens of thousands of them and...' Freddie snapped his fingers. 'Silence. Like that. Some damn signal, rapport, magic we don't understand, I suppose.'

Lorimer sat unlistening. Connell looked with affection at Freddie who, behind sudden command and bluster, was a gentle person. His hour with Lucy had drained off his optimism, his confidence, and he stood showing his age for a moment.

Jane said, 'Fever is always a raging thirst, isn't it?'

'Yes,' Freddie said, dismissed it. 'The rain is almost here. I can feel it.' The lightning forked a few miles away and the thunder was a single cannon shot.

There must be a gentle way of telling him, Connell thought, an easy careful way now that he was distracted, in doubt.

'Yes,' Freddie said. 'A raging thirst.' He drank his whisky.

Connell waited a few moments and out of the silence he said, 'It's days since she drank anything. Days. Anything.'

But Freddie was racing away from him. 'I know, I know. No rules of the road on the Coast, nothing hard and fast.' Freddie raised his glass. 'Up in the villages they blow smoke up your rectum to cure blindness. And it works! Right, Connell?'

'Sometimes,' Connell said.

Freddie was in motion, pacing about, managed even a shadow of humour in old dry reminiscences. 'A customs fellow I knew down on the coast,' he said, 'brought his wife out when she was forty-two. A holiday! Forty-two, bloody awful to look at and barren as a salt swamp. In six weeks she was pregnant! Some damn randy Lebanese quack told him it was Harmattan: "The wind blows that damn sand down from the desert everywhere."' Freddie smiled and said, 'By God, we used to raise a laugh.' He paused, looked at Connell. 'Lucy enjoyed it then, you know. She seemed to. Everything. Bougainvillaea along the eaves out there, sunflowers twelve feet high, little pint-sized students shiny as chestnuts out of the pod, off to the mission school, copybooks and ink perched on their heads, pens in their hair. Everywhere heads loaded down. Kerosene cans, bales, basins, even bloody bedsteads. She used to stare. And there was a joke. Someone's steward boy wore his hat upside down when he carried it. A Greek fellow used to tell it, night in, night out, down at the club, I remember. We always laughed. A good crowd. Good times.'

Freddie had wandered to the verandah, taken up his old crouched position at the rail.

'Yes,' Connell supplied.

Lorimer sat in controlled anxious rage that this felon of his land could breathe their air, drink, stand in the shelter of civilized people. Well, by God, Lorimer thought, he'd see him off, he'd be in the UK for his hanging because hang him he would. Troops, troops. How much did Freeman know, he wondered? A telephone? The village was burned out. Or it was unsound, unstable, dangerous.

The mines, he thought, had their direct lines to the coast. The mines!

Freddie said from the verandah, 'The village. It's quieter in there, isn't it?'

'Well,' Lorimer said. 'The wog is dead, I told you.'

Freddie thought for a moment of Connell's tight hold on his

anger and the near ridicule of this, his Ulster lord and master.

'His people,' Jane said. 'They came for Josiah's body.'

'Ah,' Freddie said, and for an instant saw him clearly as in life. 'He was a good fellow. I'll miss him.' Lucy was ill, he knew. Fever and festering bites weren't illness. But Lucy was ill. Was she dying? he wondered. He remembered her young beautiful face on the wet sidelines of rugger pitches. Her warmth. 'September,' he said, 'is a stinking month. Heat, heat, stifling. And now October rain. Up in Freetown when it rained you couldn't go out. A solid wall. Lightning wide as a house. Thunder coming down from the mountains used to rattle the beer glasses. Frightening bloody place, full of mist and disease. The Whiteman's Grave.' In '37 they'd been anchored in the Bay for three days, drinking, throwing pennies over the side for teenage divers in their canoes to slip like seals underwater and surface with coin and grinning teeth. A tender took a couple of dozen ashore once. An awful weathered hotel and steps rising to it. A group of fat blackmen, barely contained within their morning suits, bowler hats sitting above glistening sweaty faces, patent shoes, passed through to some inner sanctum. Chiefs, someone had said, down to make obeisance to the White Masters. It seemed another age. 'Sierra Leone means Mountain of the Lion,' he said, and smiled his apology. 'I was miles away,' he said. 'Up in Freetown in '37.'

It was Lorimer's moment. 'You know we have a murderer here, don't you, Freddie?' He looked from Connell to Jane's incredulous stare.

Freddie paused for a little while, didn't look at Connell. 'Of course,' he said to Lorimer. 'An alleged murderer. There's an arrest party on the train from the coast. If the rains don't slow it down.'

He thought of Jane living at close quarters with Lorimer or Lorimers. Christ! The rains would last for weeks, torrential opaque downpours, coming, going, ceasing only to let the leaden heat drain up the dampness from the ground in breathless humidity. Alternating deluge and drying out for weeks. And storms above your head that could loosen the bowels. Weather for a fugitive.

Let them come, for Christ's sake, Freddie thought. Let it rain.

'You told him they're coming to take him, didn't you?' Lorimer said. 'You'd like our Commissar to run, I think, Freddie.'

'Connell told *me*,' Freddie said.

Lorimer thought about that; he said, 'And if he runs you'll shoot him?'

'He can bloody run and good luck to him.'

'The bank wouldn't like that, Freddie.'

'The bank can kiss my arse.'

Freddie stared at him with undisguised contempt, saw him glancing towards the hanging revolver. Freddie took it and threw it across the room with Connell's cache.

'It isn't part of your contract to detain suspects, is it?' Freddie asked.

'Oh, he confessed.'

'We didn't hear him,' Jane said.

Lorimer smiled and shrugged, let the outside world creep into their silence. When this bust-up was over, there would be time for everything. He would watch the Commissar. Let him run, pay his minders to keep an hour behind him, raise the alarm. The long arm of loyalist justice . . .

Lucy cried out in the house and was silent again. In their own silence they could feel the searing pain of it. Freddie and Jane turned to go.

'No,' Connell said. 'Later, later, we'll know when it's time.' When she was conscious, he thought; when the pain and convulsions awakened her for death. When the rains came. Dear God!

Freddie poured drinks and distributed them; even for Lorimer. 'Happy landing,' he said.

Lucy's scream had set Lorimer thinking again: the mines, a line to the coast, troops at the mines. Connell would avoid the mines, he knew. But with four armed men he could make the pursuit, take him alive. He, Lorimer, could take him. He took the glass from Freddie and drank.

'Good,' Freddie said. 'Welcome to the Coast.'

Lorimer felt confidence; he said carefully, 'There's a sickbay at the mines, do you know? Doctor, nurse, pharmacy, beds.'

'Yes, I know.'

'Your wife should be there.'

Freddie studied him for a few moments. 'In the morning,' he said. 'When there's daylight. Between rainstorms. I'll see to it personally.' He tried to dull the edge of his voice. 'Don't interfere, Lorimer, like a good fellow. I get angry about things like that. You understand?'

Lorimer stared in silence at the darkness.

'Do you? Understand?' Freddie asked.

'Yes,' Lorimer said.

'It's eighteen miles up to the mines . . .'

Lorimer concluded it, 'And if the rains break we'll be sitting like ducks in a pond. You told us, Freddie.'

Freddie moved away from him, exasperated, suppressing anger. 'Damn it, we're all jumpy, Lorimer. It's nothing to be ashamed of. And Connell's not your business.' He said to Jane, 'Top up his drink.'

Lorimer stared at her. 'I'm talking about your wife, Mr Freeman. The cars are out there. Three guns, no rains for an hour yet.'

Freddie said, 'It's dark, Mr Lorimer. Pitch. Has been for a long time. No rains for an hour? Ten minutes, maybe. But dark, Mr Lorimer.'

'Commissar Connell,' Lorimer said suddenly. 'You'd steer us through, wouldn't you, Commissar? For a price?'

'She can't be moved,' Connell said.

'An hour, two, three hours ago?'

'She couldn't be moved.'

Lucy's hacking cough interrupted, an animal sound: a choking long moan of pain came and faded. In a few seconds it came again.

'The mines. Troops, safety too,' Lorimer said and watched Connell. 'You could drop us there. We'd give you an hour's head start. Fair, I think.'

'By God, Lorimer,' Freddie told him, 'I think you're an empty pisspot. You're a windy bastard. In a corner we need guts, not gab.'

'Murderers shouldn't be here,' Lorimer said. 'And maybe you should have a gust of smoke blown up your rectum, Freddie. Your wife won't last till morning.'

Freddie and Lorimer were at opposite ends of the room. Connell stood between them. He wanted calm. For Lorimer he had bitten back anger from minute to minute; it wasn't a night for anger and frustration. Jane watched him and understood. But Freddie was dumbfounded, trembling in anger at Lorimer's pronouncement on Lucy.

Connell told Freddie, 'Strap on your gun, put the bullets in your pocket, sit, keep the cartridges beside you.' He took the first-aid box. 'I brought something that might help for a little while. Sit and rest. I won't be long.'

'I'll come,' Freddie said.

'There's a job to be done here too and you're doing it,' Connell said. He went through the house doorway, left the door open. They could hear the mounting rage of Lucy's illness and Connell's footsteps on the parquet floor of the corridor. The opening of the bedroom door released the full crescendo of sound for a moment, and then again it was muffled.

Connell stood in the almost total darkness of the room: a dull tilley lamp was behind a screen and seemed to cast a creeping light on the floor. It reached the edge of the bed. He put his open box with ether and pad on the locker. He had packing needle and string too. The mosquito net had been pulled away and the still, then suddenly writhing, flailing body of Lucy Freeman took shape. Connell waited for it to stiffen in rigor, could see the terrible wells of pain in her eyes. He ripped and cut up sheets, flipped her face downwards and pinioned her hands. And then the grip of rigor broke and she was supine, a kicking savage mass again. The mucus gurgled in her throat, formed, frothed, overflowed her mouth and hung stretching on her cheek; her struggle for breath was a harsh drowning sound, a cough, a bark. A wave of terrifying anguish, visible, a kind of peristalsis of pain, passed through her body and she howled in terror. A dog. She stiffened in rigor again. Connell planted the pad of lint across mouth and nostrils and let the ether from his bottle drip on it. The spasms came and went, lessened, until she was still, for a short time, he thought. He tied her at the ankles. He wound two long lengths of linen rope. He tied her to the bed frame, beneath the arms and at the waist.

In the adjoining bathroom he washed, found disinfectant to rub on his skin. He was intact, there was nothing to be feared, but it would banish the smell of death.

He went back to the lounge.

Freddie and Jane faced him as he walked up to the sideboard. He took a lot of whisky and drank most of it. Lorimer sat, his back to him, aware, listening.

Freddie said, 'How is she, Connell?'

'I've made her comfortable for a little while,' he said. 'That's all.'

'She's quiet.'

'She'll be quiet for a little while.'

'Till daylight?'

Connell looked at Freddie. 'Perhaps,' he lied: all of them would have to know before long. Before the rains.

Freddie showed the flushed signs of drink; it had been a heavy evening, a heavy night. Jane was pale, silent. Lorimer might be thinking of a papish killer and how he might trip him.

'Sit, sit,' Freddie said. 'We should all sit. Lucy is quiet. We should rest while we can. We're grateful, Connell.'

They sat in a rough semi-circle, in stillness, listening. Everything had been said since darkness and before it and there would be a few silences to come.

But Lorimer broke the spell. 'What did you do, Commissar? What ju-ju did you bring?'

'Just ether,' Connell said. 'I put her out for a little while.'

'Good, good!' Freddie said.

'You didn't shoot her at any rate,' Lorimer said. 'We'd have heard it, wouldn't we?'

It was a tasteless aimed projectile that left a vacuum of silence in its wake, confused silence.

Freddie drank and said, too quietly, 'You'd better go now, Lorimer. You've insulted my house, my wife, Connell, everybody, everything. Pack up and go. Now. You'll make your way to the mines, I hope.' Bitterness and anger were ready to flow. Freddie was breathless, drank whisky awkwardly and it dripped from his chin. 'I hope you're out of earshot before they lay hands on you, you bastard!' He was tiring. 'Well then, come on, let's have you. Get moving!'

'Jildi, jildi?'

'Yes,' Freddie said.

Lorimer unhurriedly moved about, put his glass on the sideboard, took and arranged his jacket. Jane watched him from the window, Connell from the verandah. He didn't want to lose Connell. He had pushed too hard. But he could see Freddie's unhappiness now, his doubt. No steel. Freeman was a fool. He waited.

Freddie said, 'Lorimer, you're giving us a rough ride, aren't you?' He paused. 'Oh, drop it for Christ's sake,' he said. 'You can't go out there. Not even a gun, have you? Sit down, sit down.'

Lorimer looked at Connell, spoke to Freddie, almost with charm. 'If you want me to go ...'

'No, no. Sit down. Drink.' Freddie paced about, trying to find the special balanced words of advice, of admonition, calmness. 'When these johnnies are letting off steam,' he said, 'we sit it out. Ignore the blighters. Like Marble Arch on Sunday mornings. Fellows shouting everything from high treason to sheer lunacy. Ignore them. Leaves them puffed out, puzzled. That's the idea, you see?' Freddie turned to Jane.

'Get him a drink,' he said.

'He knows his way to the sideboard,' Jane said.

Freddie could see her anger and tried to smile. 'Yes, help yourself,' he told Lorimer.

Lorimer sat and watched Connell for a little while, said to Freddie as he passed, 'You said I was windy, Freeman. Or something like that. Didn't you?'

Lorimer waited.

Freddie held out his hands, said eventually, 'Yes, I'm sorry about that. Not my usual form, old man.' He paused. 'Well, you roughed me up a bit, you see.' Freddie tried to pass it off. 'Look, we all drink out here. The Coast. We need to. And women? Women have a lot of time on their hands, long day . . .'

Jane said, 'I've explained that.'

'So you see,' Freddie ploughed on, 'it complicates things, blurs the edges, makes it difficult to pinpoint something. Lucy. She'll sleep now. Connell's seen to it. I'll get her to the mines in the morning.'

'I'll tell them to expect you,' Lorimer said.

But Connell was his target. He thought, an escort from the mines and he could be back to take him here among his friends. Freeman and his whore-minded daughter. He might even bring a doctor. And he'd fix Freeman with his bank too: open-house to black smelling trash. A murderer.

'You're going?'

'Of course I'm going. I deal with wogs every day.'

Jane said, 'Your minders deal with them.'

223

'Oh Christ,' Freddie said. 'You're mad. You won't make it. Not two miles of it. Not a hope in hell. Not even a gun.' He suddenly seemed to lose interest; he said flatly to Lorimer, 'They don't care very much for you, Lorimer. There are ways of kicking them, you see.'

'Finished?'

'Yes,' Freddie said.

He turned to Connell. 'Commissar?'

'You can have my gun,' Connell said. 'But they'll kill you. You won't even see them.'

'I'll drive through them, Commissar.'

'Between cloudbursts and in darkness? When it rains you sit. A grey teeming wall in front of you. You sit. They'll cut you to little pieces.'

Connell held out the gun and Lorimer, sudden enthusiasm suddenly waning, looked at the motionless black masses of shrubs and brush.

'Oh, for God's sake,' Jane said. 'We're stuck with you. We should push you out there, drink our whisky and draw the curtains. We don't have to carry you on our backs. Have the spunk to get up and go, Lorimer!'

'No!' Freddie shouted: it seemed a great explosion of sound in the silence of the house, the compound. He held out peace-making hands. 'You can't go and that's an end to it. And if they come for us, if they come for you, we'll fight them off,' he reassured. 'Kill them, I suppose.'

Freddie looked at Connell.

Connell said, 'Yes, we'll kill them.' He was listening for Lucy. Only a flimsy tissue of anaesthetic wrapped her from pain deep as the darkness. And then? Freddie had to be told. Freddie and Jane.

'The gun,' Lorimer said.

Connell held it out to him and he took it to the window, a lighted stage, to display it, turn the chambers, aim it at the bush. A kind of drill exercise.

Jane watched him, turned to Connell. 'Will they come, do you think?'

'I don't know.'

'Should he stand there playing with that damn thing?'

'No.'

Lorimer was hiding his fear, his uncertainty, with a kind of childish bravado. 'It's fair bet they haven't got guns, isn't it, Commissar? Just so they can see the colour of gun metal.' He let the barrel range the bush again. 'They might be a windy bunch, eh Freddie? Well, if they want to get shot at, they'll have to make up their minds.'

Connell said, 'They're afraid. We're afraid. They have palm wine to drink. We have whisky. The moment will come.'

'Pump a half-dozen bullets into the bush,' Lorimer said. 'Send them flying with their hands up their arses. They haven't got guns, have they?'

'We don't know,' Freddie said.

'And we don't want to kill them, Lorimer,' Jane said. 'Tell him, Connell.'

Connell had moved across to the window and, without hindrance, had taken the gun from Lorimer. He calmed her. 'Unless we have to,' he said. 'Even rebels have law and order. Like in the villages. They kill each other when they have to. Yes,' he said, looking at Freddie, 'the weak ones too sometimes. When they have to. They understand.'

'Yes,' Freddie said, hurried on. 'The Indian used to die in the gutter, still dies there. Eyes open, mouth open. Skin and bone. In the gutter. Worse off than these johnnies, I can tell you. We could handle the Indian, make him do bloody somersaults. It lasted a long time. "Don't love, hate or dread him": a simple commandment, that's all. Get on with the job. Jildi, jildi. Love, hate, dread. Slow poisons. Get them in the system and you're dead from the word go.' Freddie was looking in relief at the gun in Connell's possession again. 'Yes,' he said. 'It lasted a long time. Three hundred and fifty years, you could say.' He wandered about. 'The Dutch put up the price of paper or something. They got there before us. So we went out to get our own, pushed them out. 1600, I think.'

Lorimer said, 'We were fifty years in Ulster then.'

'You were?'

'We're still there.'

'Well,' Freddie said, 'it's a good run.' He turned to Connell. 'The Dutch never forgave us. We're a bit tricky, they think. South Africa too, you see. The Boer has the blackman where he wants him and we keep butting in.'

It was almost spent now, the Empire, the colonies: port out, starboard home for India; gunboats on the Burma rivers; Malaya, Singapore, the Chinese Station; out of Liverpool for West Africa, fourteen days aboard from winter maybe into burning sunshine and running damp; the endless golden pier at Las Palmas; the Africa coast, Freetown, Takoradi, Accra, Lagos, Port Harcourt. Approaching a glittering wonderland and finding dirt roads, shanties and disease. It couldn't last, Freddie thought, you could only leave a mark on sand, a calling card of your visit. Some good things done. Bad ones too.

'We keep butting in,' he repeated, almost inaudible.

But Lorimer had heard. 'A game, Freddie,' he said.

Freddie shrugged off the gibe. 'A game,' he confirmed.

Jane crossed and took his arm and his gratitude showed for an instant. He could see that old battle glint he once had in her eye. She was proud of him: a redundant middle-aged pen-pusher, fighting back a creeping jungle of years. The Med, he thought with regret. Lucy might have been happy up there, love and closeness might have crept back to them. She was ill now. He pushed it out of mind.

Jane said to Lorimer, 'We're going to live at the Cape.' And to Freddie, 'We enjoy a good game, don't we? A hundred years of colonial carpet-baggers: the Freemans, colonials, men-at-arms, soldiers of fortune. Aren't we?'

Freddie smiled: the Cape was his haven. 'Yes,' he said.

'And we know you'll mind shop, Alec.'

Freddie said with fair conviction, 'It'll last a while longer down there, I think.'

'Longer than Ulster?' Jane asked.

'Well,' Freddie said, 'long enough for us. What do you think, Connell? You could get lost down there, you know.'

Connell said, 'I'm an African.'

'You're more than that, Commissar,' Lorimer told him.

The limp curtains stirred.

It was the first breath of storm and rain. Lightning floodlit and flickered on the compound and went to earth, the thunder was head-splitting. The village, Connell saw, was a plume of smoke above the drenched ground. The rain had reached it. And then it too faded into the black-grey approaching cataract.

'A few minutes,' Connell said, almost feeling the darkness.

The lightning and thunder struck again, brilliant, awesome in its power, and left a vacuum of silence. The village, the crickets, were still. Lucy cried out in the paralysing noise of thunder, was coughing out the choking mucus that strangled her.

Lorimer said, 'From the house that, was it? Or the bush?'

Freddie ignored him. 'The curtains moved,' he said. 'The first breeze. The rains are pushing the breeze at us, you see.'

'The wogs have a dog somewhere,' Lorimer said. 'It was like a dog.'

'No damn fear,' Freddie told him. 'These johnnies give dogs a wide berth, I can tell you.'

There was the magnesium flare of lightning again and the rip of thunder, the tinkle of bottles on Freddie's sideboard; and Lucy's smothered barking. Then silence.

Connell said, 'Rabies, Mr Lorimer. The African is afraid of rabies. We all are.' He examined Lorimer's face: the arrogance, the uncertainty, the bravery, the fear. 'Little obedient dogs carry it in their spittle,' he told him. 'If you want little dogs to lick your hand, have a tough hide, they say.'

Connell suddenly took their glasses, poured drinks, asked

them to sit. He took a chair, almost facing them. 'We have a few minutes before it breaks,' he said, raised his glass. 'What was I talking about, Mr Lorimer?'

'Rabies, Commissar,' Lorimer said.

Connell drank. 'Yes,' he said. 'It's a fear of water, you see, Mr Lorimer. Hydrophobia. It goes back a long time. To Aristotle, Homer, Xenophon. Timeless. Dogs and their kind carry it, pass it on. It poisons the system. Water is life. But the sound of water, even the thought of it, can seize the throat muscles like a strangler, leave you fighting for breath. Fear, Mr Lorimer.'

'I know about mad dogs, Commissar.'

Connell said, 'I want you to listen.' He held out the back of his hand, put a finger on it. 'You have a scratch, almost invisible, Mr Lorimer, and a little infected dog, up in the hills, gently licks it. You're poisoned. The scratch heals but you're poisoned. Four, five weeks, maybe months, and where the scratch was, a little sore festers, like an ulcer, sending out pain in waves. Muscles tighten, you're in a vice, trying to scream; mucus blocks the air passages. Unbearable pain, delirium until the system collapses. That's rabies, Mr Lorimer.'

Lorimer nodded.

'Your wife, Freddie, has rabies,' Connell said.

It was a strange silence. Freddie sat looking at his drink. While Connell had spoken it was impossible not to see Lucy in every symptom. And still some flimsy defence of incredibility had remained. There was nothing now. Jane wept without tears, shocked. Lorimer was agape.

'Dogs,' Freddie said meaninglessly. Reality had slipped out of reach again; he needed to hear his own voice. He drank back his whisky. 'Oh Christ!' he said.

'Well?' Lorimer, recovered, waited. 'We're not afraid, are we? We can get her out of here. Medicine, a doctor. Eighteen miles up the bush tracks in rain and muck and damn the bloody wog and his long knives.'

Connell said, 'It was too late to take her anywhere weeks ago.'

'Today, Connell! Before sunset. You're the bloody expert.'

'A few hours ago it seemed another fever. Headache, pains.'

Freddie walked about, unseeing, nursing his drink, avoided their faces. He trembled a little, spilt whisky.

Jane said, 'She's dying?'

'Yes,' Connell said. 'Wherever she is, here, the mines, the coast, she's dying. Dying for weeks. No one can halt it.'

'How long?'

'Hours.'

Jane nodded towards the doorway and the house. 'Is that pain?'

'Yes,' Connell said. 'It's only beginning.'

Jane stared at him.

Connell took Freddie's arm, held him in his grip. There was the sound of wind, the storm was almost overhead. The curtains billowed out. 'Close your doors and windows,' Connell said. The crash of thunder almost blotted him out. 'The door and windows! Close them. We'll go to her, stay a while,' he said. 'You'll keep watch here. And sit, Lorimer. You're a smaller target that way.' Connell nodded to Jane. 'Drink the whisky, draw the curtains,' he said.

'Yes.' She watched them move down the lounge to the house door and suddenly the whole dreadful horror of it was apparent. 'Connell,' she called out.

'Yes,' he said; she would weep tears soon and it would be better.

'Connell, she couldn't drink. I held a glass out to her. Water, ice clinking in it. I thought she was mad. Mad. She tried to scream, to tear at me but she was powerless, rooted. Connell!'

Connell came back to her.

'Water. Even the sound of it.'

He saw Lorimer was drawing the verandah doors; Jane's voice was climbing in pitch with every word.

'When the sky opens, Connell, the sound of water. The whole bush swamped in sound! . . .'

229

Connell held her in his grip until calm returned. She slumped a little, he steadied her. 'You're all right, aren't you?' he asked.

In a few moments she said, 'Yes, I'm all right.'

He looked at her. 'You're in charge here,' he told her.

When he went back to join Freddie he saw that he had been weeping. He brought a whisky bottle and glasses with him. As they closed the door behind them the first drops of rain, like pebbles, fell on the roof, the parched earth and shrubs.

The tilley lamp in Lucy's room had been on glimmer pressure for hours and now it flickered in weakness. Connell crossed behind the screen and pumped it until the mantle was an incandescent white glare. He folded the shading screen and left it standing free. Freddie closed the windows, was drawing the curtains. The storm broke with a rush of wind that slapped the glass, flung the rain of open heavens against them; the curtains could only dim the flare of lightning; the thunder whip-cracked and seemed to fall on them like an avalanche of tumbling stone. Even Lucy's strangled screams were muffled.

'A towel?' Connell said.

Freddie looked at the awful dying shuddering frame on the bed; he tried to remember its beauty. He could see her pinioned wrists and ankles, the wound sheets tying her down. Connell had been good. The rain fell in torrents now, the plash of it everywhere; it shot down the pitch of the roof on to shrubs and pools forming in the compound, a great univeral sound, torturous unbearable sound. The seizures and releases must kill her in moments, he thought. But Connell had said 'hours'.

Freddie brought the towel, looked at the coughing ooze of froth and mucus creeping, congealing, spread across her lower face, matted in her hair.

'I'll have a drink, Connell,' he said.

'Yes, take a drink.'

230

'And you?'

'Later.'

'Can I help?'

'No,' Connell said. 'I had to tie her down, Freddie. It's like madness in her mind now. Dangerous.' With the towel he pushed away the mucus. She found voice for an instant and screamed a thin shattering thread of sound.

'That was madness, Connell?' Freddie stared at him.

'That was pain.' Connell didn't spare him. 'Pain causes madness too.'

'Christ . . . pain!'

Connell took a fresh pad and remnants of ether, covered her mouth and let the ether drip. The body movement lessened, slowed only a little, Connell knew; she moaned a strange snarling sound. In a few moments he stood erect, took a drink from Freddie, swallowed it back, held out his glass again. There was an awful deed to be done, he knew.

'You too,' Connell said.

Freddie drained his glass, filled it again.

'She's quieter,' he said.

'For a few minutes.'

The ceaseless sluicing hammering rain fell outside; the overhead storm was still there, but moving a little. It would take its message elsewhere and leave the torrential rain. The bush would be alive with movement now, things stirring, following some timeless plan of procreating, consuming, dying. The rain was death for some, life for others. The rivers and creeks would be brown-yellow races of current . . .

'How?' Freddie was saying. 'How, Connell?'

'The hills,' Connell told him. 'Dogs. It must be the hills, mustn't it? You sent her up there, remember? There were dogs, she told me.'

'Six, seven weeks ago. She needed it. A break, I thought. A bit heavy on the gin, you see. Not much. Starting too early, finishing late, that was all.'

'Up in the hills,' Connell said, 'you see dogs. White people, not too many, just a few, keep dogs. Reminds them of home, I suppose.'

'Home,' Freddie said. 'Yes, it reminded her of home, up there.' He stood motionless for moments. 'She wanted to go, Connell, and I wanted her to be happy.'

'Yes.'

Connell became aware of her bedroom. It was Lucy's piece of home that he had never seen: a corner cabinet of family pictures, statuettes, bric-à-brac; her young lady's writing desk with blotter, a drawer, pigeon-holes, even a jar of pristine paintbrushes; Landseer prints elegantly mounted on the walls; a framed embroidery word, BLESSING. And where the folded screen would have covered it, a prie-dieu facing a black untenanted cross.

Freddie followed Connell's gaze. He explained, 'I've never been in here until today, Connell.'

Connell was silent.

'It was always locked, you see. Her piece of home.'

She might have heard him. A great rolling breaker of pain seemed to pass through her; she strained against all the bonds that held her down, made the awful barking noise. Then almost silence.

'How long?' Freddie asked.

'For what?'

'The end of ether.'

'Minutes.'

'And she'll battle her way to the end in pain?'

'Yes.'

'Scream her way?'

'Yes. And silent screams too. And barking sounds.'

'For how long?'

Connell shrugged. 'Hours, I don't know.' He raised his glass. 'I'm sorry, Freddie,' he said. 'And sorry for Lucy and her home.'

'We all belonged somewhere once,' Freddie said.

'Yes,' Connell remembered.

'We're lonely people, Connell.'

The storm lingered, the wind came in great charges against the windows. Only the sound of water deluging on the trees and shrubs and the iron ground. They drank in silence.

'We're cornered, aren't we, Connell? I don't seem to care any more.'

'The Cape?'

'It seems far away.'

'Jane's your responsibility now.'

'We're going to die here, Connell, aren't we? All of us?'

'I don't know.'

'Listen to that rain.' The storm rumbled farther away now, the lightning no longer a blinding flare. The wind pulled the storm farther afield. But the rain stayed with them, vertical rods, sheets of rain, spattering, flooding, before it was pulled into the burnt-out ground; hammering on the roof and shooting down on pathways and shrubs and verandah. The sound pierced the evaporating film of Connell's ether and Lucy suddenly struggled in and out of rigor, sent her gurgling howl of pain into a world of falling water. Within a minute pain had enclosed her: a falling downpour of agonizing pain. She was a choking, groaning, barking animal.

Freddie and his whisky had kept fear at bay; but now his powerlessness to relieve what he loved most slapped him to sobriety.

'Oh God,' he said to Connell. 'I dragged her out here, you know. To drink, boredom, and now this. She didn't belong, Connell. London imprisoned me. Buses, undergrounds, suits, overcoats, soft hats, bowlers, mackintoshes, getting old, a few pints and a whore on Fridays, promotions, demotions, stagnation, Sunday lunches in Muswell Hill ... Oh Christ!'

Lucy was at war with flooding pain and constriction, without break now. No longer human, even for a moment, Freddie thought.

'Why?' he asked Connell.

'If you believe in God, it is His will,' Connell shrugged. 'If you don't, like the African says, it's her turn.'

'What does he do? What does the African do? What do I do, Connell?'

'The African?'

'Yes.'

'Down on the coast he would give her to the hospital and forget her. Morphine. Keep her in pain but quiet until she choked. Ethics, they call it. A kind doctor might give her a single shot and draw the sheet over her.'

'A shot?'

'A jab.'

'What do we do?'

'Stay with her until it's over.'

'Daylight?'

'I don't know. A long time at any rate.'

'Hours?'

'Drink, drink, drink,' Connell said.

Freddie poured drinks and they sat on a bedroom settee that might have looked at home in a suburban semi. In minutes, the heaving repetitious agony on the bed, the animal sounds, the cascading rain on the world outside, had rubbed Freddie raw. He stood, paced the room, held back the curtains to look aimlessly at a veil of rain between him and the familiar shapes of the bush.

Lucy suddenly howled her pain in a choking climbing shriek and he shouted, 'Connell!'

Connell brought the whisky bottle, placed it beside him, waited for some calmness. 'Yes?' he said.

'You've seen it before?'

'Once,' Connell said. 'Once only. Villages deal with it, have their own customs.'

'How?'

'Make a pit. Open an artery.'

'Jesus.'

234

'It's kind,' Connell said.

'And you?'

'He was a young boy. I shot him. He's buried down there somewhere.'

Freddie closed his eyes and looked into the blackness and grey amorphous changing shapes. He took his gun and cocked it, went and stood by the bed. The face, he thought, that had been so beautiful . . .

At a Christmas dance she had worn what Freddie called a Charleston frock, drop-waisted, and golden shoes and earrings that swung with her long hair as they went da–da da–da; the tune hummed itself in his mind. She was a picture, looking at him in admiration. He had said, 'I haven't got much, Lucy, but I'm bound for the Med. Good money, good places out there. Would you marry me? Or even think about it?' 'I'd rather marry you,' she had said . . .

Freddie pulled himself back, looked at the tangled frantic head of hair and mucus. He even aimed the gun but stood there powerless.

'Connell,' he said. 'I can't do it.'

'But you want to?'

'Oh yes, Christ yes!'

'Then sit far away where you can see my back. Not her face.'

Connell heard him pull a chair and the creaking sound as he put his weight on it. He took the gun from his belt and shot her through the head. The sound was a huge blast in the confines of the room but it wasted away and there was stillness. No more breathing, choking, writhing, only endless rain outside.

'Just sit there and drink,' Connell told him. Freddie sat, head in hands; he might be in tears.

He put Lucy's head between pillows. She lay on a tangled sheet and underlay. Connell pulled and smoothed them out, parcelled her in them. With the packing needle and string he sewed her in her shroud. He had sewn a lot of shrouds in a quarter of a century.

'Come,' he said to Freddie.

The storm had passed. Connell could see the distant flash of lightning even through the curtains and then in seconds the thunder was a great growling roar. The rain had settled to a steady downpour now.

'A waterproof. A big one. Your own,' Connell said.

Freddie brought it and Connell wrapped the remains, pulled the belt tightly about them. With Freddie he went down the passageway to the lounge. Freddie went to Jane. She had done her weeping for now and he put his arms about her.

There was work to be done, Connell knew: he looked out at the steadily falling rain, pulled back the curtains so they could see the night; so that what was in the night could see them. He turned back to the lounge, saw Lorimer rigid as a guardsman, staring at him. Connell took the weight of the gun from his belt and put it on a drinks table; he sat on the armrest of the chair and gave them moments of respite.

Lorimer said, 'You shot her, didn't you?'

'Yes,' Connell said; he stood and opened the verandah doors. Rain splashes reached into the fringes of the lounge. A little coolness came too.

Lorimer said, 'You let him shoot your wife, Freeman?'

'I told him to,' Freddie said.

'You're God, are you, Connell?'

'In the bush everyone is God. Even you.'

Connell turned and saw that Lorimer had taken and aimed his revolver. It was a kind of ridiculous charade. 'Drop your gunbelt on the floor, Freeman.'

Freddie loosened the buckle and let it fall to his feet. He was tired.

'Now move away from it.'

Lorimer took Freddie's revolver from its holster and flung it into the rain and blackness. He opened the window, took up and smashed the shotgun on the steel frame.

'I'll leave you to grieve with your wife's body, Mr Freeman,'

236

he said. 'And Mr Connell and your...' He had second thoughts about his words of abuse for Jane. He felt dirty. He looked almost with sadness at them. 'Your daughter, Mr Freeman.'

It struck Connell that Lorimer had forgotten the gibing 'Commissar' tag. And spare shells too. Mr Lorimer would leave with confidence on his final mission.

Connell said, 'Safe passage, my friend.'

Lorimer motioned him away from the verandah, backed out towards the night. 'You won't get very far, Connell,' he said. 'I'll see to it.' He was gone.

Freddie's car was out there in the darkness; and Lorimer's. A bullet in Freddie's tank. That would maroon them. Or he might not even fire a shot.

Lorimer was killed in silence. A single swinging knife-blow almost severed his head. His body was mutilated.

They stood in silence in the lounge and waited for gunshot or some sound of battle. There was nothing but the interminable vertical rain.

Connell said, 'We should go now.'

Freddie stood listening, puzzled, confused. The immense explosion of Connell's gun, the single twitch of Lucy's feet which were in his sight line, were an unreality of a long time ago. He couldn't do it. How could he? He remembered the intense happiness of premarital days – the only real happiness he had ever known, he thought – and the sound of her laughter at his old, old jokes. It would have been shooting a loving eager face that he had never forgotten.

'I'm sorry, Connell,' he said. 'I wasn't listening. I wanted to say...'

'Yes,' Connell said.

'I wasn't listening.'

'I said it's time to go.'

'Lorimer?' Freddie said. 'No car engine. No shots. He might be out there.'

'He is.'

Jane said, 'And very dead, I imagine.'

'Dead,' Freddie said and pondered it, looked to Connell.

'Yes, probably dead,' Connell said.

Freddie looked at the black rain and showed all his emptiness. 'And it's time to go, Connell, is it?' he queried.

'We'll be carrying the dead. There's respect for grief. You are respected, Freddie.'

Freddie's gratitude showed. 'Lucy?' he said.

'She must be buried.'

Jane said, 'And then?'

'That's as far as I can see,' Connell said. 'Get a box, a trunk. Pack them. A couple of blankets, coats, long boots, a flashlight. What you can wear or carry.' He said to Freddie, 'Money?'

'Money?'

'From the bank. Your bank is razed, your breeze-block strongroom. Almost nothing stands down there. You sent them their gold and diamonds. The paper notes are yours, Freddie. Where?'

'The sideboard,' he said.

Connell found the holdall and pushed it towards Jane. 'That and whisky. And passports. And hurry.'

He took Freddie back to the silent bedroom and its tied shapeless bundle. There was still whisky and glasses. 'Pour it,' he said. They drank. 'There are people hidden out there. Friends, enemies, I don't know. But walk tall, Freddie.'

'Yes.'

'Your car keys?'

'Yes.'

Connell picked up the bundled waterproofed Lucy and let her hang back across his shoulder. Freddie opened a side door and for a moment they looked at the rain, settled into a monotonous flow.

'She goes on the roof rack,' Connell said. 'You have straps. In the boot?'

'The roof rack?'

'It's a funeral, Freddie. But safer, that's all. They can see the dead. A short journey. And the blackman fears poison too.'

'But where?'

Connell said, '*My* coffin, *my* grave, *my* ground.'

They stepped out across the compound. The rain was without sting, almost warm. It was clean, Freddie thought. They found his car and Connell raised Lucy up to rest on the bars.

'The straps,' he said. 'Don't lock the boot.' Freddie was a drenched ghost of his old confident self. 'Jane needs you in there,' he told him.

'Yes.'

Freddie took the image of the car with him. He had grown old, he felt, since he had come up from the club complaining of the absence of servants, of saluting steward boys. And Lucy sitting there, holding her poisoned hand, looking a bit 'down' as she might with mild fever or a hangover.

Connell made the bundle of Lucy secure and let the rain wash down his body. He walked to Lorimer's car and saw his almost decapitated remains: his legs, arms and genitals hacked. A loyal forgotten man, Connell thought without rancour, like skeletons deep down in French mud. Connell's gun was beside him. He picked it up and put it in his belt. Sounds of Freddie and Jane reached him and he went to meet them, loaded the boot, slammed it.

He said to Freddie, 'You'll drive. I'm beside you.' He opened the rear door for Jane.

'Lorimer?' she asked.

'A few feet away, behind his car. You wouldn't want to see it.'

'The long knives?' Freddie asked.

Connell was silent for moments. 'This is a funeral,' he told Freddie. 'You drive at crawl pace. We're not running from

239

anyone, remember. That's important. On the road, by the commune, you stop.'

'Yes.'

The windscreen wipers pushed against streams of water, fought almost a losing battle, showed a patch of road, lost it, found it. Rain swept against the side and rear windows, hammered the bonnet, the roof. Freddie's car leant against its gears on the steep gradient of the hill from the plateau. He saw that Connell's gun was on his lap, his hands resting on it.

'They didn't take it,' Freddie said.

'No.'

'They knew it was yours?'

'They probably didn't see it,' Connell said.

It was a strange floating sensation in Freddie's car, darkness, light, water coursing down the steep gradient, imprisoned water, the slow crawling progress; the roof was pummelled and the bundle of Lucy's body too ... had a drink with a fellow at lunchtime, Freddie had said, was at his funeral before sundown ... he might have gone on leave. Freedom would come, new masters for old, a great tide of blood. Black masters with the whiteman's paradigm of progress to be mimed, superimposed on the old old sleeping culture. There would be battles always, peace was a brittle transient word. In Africa, India, in Lorimer's land, wherever there were great blind beliefs, certainties. Always battles.

He heard the small sounds of Jane weeping behind him; his regrets were for her loss. He was glad he had been with them at the end.

They reached the flat road, almost a tangent, crawled the mile of darkness to where it passed by the bush that was the palisade of Connell's commune.

'Stop here,' he said to Freddie. 'Don't lock your doors, switch off, leave your keys.' They stood out again in the warm rain, let sweat and fear wash away. Connell unbuckled the roof straps.

'Connell?' Freddie said.

Connell turned to look at his worn face. 'Yes?'

'Not with the sick ones. She was so beautiful, Connell.'

'Not with the sick ones,' Connell said. 'Take care of your daughter.'

He lifted Lucy on to his shoulder, found his tunnel through the bush; they followed, a single file. The rain beat against the weave of branch and leaf and creeper above them and poured in from a hundred spouting falls. The darkness was total.

'Not long,' Connell said.

They emerged into the real world of falling rain; heat had still been entrapped in the bush but in the openness there was the illusion, momentarily, of cold. Eyes had adjusted to the darkness too: they could see each other, the ground ten feet ahead. Connell knew it, every square inch he had cleared and tilled in all his years.

They climbed a hillock and were confronted with his cabin, its small roofed verandah wet from sweeps of rain. He laid Lucy down on her bier. Freddie and Jane stood at head and feet in gathering pools of water; Lucy's cerements too wept all round her. Connell had gone in his cabin, was dragging something from beneath his bed. It was a coffin, shaped, panelled, moulded; grained wood varnished to a high gloss. Its furnishings were brass, from far far south, solid metal, cast in village furnaces, with native beauty, cracks and faults.

Connell removed the lid. 'I made it a long time ago,' he said. His womenfolk had lined and beautified his last resting place. 'And give it in sadness, Freddie.' He lifted and laid Lucy in the softness, pulled across the sidesheets, screwed down the lid.

Connell stood listening for moments, listening to the ceaseless pelt of rain above him, on the roof of his verandah. His light-weight clothes hung drenched on him, stuck against his iron frame; his face was an unfinished daub: they were a lost pre-Raphaelite group, banal, pitiable.

Connell had brought a small leather-bound missal from his cabin. He read: an almost inaudible muttering.

'Out of the depths I have cried unto thee, O Lord.
Lord hear my voice.
O let thine ears consider well
The voice of my supplication.
If thou, O Lord, will mark iniquities,
Lord who shall abide it? . . .
For with the Lord there is mercy,
And with him is plenteous redemption.'

Connell put away the book. His grave had been dug and timbered behind his cabin for as long as the coffin had been made: the excavated earth framed it and a pitched cover sealed it from weather. Lucy was a light burden. They carried her there. Connell opened the grave. There was a shovel and ropes. The coffin was lowered. He back-filled enough earth to cover it from sight, six inches of graveside earth above coffin level, settling with the fall of rain.

'Come now,' he said.

The unceasing rain, Freddie thought. He took a fistful of sodden earth and let it fall in the darkness. They followed him back across the open ground and the tunnel through the bush. Connell stopped, put a hand on their shoulders. They could see the bare glint of the chrome from their car.

Connell said, 'There are three men in your car now. Good men. Armed. African men. It's two hundred miles to the border, two hundred more to the airstrip. They'll get you there. And from there to the Cape the world is at peace. For a while. You have money, Freddie. A pension too.' He paused. 'Your car. That's the price. They must get back. A small price.'

Freddie said, 'Come with us, Connell. There's nothing here. The jig is up. A squad of johnnies from the train and some damn white spycatcher with a warrant. Come with us.'

'The bush is endless out there,' Connell said. 'Getting lost is easy.'

The rain coursed down, drenched hair and bodies. Connell

hustled them to the car, opened the rear door; he saw Sten guns and side arms, two militia, a driver. They spoke in patois.

The village was lost, they said; burnt, most of it, but in the hands of His Majesty's black army. The post office stood, the railway lines were intact, the gaol and the body of James Connell were untouched. They would be fighting for the village again.

Connell nodded.

A militia man said, 'The train come, sah. It arrived with first fall of rain. Two hundred men, they say. Some dead now. But many of us. Troops and whiteman come here for you, the Letter Writer say. You go now for bush. Very soon, sah.'

'Yes.' Connell thanked him, nodded to the driver. Jane gripped his arms, kissed him on the mouth.

'You'll watch over her grave, Connell?'

'Every day,' he said.

Freddie held his hand, said, 'We're still carpet-baggers, Connell. For ever on the trot.'

Connell nodded to the driver, slammed the door behind Freddie, watched the headlights and luminous rain out of sight. He stood there in silence, could hear faintly the distant muffled noise of a truck, its four-wheel drive pushing through the rain.

He walked back through the bush, across the compound, to his cabin, thought of the blood of all his black family soaking into its native ground; and the Freemans following tracks and open plains still hard before the rains dissolved them. It was the end. Too late to start again.

From his cabin he brought a chair, a bottle of whisky, a flashlight, sat in the doorway beneath the shelter of the balcony roof; he checked his gun, spun the chamber, counted five shells. He cleared away the embedded mud. Then he drank. Again and again. A quarter of the bottle. Thank God for whisky, he thought, in this awful place. On impulse he went inside his cabin and washed and changed. He wore a dark shirt and slacks, toe-grip sandals. He brushed back his streaming hair, sat and waited.

It would be autumn now in Ireland, falling leaves, chestnuts on the roads, he thought, the breeze stirring stiffening leaves, bronze evenings. His seed had gone from Antrim now. And in Belfast, Elizabeth Orr. She hardly remembered, he supposed, a passing fancy of youth. He was glad he would remember her always as young and beautiful. As Freddie remembered Lucy.

He could hear the escort coming now, the growing nearness of the diesel truck, the silence when it stopped.

He took his chair around the back of his cabin, his whisky, his gun, his flashlight. He planted his chair on the frame of earth around the grave, its back to it, sat and heard their sounds, pushing, hacking through the bush. Six, eight, ten; more, less. Now they were in open ground, only the sound of metal: guns, buckles. He drank from his bottle and broke it against an outcrop of rock. They would be soft-footing it now towards the sound of broken glass, behind the grey curtain of rain.

They emerged in a shallow arc. The whiteman, in oilskins reaching the ground, a helmet, a service pistol, had a foursome on each flank. Sten guns at the extremities, Connell saw, the rest, rifles, fixed bayonets. They had come closer than he expected, he thought, heads forward, squinting into the rain.

Arm outstretched, he took aim at the whiteman, shone the flashlight on his own gun, sent a bullet high above the whiteman's head. The whiteman was shouting, 'Fire, fire, fire!' as he dived for cover, splashed on the liquid ground. The Sten guns sent twenty, thirty rounds into Connell's chest and stomach. He felt nothing. The force toppled the chair and he lay on the mound of graveside earth.

The squad slowly closed in, stood looking down at him. The fat gaoler leaned over and peered.

'Is that Connell?' he was asked.

The rain pelted down on Connell's open mouth and eyes; on the gaping holes the Stens had left.

'That's Connell.'

The whiteman, with his revolver, knelt on the graveside earth and shot Connell through the head. A kind of ceremonial coup de grâce.

'There's a shovel. Use your boots, rifle butts,' he said. With his foot he pushed Connell and saw him drop into the grave. 'Fill it in. Idiots in Belfast wanted him alive but we'll send our regrets. Shot while resisting arrest. Two of you,' he said. 'Bring petrol. Jerrycans from the truck. Burn every cabin, every stick.'

'The sick ones, sah?'

'Let them do their own dying.'

CO walked round into Connell's cabin, with his flashlight found whisky. Malt. The very best, he thought. He stood on the verandah and sipped. He was thinking of the awful tedious journey back to the coast and the comfort of his Secretariat office. He wondered if the hole behind Connell's cabin had been fashioned for a grave or a dug-out.

Discover more about our forthcoming books through Penguin's FREE newspaper...

Penguin Quarterly

It's packed with:

- exciting features
- author interviews
- previews & reviews
- books from your favourite films & TV series
- exclusive competitions & much, much more...

Write off for your free copy today to:
Dept JC
Penguin Books Ltd
FREEPOST
West Drayton
Middlesex
UB7 0BR
NO STAMP REQUIRED

READ MORE IN PENGUIN

In every corner of the world, on every subject under the sun, Penguin represents quality and variety – the very best in publishing today.

For complete information about books available from Penguin – including Puffins, Penguin Classics and Arkana – and how to order them, write to us at the appropriate address below. Please note that for copyright reasons the selection of books varies from country to country.

In the United Kingdom: Please write to *Dept. JC, Penguin Books Ltd, FREEPOST, West Drayton, Middlesex UB7 0BR*

If you have any difficulty in obtaining a title, please send your order with the correct money, plus ten per cent for postage and packaging, to *PO Box No. 11, West Drayton, Middlesex UB7 0BR*

In the United States: Please write to *Penguin USA Inc., 375 Hudson Street, New York, NY 10014*

In Canada: Please write to *Penguin Books Canada Ltd, 10 Alcorn Avenue, Suite 300, Toronto, Ontario M4V 3B2*

In Australia: Please write to *Penguin Books Australia Ltd, 487 Maroondah Highway, Ringwood, Victoria 3134*

In New Zealand: Please write to *Penguin Books (NZ) Ltd, 182–190 Wairau Road, Private Bag, Takapuna, Auckland 9*

In India: Please write to *Penguin Books India Pvt Ltd, 706 Eros Apartments, 56 Nehru Place, New Delhi 110 019*

In the Netherlands: Please write to *Penguin Books Netherlands B.V., Keizersgracht 231 NL–1016 DV Amsterdam*

In Germany: Please write to *Penguin Books Deutschland GmbH, Friedrichstrasse 10–12, W–6000 Frankfurt/Main 1*

In Spain: Please write to *Penguin Books S. A., C. San Bernardo 117–6° E–28015 Madrid*

In Italy: Please write to *Penguin Italia s.r.l., Via Felice Casati 20, I–20124 Milano*

In France: Please write to *Penguin France S. A., 17 rue Lejeune, F–31000 Toulouse*

In Japan: Please write to *Penguin Books Japan, Ishikiribashi Building, 2–5–4, Suido, Tokyo 112*

In Greece: Please write to *Penguin Hellas Ltd, Dimocritou 3, GR–106 71 Athens*

In South Africa: Please write to *Longman Penguin Southern Africa (Pty) Ltd, Private Bag X08, Bertsham 2013*

READ MORE IN PENGUIN

A CHOICE OF FICTION

Father Melancholy's Daughter Gail Godwin

A young woman's poignant search for self-discovery, *Father Melan-choly's Daughter* eloquently exemplifies the struggle within us all to attain grace, inspiration and wisdom in our daily lives. 'Skilfully written, accessible, funny, discriminating, readable and thoughtful' – *The Times Literary Supplement*

The Message to the Planet Iris Murdoch

'I suspect that when the intellectual map of our own times comes to be sketched out, Iris Murdoch will occupy a position analogous to Tolstoy and Dostoyevsky ... Her vision of the world is heart-rending, but ultimately celebratory' – A. N. Wilson in the *Guardian*

Hemlock and After Angus Wilson

'He was a very acute observer ... and it was this vigilance, allied to a profound curiosity about the world, that gave his fiction its zest and its social accuracy ... a great novelist' – Rose Tremain in the *Guardian*

July's People Nadine Gordimer

'So flawlessly written that every one of its events seems chillingly, ominously possible' – *The New York Times Book Review*. 'This is the best novel that Miss Gordimer has ever written' – Alan Paton

The Slave Isaac Bashevis Singer

The Slave is a powerful drama set against the exotic background of seventeenth-century Poland with all its superstitions, witchcraft and witchhunts, abundant life and appalling prejudices. 'The tale is tragic and warmhearted, full of mellow wisdom learned through suffering' – *Yorkshire Post*

A CHOICE OF FICTION

My Son's Story Nadine Gordimer

'*My Son's Story* is a novel of conviction – a passionate novel. But if that passion moves and convinces, it is because we have seen it pass through the checks and balances of a rigorously sceptical, ice-cool intellect' – *Independent*

A Natural Curiosity Margaret Drabble

'This book, like its predecessor [*The Radiant Way*], is a remarkable mixture of rambling but compelling narrative, psychological insight, generous human portrayal, acute observation, humour, horror, beauty and disgust' – *The Times Literary Supplement*

Love in the Time of Cholera Gabriel García Márquez

'A powerful, poetic and comic long-distance love story set on the Caribbean coast … Unique Márquez magic of the sadness and funniness of humanity' – *The Times*

My Secret History Paul Theroux

'André Parent saunters into the book, aged fifteen … a creature of naked and unquenchable ego, greedy for sex, money, experience, another life … read it warily; read it twice, and more; it is darker and deeper than it looks' – *Observer*

Age of Iron J. M. Coetzee

'Coetzee's vision is incisive and yet tremulous, poetic. His intelligence is scabrous, but his prose is aerated and expansive when it needs to be' – James Wood in the *Guardian*

READ MORE IN PENGUIN

A CHOICE OF FICTION

Our House in the Last World   Oscar Hijuelos

'Virtuoso writing that describes immigrant life in New York ... a novel of great warmth and tenderness' – *The New York Times Book Review*. 'Told in an oblique lyric voice, with an air of absolute authenticity and assurance' – Joyce Carol Oates

Crucible of Fools   M. S. Power

'It has a haunting, lyrical and emotional intensity. Graphically macabre, it is overlaid with the blackest of black senses of humour' – *Scotland on Sunday*

Stars of the New Curfew   Ben Okri

'Anarchical energy with authoritative poise ... an electrifying collection' – Graham Swift. 'Okri's work is obsessive and compelling, spangled with exotic magic and haunted by shadows ... Reality re-dreamt with great conviction' – *Time Out*

The Stories of Eva Luna   Isabelle Allende

'Vibrant and colourful ... twenty-three magical tales, of anger that changes to laughter and revenge that turns into love' – *Literary Review*. 'Like a plate of hors-d'œuvres, each one tempting, some as exquisite as caviare ... stunning' – *The New York Times Book Review*

The Inn at the Edge of the World   Alice Thomas Ellis

'Peopled with marvels ... A fine balance between comedy and tragedy ensures the reader a sense of deep satisfaction after the last page' – Ruth Rendell in the *Daily Telegraph*